MURDER

at the

MAPLES

by
Joanne Phillips

Mirrorball Books

MURDER

at the

MAPLES

by
Joanne Phillips

Mirrorball Books
An imprint of Bostock Publishing
Bostock Hall, Shropshire
SY13 2RN

www.bostockpublishing.co.uk

Paperback Edition 2013
ISBN 978-0-9573094-2-5

Typeset in Sabon, printed and bound in the UK by Lightning Source
Cover design by Blondesign

Praise for Joanne Phillips

'Fear is the tax that conscience pays to guilt.'
George Sewell

Chapter 1

Are you sure it's safe?' Flora looked out of the window and up the cliff face. The other carriage seemed suspended above them. How on earth had she let Joy talk her into this?

'Oh, Flora, you're such a wimp.' Joy sat back with a smile and patted the bench by her side. 'Come on, it only lasts a minute.'

So does plummeting to your certain death, thought Flora, but she tucked herself in next to Joy anyway and began a head count of the other passengers.

Visiting the cliff railway at Bridgnorth was a special treat for her friend's eightieth birthday – Flora's idea of a fun day out was shopping for vintage clothes or taking to the hills with a backpack. Not risking life and limb for a trip down memory lane. Flora stowed her tote bag between her sandaled feet and began to read the guidebook with determined interest.

'It was right here,' Joy said dreamily, 'where Eddie proposed to me. The fourth of May, nineteen fifty-one. The happiest day of my life.'

'It says here that the passenger cars were replaced in nineteen fifty-five, so it wasn't this actual carriage, in fact.' Flora looked up in time to catch Joy's withering glare.

'Flora, sometimes I despair of you. You are entirely devoid of romance.'

While Joy continued her reverie, Flora dropped the book into her bag and absently chewed on a bitten-down nail. She'd counted eighteen people squashed into the tiny carriage, and presumably there were another eighteen coming down the cliff at the same time. Thirty-six lives in the hands of a couple of ambitious Victorian engineers.

'How does it work, exactly?' she asked the conductor. He was standing in the wooden doorway, his hat placed at a jaunty angle. He shrugged his shoulders. 'Beats me.'

Oh, very reassuring, thank you. Flora craned her neck to get a better view of the steep track that climbed up the cliff, and then immediately wished she hadn't bothered. She ran a hand through her cropped brown hair – back to its natural colour now the bleached blonde had grown out – then placed both her hands very carefully on top of her tensed thighs.

'It's something to do with wheels and pulleys,' said a voice by her side. A bespectacled child with a Hello Kitty rucksack perched on her lap was looking up at Flora with a serious expression.

'Pardon?'

'You were wondering how it works. We did it in a school project. The Victorians.'

'You mean ropes and things?'

The girl nodded solemnly.

'Great,' said Flora under her breath.

Joy laughed and bounced in her seat. She laid a white-gloved hand across Flora's clenched fists and stage-whispered, 'Hold on tight.'

The carriage lunged forward with a sickening jerk and began to trundle up the rails. Flora watched layers of carved rock slide past the windows as they rose higher and higher up the cliff.

'Wave hello!' someone called out, and Flora turned in time to see the other carriage pass them on its way down. A fleeting glimpse of expressionless faces, and then they were gone. The little girl with the glasses was rummaging in her rucksack, oblivious to the entire journey, while Joy sat on Flora's other side with her eyes closed, a secret smile turning her lips up at the corners. Flora began to hum, blocking out the rumbling of the silly train as it was pulled up and up by ropes and pulleys and, by the looks of it, blind faith. The carriage smelt of hot wood and oil. She focused on a patch of flaky blue paint above her head and imagined herself elsewhere. Anywhere else would be fine.

And then, with another stomach-churning jolt, it was over.

'That wasn't so bad, was it?'

Flora waited until they were clear of the ticket station at the top of the cliff, then she leaned against the wall with her back to the view and said, 'I am never bringing you on a day out again, Joy it's-nothing-like-a-cable-car Martin.'

Joy snickered and rolled her eyes. 'For a young person, Flora, you aren't very adventurous. You're twenty-nine, not ninety-nine! Anyway, this is nothing by today's standards. These days you've got all those roller coasters and white-knuckle rides for excitement. When Eddie and I first came here, oh, it was considered very daring. We would just stand and watch the carriages going up and down for hours.'

'And they say there was nothing to do before TV.'

'Flora, don't be a wet blanket. Come and look at the view.'

'I'm not being a wet blanket, Joy. I don't like heights, okay?'

'Well, that's plain silly. You can't fall from here. Come and have a look.'

'No.'

Flora could feel her friend's eyes upon her, but she

didn't turn her head.

'I had no idea you were afraid of heights. I guess the funicular railway wasn't much fun for you, was it?'

You think? Flora shook her head, smiling in spite of herself. This last six months she'd grown to care about Joy like a surrogate grandmother, but you couldn't deny the old woman was in a world of her own. When Shakers Removals had moved Joy into her new home at the Maples Retirement Village last November, Flora had been blown away by the older woman's resilience. Never mind that she'd buried her husband of nearly sixty years the month before – never mind that she was moving out of her beloved family home and into a one-room unit with no garden – Joy Martin had remained cheerful and spirited throughout.

'The next time I move house it'll be me in a box, not ornaments and picture frames and knick-knacks,' Joy had joked, nudging Marshall in the ribs for good measure.

Marshall's face had been a study of embarrassment, much to Flora's amusement. He still struggled with the British sense of humour – especially the morbid kind.

Which wasn't the only thing he struggled with, of course. Having to work for Flora had to be top of the list.

Joy pulled Flora's attention back to the present with a sharp tug on the strap of her bag. 'You really should take a look down here. It's amazing. The people are so tiny they look like toy soldiers, and that man there ... Why, what on earth is he doing?'

Flora swung around, her curiosity captured, and found Joy leaning out dangerously over the low wall.

'For God's sake, you crazy old woman, get back will you?' Flora grabbed Joy's arm and gripped it tightly. Joy gave a mischievous laugh.

'Made you look though, didn't I?'

4

The girl with the glasses skipped past, holding an ice cream in one chapped-looking hand and her mum's sleeve in the other. She stared at Flora's shoulder, openly curious. Flora tugged down the cap sleeve of her T-shirt, but not before the child's mother had given her the once-over, taking in the skull-and-hearts tattoo and the beaded jewellery and the many-patched vintage jeans with fraying hems. She pulled a face of disapproval, then the two of them skipped away along the walled path, leaving Flora feeling suddenly and unaccountably annoyed.

She knew people made judgments about her based on how she looked – her dressed-down style and the tattoo; the spiky hair she used to dye a different colour every month; her vintage skirts and jewellery and wacky floral bags – but all this said nothing about her as a person. If they thought she was tough they were right to a point, but they were also dead wrong.

'Do I look like a freak or something?' she grumbled, turning back to Joy. 'These jeans were actually really expensive.' But what a person to ask: Joy was hardly a fashionista in pale blue comfort-fit old lady trousers and a matching flowered blouse, her white fluffy perm showing pink scalp with every gust of wind.

'You look very lovely, dear,' Joy said, peering at Flora's face. 'Although you'd look even more lovely if you wore a little make-up from time to time.'

Flora shrugged and looked around to get her bearings. She was starting to regret bringing Joy out, birthday or not. Of course, she should have known that with a name like the funicular railway it wasn't going to be just any normal train journey. She should have known, with Joy involved, that there would be a catch.

Marshall was right: she was a soft touch. 'You treat these old people like they're family,' he'd said when Shakers Removals got the contract for the retirement village. 'You get too attached to people, Flora. That's your problem.'

Well, it was true. She did. But look at them, she'd argued. Look at them with their crinkly eyes and their cardigans in odd pastel colours, their ugly pets and their ancient, dusty furniture that they just would not admit was surplus to requirements. Not even now that they had moved from their vast family homes and would be living in a room – one room – with a kitchenette and an en suite shower for the rest of their lives. If they were lucky. If they didn't get carted off to the third floor for Special Care: Joy's biggest fear these days.

And look at Joy, leaning over the wall to see down the cliff as if she could lean back through time and grab her dead husband by the hand and wrench him back to life again. She was full of energy, incorrigible, never moaning about being lonely, although Flora knew she must be, deep down. What sacrifice was a day off, really? For someone as special as Joy.

Flora sighed and tapped her friend on the arm. 'Come on. Let's go and have a cup of tea.'

'Oh, can we? I know you prefer your coffee, but in the tea rooms just here you can see the winding gear with the ropes and everything. I read about it on the internet.'

Flora smiled. 'Fine. But I'm not going back down the cliff in that thing, okay? I'm walking back to the Low Town – next time you're on your own.'

***

Joy fell asleep on the bus back to Shrewsbury. Not five minutes into the journey she was snoring softly, her thin lips parted, the lipstick she'd worn especially for today worn off around the edges but still bright pink in the middle. A thin sliver of drool crept down to her chin, following the creases in her papery skin. Flora smiled, her eyes soft with concern. Lately Joy had been on her mind a lot, and not just because it was coming up to what would have been Joy and Eddie's sixtieth wedding anniversary. She was, Flora feared, starting to lose it a bit. Just the odd comment here and there, things that didn't add up.

For example, she'd completely taken against a new resident, a Mr Felix, who Flora and Marshall had moved into the Maples only a month ago. Mr Felix was a harmless little man in his seventies, short and starchy-looking with pale ginger hair swept across a pink and freckled bald patch. He used a mobility scooter, or else hobbled around on Maples-issue crutches.

'He's got shifty eyes,' Joy said when Flora pressed her to explain why, that very morning, she had turned full circle and refused to walk through the communal area until the poor man had gone. 'And his trousers are too long.'

Well, that may be true, but was it any reason to act so disgusted? Flora felt embarrassed for him, although it was a fact that he hadn't been overly friendly on moving day. When Flora had offered to set up his kitchenette for him, and maybe even cook his dinner if he was very tired, he had looked affronted and told her no, thank you, and would they mind hurrying up, please. Flora hadn't been able to meet Marshall's eyes the entire rest of the afternoon – she just knew what he was thinking.

That was the trouble with Flora's line of business: it was hard not to get personal with people. You came across them at times of such importance: moving into their first homes, with barely a stick of furniture but so proud of their boxes marked "Kitchen!" and "Bedroom!", all jaunty writing and exclamation marks. Or moving up from their first home to something bigger and better (and more expensive, a drain and a burden, Marshall would say), with tiny babies bundled up in blankets and flustered-looking mothers saying, 'Now, where did I put those scissors exactly ...?' Or simply walking from room to room with the baby on a hip, their faces blank and bewildered.

'It'll be all right,' Flora always wanted to tell them. 'Once you move in it'll all get sorted in no time.' And often she did say this, or something similar, and the customer would turn to her with a face so bright and hopeful. 'Do you really think so?' they'd ask. 'Really? Will it?'

It was no wonder she got so involved. Her dad should have known better than to leave her the business. When had she ever been able to remain detached?

The bus pulled into the terminal with a screech of brakes and Joy lifted her head from the window and yawned. She had a crease down one cheek and smudges of black under her eyes. Flora said nothing. She took Joy's arm, gave it a little squeeze, then steered her towards the zebra crossing, the river, and home.

***

The Maples Retirement Village was a sprawling maze of blocky, low-roofed units with a three-storey weather-boarded building at the centre. Its resemblance to a prison was uncanny, and unfortunate, because the Maples was in fact a highly desirable place to live out one's retirement. Or so the literature claimed. Desirable or not, it was certainly expensive – when Joy had confided in Flora how much her own tiny unit cost per week, Flora was stunned, and she made a mental note to look into her own pension as soon as possible. She might be only twenty-nine, but it would take a lifetime to save enough to cover just a year of care in a place like the Maples.

Or, as Marshall called it, Sleepy City, where the residents' every need was catered to, and there was no requirement to go "off site" at all if they chose. Sleepy City had it all: medical centre, hairdresser, general store, mini library, mobility shop. There was a communal lounge with a bewildering array of entertainment and craft activities on offer, a coffee shop and a travel agent called Coaching Dreams. Marshall said it made him feel ill: he had been against taking on the contract from the outset – Shakers, in his opinion, should be moving into a completely different business area. Flora had overruled him – he might be the manager but she owned the company. Besides, Flora loved the place. There was something so other-worldly about it, and she imagined it to be very American. Marshall, who actually was American and therefore not so impressed by all things USA like Flora, looked at her with a combination of pity and despair when she said this. Which was just about his usual expression anyway.

'I can't stay,' Flora told Joy when they arrived at the Maples' incongruously grand entrance of faux marble columns either side of a topiary arch. 'I've missed about twenty phone calls from Marshall. There must be a problem back at the office that he simply can't cope with. Being a man and all.'

Joy tutted. 'You know, that's just sexist, Flora. There's no reason why being a man should affect his ability to do his job.'

Flora let the comment pass with a good-natured shake of her head. Joy had feminist views which went way beyond those usually held by women of her generation – it was one of the reasons they'd struck up a friendship in the first place, with Joy surprised and impressed by Flora's unlikely status as the owner of a removal firm. 'And you do all the lifting too?' Joy had asked. 'You don't leave that to the men?'

'Of course I don't!' Flora had heard this question far too many times. 'I can shift a wardrobe down a flight of stairs single-handed. It's all in the technique,' she'd added when Joy eyed Flora's slight frame dubiously.

Joy wouldn't hear a word against Marshall, although Flora had her suspicions that this had far more to do with Marshall's rugged good looks and undoubted sex appeal than Joy's own personal equality affirmation programme.

'Afternoon, ladies.'

Flora smiled at the old man who'd stopped outside Joy's unit. The Captain was one of the Maples' oldest residents, and also the most dapper. His neatly combed moustache emphasized a slightly hooked nose, and the medals on his left breast pocket shone proudly.

'Happy birthday,' he said, holding out a crisp white envelope. Joy took the card with a warm smile, and promised to join him later for "the play".

'Amateur dramatics?' Flora asked, watching the Captain walk away, his erect posture making her straighten her shoulders.

'Radio Four. Anyway, you should have told me you needed to get off.' Joy rooted in her stiff leather handbag for her key. 'I could have walked back here alone.'

'Of course you could.'

Joy's unit was identical to all the others except for bright red Venetian blinds and a hand-printed sign on the door which read: *Beware of the dog!* Flora leaned against the breeze-block wall. 'I wanted to see you back safely. And don't think I haven't noticed you're wearing your gloves again. Eczema playing up, is it?'

'A bit. But before you start, I've still got plenty of tablets. It will clear up again in no time.'

'You know what I think about all that. And what about your asthma? I just don't think it's right that you–'

'Well, anyway.' Joy cut her off with a wave of her hand. 'If I can just find my key your duties are over for today. And I've got Otto to protect me, of course.'

Flora waited for her to open the door and for Otto, the pug with as much bounce as a saggy mattress, to start his customary yapping around their ankles. She liked dogs, she really did. Just not as much as she liked people. And she definitely preferred dogs when they were quiet.

But not this quiet. Joy called out Otto's name and stepped inside. She stood in the centre of the small room, turning around in a slow circle, her face beginning to take on a puzzled expression. Flora followed and closed the door behind her. The silence was unexpected, but not inexplicable. Maybe the mutt was taking a nap. Or chewing a particularly tasty bit of slipper.

'Otto! Otto, no!' Joy clapped her hands to her cheeks and let out a piercing scream.

Curled up on the floor, close enough to Flora's feet that she might have stepped on him, Otto was writhing in a desperate, choking panic, tangled up so tightly in the long cord of the blind his eyes were fairly popping out of his head. Joy lunged forward but Flora was closer. She dropped to her knees and tried to loosen the cord from around the little dog's neck.

'Get some scissors,' she shouted. Joy veered off towards the kitchenette. 'Come on, little man. Try and stay still. You're only making it worse.' But Otto was beyond hearing, his pitiful yelps cut off by the tightening band.

'Is he bleeding? Has it cut him?' Joy handed her the scissors, sobbing. Flora shook her head.

'I thought that too, but it's just the red cord.' She snipped carefully, first releasing the animal's neck then moving down to his paws. As soon as he could, Otto began to bark, which Flora took as a positive sign. She held him still with one hand and worked the scissors with the other. Joy stood by with a crocheted blanket, poised and ready to pounce.

'That was close.' Flora sat back on her heels and watched Joy cradle her baby. 'How the hell did he get tangled up like that?' She looked at her friend and pulled a face. 'Joy, you should have those cords tied up. It's really dangerous to leave them dangling.'

Joy glared at her, clearly rattled. 'Well, I know that, thank you very much. And I did have them tied up – look, they wrap around that bracket there.'

Flora looked at the two-pronged bracket on the wall. 'It must have come loose.' She shook her head. 'We'll have to ask the warden to get someone to look at it. Poor Otto.' The dog was panting in Joy's arms, but apart from a slightly disgruntled countenance and a patch of missing fur where Flora had accidentally snipped it along with the blind cord, he didn't appear to have suffered any serious injury. 'You should get him checked out at the medical centre. Do they look at pets there?' But when Flora turned back to Joy she found her friend staring fixedly at the wall.

'Flora, I don't think this was an accident at all.'

'What do you mean?' Flora pushed herself up to standing and gave Otto a little tickle under his chin. He closed his bug eyes in delight.

'That cord didn't come loose by itself. It was tied up this morning when we left. Someone must have been in here and let it down. Which means …'

Flora raised her eyebrows. 'Which means what?'

Joy mimed wrapping a cord around her neck with her free hand and tipped her head to the side, tongue lolling. Then she pointed to Otto and put her finger to her lips.

'Joy, Otto can't understand what you're saying. You can speak out loud.'

'He understands everything,' she whispered, kissing him on his head.

'Well, it's a shame he can't talk as well, because then he could tell us exactly what happened. But you can't be serious. Who on earth would try to hurt Otto?' Flora looked at the pieces of red cord scattered on the beige carpet. For a second she imagined the dog up there still, wound even higher, dangling like a parachutist caught in a tree. She shook the image away with a shudder. Joy was regarding her with narrowed eyes.

'I am deadly serious. And it proves I was right about him, Flora.'

'Who? Right about who?'

But Joy wasn't listening. 'I knew it from the moment I saw him – it's him and he's come back to get his revenge. Otto is only the beginning.' Her friend clutched the pooch to her chest so tightly he peered out from the blanket in alarm.

'I've got no idea what you're talking about, Joy.' Flora reached out and loosened her friend's grip. 'Let's have a cup of tea and calm down. Joy?'

But Joy was staring out of the window, her shoulders and neck suddenly rigid with tension. The slats of the blind threw striped shadows across her pale face and her breath quickened, coming out in small pants, mirrored by the pug. Outside, the motorised buzz of a mobility scooter caught Flora's attention. As she followed Joy's gaze, Mr Felix looked up and lifted his hand in a tentative wave. Joy hissed and swept the blinds closed, plunging the room into darkness.

Chapter 2

'Where've you been? I've been calling you for hours.'
Flora flopped into her worn leather office chair and spun it away from Marshall's accusing face. What a day. And it looked like there wasn't going to be any respite yet.

'What, then?' she said, spinning back to glare up at him. 'What's so urgent that you have to phone me on my day off? You're always reminding me that you're the manager, you're responsible for the day-to-day running of the business, not me. But now there's a problem you can't cope with? Super-man Marshall? Surely not.'

Flora clamped her mouth shut and let the sudden silence wash over them. Had she just said all that out loud? Evidently if you imagined saying something often enough it would come out on its own one day.

Marshall's eyes narrowed and he took a step back, glancing over his shoulder before crossing his arms in front of his chest. It was the briefest gesture, but Flora knew him too well.

'Stuart and Steve can't hear us, don't worry. You're not going to lose face in front of the lads.'

Oh, now he was angry. For just one second, just the tiniest second, Flora enjoyed the way his broad shoulders tensed and his lips, usually so full and smiling, became thinner as he stuck out his jaw. Damn, but he was good looking when he was angry. Such a shame he was also a complete pain in the arse.

'I do not, nor will I ever, give a crap what those two think of me, but I'd appreciate it if you could restrain yourself from balling me out.'

Flora gritted her teeth, willing herself to keep her mouth shut. Sometimes it felt like Marshall was forcing her hand, trying to push her to do something about the intolerable situation they'd found themselves in. Her father had taken Marshall on just after her mum got sick, when he couldn't keep running the business and look after his wife. But when Peter Lively had died only six months after Flora's mum lost her fight with cancer, the business had passed to her. Flora knew her dad had trusted Marshall like family, but even though Shakers' "manager" might be her Uncle Max's stepson from a long-ago marriage, he sure as hell needed to try and remember who was really in charge.

She relaxed back into her chair and laced her fingers together. 'Look, I've not had the best of days. So why don't you just tell me what the problem is.'

'It's Rockfords.'

Flora's stomach did a somersault for the third time that day.

'What about them?'

'They're coming. Here.'

She looked around the office. Shakers Removals had premises under a section of Shrewsbury's railway arches, one of five down-at-heel units tucked out of sight – and often out of mind – of the town's more successful businesses. The glass-walled office sat at the top of a set of metal steps, perched above the warehouse below. It had been a hive of efficient activity back in the days when her dad was around. Now the whole place had an air of neglect.

'Here?' she said.

'To Shrewsbury. They're opening a branch right on our doorstep. This is bad news, Flora, the worse kind.

We can't compete with a multinational like that. No way.'

'I don't believe it.' Flora pushed her cropped fringe off her forehead and rubbed her eyes. They felt gritty and sore. The bitten-down fingernails of her right hand found their way into her mouth again. Marshall rolled his shoulders and pulled a stacking chair across the room, positioning it on the other side of the enormous, paper-covered desk. He looked at her, his head on one side. He was wearing his fraternity sweater, the one with the eagle on it and the frayed cuffs, and his hazel eyes were concerned now, not angry. Flora forced a smile. Tears threatened, but she would not cry, especially not in front of Marshall. She looked up at the photos on the noticeboard. This business had been her father's pride and joy; she still felt the need to make him proud almost a year after saying her final goodbye.

How could she make him proud if she let his business fail?

But no, there was no way she would allow that to happen.

She focused on the calendar behind Marshall's head, willing her tears away. What she saw there brought a wry smile to her lips. Marshall, still watching her intently, raised a questioning eyebrow.

'It's funny now?'

She shook her head. 'It's Friday the thirteenth. I just noticed. The perfect day for bad news.'

Marshall held her gaze for another second, then nodded as though he'd understood far more than she had meant to say. 'Looks like you need a time out. I'll go tell the others.'

Flora noticed that Marshall had pushed the box of own-brand tissues slightly closer as he stood. He knew her so well, knew she would rather stick pins in herself than be seen crying.

'I'm sorry,' she called out on impulse as he headed for the stairs. 'Looks like I picked a hell of a day to go off on a jolly.'

He lifted his hand then let it drop without turning around. She watched him all the way out of the warehouse door, then she pulled out the diary to check for messages. Nothing. And no bookings either. Rockfords or not, soon they were all going to have to face up to some harsh truths. Shakers was in trouble. And Flora had no idea what the hell she was supposed to do about that.

***

Stuart and Steve sat on packing crates while Flora perched on a mahogany table she'd never seen before. Its presence in the warehouse was a little worrying, but now was not the time to ask which poor soul had moved into their new house minus their dining table this week. Marshall's behaviour was still bothering her. One minute he was tensed for a fight, all jutting jaw and frowns; the next he was passing her tissues and playing the good guy. He'd seemed genuinely worried about her reaction to the Rockfords news – he knew how she took everything so personally.

'You're not responsible for the worldwide recession,' he'd said during one of their many rows about the state of the business.

But Flora knew he thought *he* could do so much better if she'd only give him free rein.

Marshall returned with beer and pizza and they all tucked in, eating in gloomy silence until Flora said, 'Come on, guys, it's not the end of the world.' Her words sounded unconvincing even to her own ears.

Stuart sighed. 'Business has been crap lately anyway. It's not like this is going to make it any worse.' He shoved another slice of pepperoni into his mouth and chewed it solemnly. Flora tried to hide her exasperation. It was difficult for Stuart and Steve, they were on casual contracts – Shakers couldn't support more than two full-time employees. Even so, they'd been employed pretty consistently for the last few years, despite the recession. None of them knew that Flora paid herself a pittance so she could keep their wages flowing. She had a feeling Uncle Max suspected, but out in the wilds of Whixall he was in no position to be inspecting the accounts.

'Come on.' Flora adopted a tone of voice more jolly than she felt. 'I'm sure we can think of something.'

'Maybe you should go see David Rockford,' Marshall said, fixing Stuart with a sardonic stare. 'You could ask if there's any work going. They're bound to be recruiting soon.'

'Marshall! There's no need for that.' Flora jumped off the table and laid her pizza to one side. She began to pace around the perimeter of the warehouse, kicking boxes out of her path as she went. 'We've got to stick together,' she said. 'This is not the time to be bickering.'

Marshall kept his eyes on the wall. Stuart's expression had darkened but he continued munching on his pepperoni – Steve was keeping quiet, but there was something tense about his shoulders, and he'd hardly touched his pizza. Or his beer, which was definitely worrying.

Flora sighed and leaned against one side of the shutters. A breeze blew in and ruffled her hair. She tipped her face to the last of the sun and closed her eyes. Honestly, being in charge of three male employees was a lot more challenging than people might imagine. Keeping these boys in check was something her dad had not prepared her for. If only he'd managed to stick around a bit longer … She swallowed. While her mum's death had been expected, only a matter of time, her father's had taken everyone by surprise. He'd only been sixty-four, fit and robust, hauling furniture with the strength of a man half his age. Flora knew his heart attack was just another word for a broken heart. He hadn't the will to go on without her mother.

But he'd had faith in her, and he'd wanted Shakers to be hers one day. Most days that was enough to get her through.

'It's time to make some changes, that's for sure,' Marshall said.

Flora opened her eyes and pulled a face in the direction of the car park. There was no one to see her, but it made her feel better anyway.

'Damn right. Can't go on like this.'

Steve's contribution. Flora waited for Stuart to pipe up.

'What do you suggest, mate?' he said.

Flora couldn't stand it any longer.

'We all know exactly what Marshall's talking about, so don't come all "what do you suggest", Stuart.' She ignored his shocked expression and rounded on Marshall. 'And you – you should know better. We need to stick together, we need to keep doing what we're doing and try harder. Work harder. We don't need to change direction in the middle of the worst recession this country's ever seen, and we don't need wild ideas.'

'It's not a wild idea. It's a proven business strategy – the company I ran back home did real well out of commercial storage and I think–'

'I don't want to hear it again, Marshall. And if you were doing so well "back home", why are you still here? Why don't you go back to the States and do us all a favour?'

'Could you two, for once, for all our sakes, just give it a bloody rest? Could I just eat my pizza in peace and not have to listen to you two bickering for a couple of minutes?'

Flora turned to Steve, outraged. 'What do you mean? Just who the hell do you think you're–'

'Flora.' Marshall's hand was on her arm, his eyes twinkling. 'Leave it, okay?'

'No, it is not okay,' she said, annoyed by how shaky her voice sounded. But she left it all the same, too angry to push it any further. There was so much wrong with Marshall's plan she didn't know where to start. And as for Steve …

Stuart and Steve exchanged a glance. Their discomfort filled the warehouse the way the excess of testosterone had ten minutes ago.

Biting back her anger, Flora squared her shoulders and thought about her dad. What would Peter Lively do right now? A major competitor muscling in; dissent amongst the ranks. The pub of course! A change of scene was just what they needed, and an extra supply of beer couldn't hurt the boys' mood either.

Stuart and Steve brightened instantly, looking even more pleased when Flora said the drinks were on her. But as they were locking up, Marshall said, 'I'll give it a miss, okay? I'm not in the mood.'

'Oh. Right.' Flora tried to hide her disappointment. It wouldn't do for Marshall to think she actually wanted him around, although a team-building exercise at the local pub didn't seem like such a great idea without him.

'What went wrong with your trip out?' he asked over his shoulder, pulling down the metal shutter and slotting it into place in one smooth movement.

'What do you mean?'

'Earlier. You said you hadn't had a very good day either.'

Flora looked down at the back of Marshall's head as he closed the padlock and took out the key. Should she tell him about Otto? He'd probably only make a joke of it.

'What?' Marshall stood and saw the look on Flora's face. 'Come on. I'll walk up with you. You can tell me about it on the way.'

Flora shrugged. Annoying though he was, it would be good to have someone to sound off to. Voicing her concerns about Joy might show her how silly they were.

They walked up past the heavy commuter traffic, under the railway bridge, heading for the castle. As Flora spoke she was relieved to see Marshall's face remain serious. 'Poor old Joy,' he said when she got to the part about finding Otto. 'What a thing to happen.'

'She's convinced someone did it on purpose. I know, it's totally crazy. Do you remember that old guy we moved in?'

'They're all old, Flora.'

'Mr Felix, he was called.'

'In a wheelchair?'

'Not really. He can walk, he just uses one of those mobility scooters. Anyway, she's convinced it was him. Wouldn't say another word about it, just kept repeating over and over something about him "getting his revenge".'

'Wow. Heavy stuff. How did it happen, do you think?'

Flora pulled a face. 'Those blinds are actually quite dangerous. She had the cord looped up but it had fallen down, somehow. Accidents happen.'

Marshall nodded solemnly. 'If it was an accident, of course.'

'What do you mean?'

'Well, come on. Sleepy City is a pretty depressing place, even for a dog. And Joy was out all day with you, and Otto is there all on his own.'

Flora stopped by the traffic lights and pressed the button to cross. 'I wish you wouldn't call it that. It just sounds so … like a final resting place, or something.'

'Which it is,' countered Marshall with a shrug.

'You know, Marshall, you don't have to look for the dark side in everything. Lots of people live in places like the Maples and they're really happy.' Flora tapped her foot impatiently, squinting in the low sun. 'Anyway, what precisely are you getting at? What do you mean about Otto being there all on his own?'

He leaned against a bollard and gave her a twisted smile. 'I think, Flora, that little Otto might have been trying to, you know – end it all?'

'Oh, you are the most hateful man!' Flora swung her tote bag and whacked him on the legs as hard as she could. 'The most annoying, hateful, horrible man I have ever met. How you could take something as serious as this and turn it into some kind of a joke ... that's low even for you, Marshall Goodman. Even for you.'

'You're right,' Marshall said, trying to smother his laughter. 'You're right, Flora. I'm so sorry. It's unforgivable. I'm sure you're right, I'm sure Otto's really happy there.'

'I hate you. I really do.'

'No. You don't. And that's part of the problem, don't you think?'

While Flora stood with her mouth hanging open, trying to think of a snappy comeback, Marshall raised his arm and walked away up Castle Hill. Come back, she wanted to shout. I haven't finished having a go at you yet. But the insistent beep, beep, beep of the pedestrian crossing forced her to walk forward with the crowd and before long he was out of sight completely.

***

By the following morning, Flora had calmed down enough to almost see the funny side of Marshall's joke. But it didn't make her laugh, or even raise a smile. When she arrived at Joy's unit with her favourite chilli chicken

Subway roll, her friend looked to have aged about five years.

Which, in an octogenarian with chronic asthma, was not a good thing.

There was a chill in the air, April showers threatening, and not for the first time Flora lamented her inability to drive. The walk across the city from Sunnybank Rise to the Maples never seemed to get any shorter.

'Hey, I know,' Marshall had said last month when their driver retired, 'why don't you learn to drive? That would solve all our problems, and you'd be a bit more use around here, wouldn't you?'

Flora hadn't risen to it. She'd made her face blank the way she always did when he needled her and carried on typing, her back ruler-straight, her chin set to "get stuffed". This was a sore point, but it was one Marshall didn't even know he was prodding. Flora had to date failed her driving test seven times, and that was six times too many. But as far as Marshall was concerned, Flora had never even had lessons. Only Uncle Max knew the truth.

Flora and Joy ate their lunch side by side on Joy's tiny sofa, elbows knocking together companionably. Flora tried not to look at the window, now devoid of the garish red blinds. Otto lay at Joy's feet, surrounded by squeaky toys and wrapped up cosily in the crocheted blanket.

'How is he doing today?' Flora said, offering the mutt a piece of bread. Otto turned his head away disgustedly.

'He's a trouper, is Otto. I think he's fine. But he won't go near the window and he whimpers if I try and take him outdoors.'

Flora sniffed the air, wondering how they were managing toilet trips if that were the case. She decided not to ask. 'And how are you feeling?'

'Oh, you know. Not great. But I have to keep my spirits up or they'll move me to the third floor. Like the Captain.' Joy shook her head and sighed. 'It was so sad to see him go up there. Once they've got you in Special Care ...' She shuddered and returned to her baguette.

'Oh, come on!' Flora wiped her mouth on a piece of kitchen roll and laughed. 'What is it with you lot and this third floor business? You talk as if there are horrible experiments going on up there or something.'

Joy tipped her head knowingly. 'Or something, indeed. It's where they send you to die, Flora, pure and simple. You move in here, into one of these lovely self-contained units, and they let you stay while you're young enough and fit enough to fend for yourself. But as soon as they see you're on your way out, that's it. You're off to the third floor. Everyone who goes up there dies within three months. Or less. You ask yourself why.'

Flora pulled a face. 'I know this sounds kind of insensitive, but could it be that most of the people who move to Special Care die so soon after because they're, well ... old? And sick?'

'Ah, yes. That's what they tell you. That's what they'd *like* you to believe. They say you need to move because there's all this special equipment in the rooms, hoists and such like, and the staff are specially trained. But that just makes it worse. For us.'

'I'm not following.'

'When you're my age all you have is hope. Hope and memories. When they send you to the third floor, what is there to look forward to? You know you're on your way out. You're next. So it happens, doesn't it? You just give up and die.'

'But it doesn't have to be that way, surely? Some of the people who move up there live longer than three months, don't they?'

Joy tapped her finger to her nose and made a pretend

zip across her mouth. Flora sighed and looked around the room. She noticed a collection of doggie paraphernalia and a canvas bag by the door – Otto's lead, his spare food bowl, a couple more toys. They sat on top of a list, written in Joy's spidery handwriting. *Breakfast, 6 am,* Flora read. *Walk and poopsies straight after.*

'Are you planning a trip?' Flora nodded at the list.

'No. Why?'

'Looks like you're leaving someone instructions for looking after Otto.'

Joy's face assumed a closed-off expression. 'As if I'd leave him after what just happened. How could you even think it?'

'Well, I–'

'He's everything to me, as well you know. I have to make sure Otto is safe. That's my number one priority.'

'I know that, I was only–'

'They're for you,' Joy said suddenly, almost shouting. 'I know what you're going to say but you must, Flora, you must. I can't keep him here any longer, he's in too much danger.'

Flora looked down at her hands. She watched a vein pulse near the base of her thumb. This had to be handled very carefully.

'Joy, is this about Mr Felix again? Because if it is–'

Joy jumped off the sofa, jolting Flora's arm and knocking her Subway into her lap. The old lady's handbag slipped to the side and landed upside down on the floor. Joy ignored it.

'You're a good girl, Flora. You look out for me like family, but there are things about me you don't know. I'm sure what happened to Otto wasn't an accident, and I'm equally sure that man was responsible. And I'm sure it's just a matter of time before he tries again.'

'Joy, I can't look after a dog. Not even for you. I'm

just not … I don't know what to do with dogs.'

She dropped to her knees to retrieve the contents of Joy's handbag, noticing as she did so that her friend wasn't wearing her gloves today and that her skin was raw and peeling. It was hardly surprising that the eczema had flared up after all this stress, but Flora's heart sank. What else would be flaring up soon? This wasn't a time for secrets. Flora sat back on her heels and nodded at Joy's hands.

'Have you told them yet?'

Joy tutted and turned away. 'He's no trouble at all. And I've written it all down for you.'

'I'll take that as a "no", shall I?' Flora scooped up the rest of the contents – tissues, antique mirror compact, ancient lipstick, humbugs, a purse the weight of a house brick – and plonked them back in the bag. The blue plastic tube she held on to, waving it in the air to get Joy's attention. 'I thought we'd talked about this. You can't keep something like chronic asthma a secret, not when you live in a retirement home.'

'Village,' said Joy stubbornly. 'It's a retirement village, and I am completely independent here, as you can see.' She swept her hand to take in the room, with its bed crammed in one corner and tiny kitchenette in another.

'Joy, what happened to Otto was a horrible accident. He must have jumped up and … well, who knows what really happened? But no one did this to you, or to him. I don't like to hear you talking this way. It scares me.'

Joy looked away. She sucked in her cheeks, then picked a piece of fluff off the sleeve of her pale green cardigan. 'Well, you'd better be going, I suppose. Things to do. People to see.'

Flora sighed and stood up. She noticed she'd dropped chilli sauce on her jeans, but doubted Joy would let her stick around and mop it up now. Should she take the blasted dog, just to keep her friend happy? It was out of the question. She'd never had a pet, and right now – still living in her mum and dad's old bungalow, feeling like an impostor in someone else's home – was not the time to start. Besides, Joy needed the pug with her. They were devoted to each other – they even wheezed in unison. She grabbed her bag and headed for the door.

'We're moving a new resident in on Monday,' she said brightly. 'Vera's a lot of fun, you'll love her. She's my best friend's great-aunt – you've heard me talk about Celeste, right? The one who's travelling?'

Joy grunted and shuffled to the door behind her.

'Oh, look! How lovely. Someone's brought you flowers.' Flora picked up the daffodils and handed them to Joy. The response from her friend was totally unexpected: Joy leapt back as though Flora had tried to thrust a knife at her, not a slightly droopy bunch of flowers wrapped in brown paper, and shoved the yellow blooms clean out of Flora's grip.

'Get rid of them,' she hissed.

'Joy, what on earth …?' Flora looked at the flowers by her feet, astonished to see Joy grinding the petals into the door step with one sturdy shoe. 'What on earth are you doing?'

'Not daffodils. Not narcissus. No.' She ground and stamped until the flowers were nothing more than a pulpy smudge of yellow and green. Flora lowered her head, trying to see Joy's face. Her expression was nothing less than terrified.

'Joy, what are you doing? What's going on?'

But Joy didn't answer. She was staring at a point over Flora's shoulder. Flora took another look at her face, then followed her friend's line of vision. The brown wrapping paper had fluttered away and was wedged in a bush across the path. The young maples rustled in the breeze, and another, more insistent buzz, sounded beyond them. Appearing and disappearing behind hedges as it motored along the path on the other side of the quadrant was a bright red mobility scooter, and bumbling across the tops of the manicured privet was the unmistakable pale ginger hair of Mr Felix.

Chapter 3

What is that boy doing out there in the van?'

Monday morning and Flora was at work bright and early, determined to start the week in a positive frame of mind. She would not let this Rockfords thing drag her down. Joy's close call with Otto, and her resulting weird behaviour and obvious paranoia, had played on Flora's mind all weekend. This morning she'd woken up with her priorities realigned. Shakers was a business. It didn't have to represent her father's hopes and dreams; she didn't have to feel so responsible all the time. All they needed to do was tighten their belts and start touting for new customers harder than ever before.

As for Marshall, Flora planned to do what she always did. Ignore him.

Which was harder than it sounded. Like now, he was sitting in her chair, which he knew drove her crazy, swinging his long legs and chatting on the phone: the office phone.

'What,' said Flora again, 'is that boy doing out there in the van?'

'Hold on a minute, sweetheart,' Marshall said into the receiver. Sweetheart? By the time he turned to Flora she was as mad as hell.

'If you don't mind me interrupting your personal calls, I just thought you might be able to shed some light on the fact that there's a strange man – well, boy – driving our van around the car park. If it's not too much trouble.'

Marshall rolled his eyes, whispered something into the receiver, then put down the phone. He said, as if talking to someone very stupid, 'That's Richie, isn't it? The new driver.'

'What?' Flora jerked her head to tell him to get the hell out of her chair. Marshall eased himself up in no hurry whatsoever. 'What new driver?'

'You're gonna have to keep your eye on the ball better than that, Flora. What with Rockfords coming and all ... you're losing it, girl.'

'Do not call me "girl". And I am not losing it – can you drop the attitude and tell me what's going on?'

'Richie is the new driver. Like I said. The one we advertised for when Harry retired.'

Flora flopped down into the vacated chair, which felt uncomfortably warm. Her face reddened as she processed his words. She had completely forgotten about the interviews they'd scheduled for last week. Which played right into Marshall's I-should-be-the-one-in-total-charge hands, damn it. Clearly Marshall hadn't forgotten, and clearly he'd just gone right ahead and held the interviews without her. *And* made the decision about who to take on.

'Where was I when all this was happening?' she said, mainly to herself. Marshall had the decency to look embarrassed.

'You were in Wales,' he mumbled.

Ah, so that was it. A week ago, Flora and her Uncle Max had visited Llandudno to mark her mother's birthday. Kitty Lively, born and raised in North Wales, always went to the seaside for her birthday, and Flora had chosen to keep up the tradition.

'I was only away for two days, Marshall.' She kept her voice low. 'You could have filled me in when I got back.'

He nodded. 'Honestly? I thought I had. Maybe you've been more distracted than you realise.'

'That's not fair, and you know it. Fine, it was my mum's birthday, but I'm dealing with it perfectly well, and I'm totally on top of things here. It's about time you got that into your stubborn head and stopped trying to undermine me at every opportunity.'

'I'm not trying to undermine you, Flora. You weren't here, simple as. And last time I looked it said Manager in my contract. I don't need to consult with you over every decision.'

There was no point pursuing it. Marshall was indeed stubborn, and Flora had too much on her mind to let herself get sidetracked into another pointless fight. Besides, there was a more important issue at stake.

'Well, you'll just have to go outside and tell Richie the job's no longer available, won't you? We can't afford to take on a new driver, not with the threat from Rockfords. We'll just have to make do as we are.' Flora walked over to the window and watched the van back into a space wide enough for four cars. 'What exactly is he doing out there, anyway?'

'Practising. He's a bit rusty driving a vehicle that size.'

Flora snorted. 'So not only did you give the job – of driver – to someone without even consulting me, you gave it to someone who's "a bit rusty" at driving. That's just great, Marshall. Just great.'

She marched out of the office, ignoring Marshall's annoying smirk, bounded down the metal stairs and stormed through the warehouse and into the car park, where the so-called driver was leaning out of the van's window, trying to get a better view of the bollard he'd just flattened.

'Oi,' Flora shouted. 'You in there. We need a word. Right now.'

But when the boy jumped down from the cab – and

he really was only a boy, no older than seventeen, surely, with pimply skin and pale hair that flopped in his eyes – Flora pointed back up the stairs. 'Marshall needs a word with you,' she said with a smile. 'There's been a change of plan.'

***

Flora pressed her forehead to the window and tried to block her ears. Richie's singing was torture. Marshall was in the back, hanging on to the straps with both hands, grinning at her in the mirror. Up front, sitting between Richie and her, Steve tapped at his mobile phone constantly; how it didn't make him feel totally sick, Flora couldn't understand.

'Don't you like Pink Floyd, Flora?' said Marshall, still grinning. 'Not your kind of thing?'

What I don't like is my employees blatantly taking the piss out of me, she thought. She said nothing, just stared out of the window and watched the countryside trundle by until her eyes glazed over. Marshall was in a funny mood today. It was best to ignore him when he was like this.

Monday lunchtime and they were moving another resident into Sleepy City. Vera lived out towards Bishops Castle in a crammed four-bed detached that she had somehow managed to pack up into enough boxes for a one-way trip to Shrewsbury and the delights of retirement at the Maples.

That Marshall had intentionally conned her over the Richie issue was something Flora was not going to forgive in a hurry, but as being angry with Marshall was about as satisfying as a Weight Watchers dinner, Flora was taking her temper out on Richie instead.

Who was oblivious, of course. Not the pimply youth Flora had assumed, Richie Baker was twenty years old, as bright as a dungeon and the favourite nephew of

Cynthia Curtis, the Maples' warden. Which explained, when Flora finally managed to get Marshall to discuss it with her civilly, why he'd been a shoe-in for the job.

'You're the one who wanted the crinkly contract. I thought this would keep his aunt happy and you'd be pleased.'

'Fine.' Although it was anything but. 'So why didn't you just tell me that in the first place?'

'I didn't get the chance. And I'm sick and tired of jumping through your hoops of disapproval every time I make a decision without you, okay?'

Well, no, it wasn't okay, Flora might have told him. And it was the whole "making decisions without her" thing that was the problem.

Flora knew she would have to deal with this sooner or later. Things couldn't go on as they were. With the threat from Rockfords, and the recession affecting business so badly, they could do without the sniping and the bad atmosphere at Shakers. Stuart had found himself another casual job, labouring for his builder brother, and Flora knew full well that Stuart hated his brother. Which just about said it all, really.

But at least that meant they could afford the new driver, just about. And Richie wasn't really so obnoxious – although his taste in music could do with fine-tuning, as could his singing voice. When Van Halen's 'Jump' started, Flora reached across Steve's lap and turned off the CD. There was only so much a girl could take.

'Aw, shucks, I was listening to that,' Marshall said.

Flora ignored him. 'We'll be there in a minute,' she told Richie. 'You'll need to concentrate on the directions.'

'Sure, babe,' Richie said. 'No problem.'

Oh, Jesus, thought Flora, determinedly not meeting Marshall's eye in the mirror. Could this day actually get any worse?

Vera lived on a modern housing estate in the middle of precisely nowhere – no shops, no pub, nothing. It was as if the developers had started to build a new village and then got fed up after the houses were finished. Or run out of money, more likely. Still, retirement and extreme downsizing beckoned. In her new home at the Maples Vera would have room for a bed, a sofa and not much else. When you really thought about it, what was the point in accumulating so much stuff throughout your life, when one day you would have to pack it all up and sell it, or just give it away?

Or worse, leave it all to your daughter who had diametrically different tastes to you and wished she could chuck it all in the bin but couldn't because she'd feel too guilty.

'Hello,' said Marshall, 'earth calling Flora Lively. We could do with a bit of navigating here.'

Flora shook herself out of her reverie and read out the directions to Richie.

When they arrived they found Vera sitting on a tea chest with a vacant expression on her face. Although Flora had been friends with Vera's great-niece since university, she'd only met the old lady twice before. Celeste's aunt was tall with a big-boned, spare frame. She wore some kind of caftan in an Aztec pattern, with a large cross draped around her neck. It was clear from the half-filled boxes and cluttered surfaces that she'd either run out of steam or was finding the task more onerous than she'd expected.

'Come on, let's go and get some drinks sorted.' Flora led the old lady into the kitchen, away from Marshall who looked fit to burst with frustration at finding the job half done. She suppressed a smile, and asked Vera if she had any biscuits. Marshall could damn well sort it on his own for once.

'Have you heard from Celeste lately?' Flora said,

tipping custard creams onto a china plate. 'I haven't had so much as a postcard since she left Melbourne.'

'I think she wrote to me last month, I'm not sure.' Vera began to search in a drawer overflowing with papers and magazines. Flora pursed her lips.

'I tell you what, why don't I get some boxes and help you pack up the kitchen while the boys are loading up the rest of the house?'

Vera nodded gratefully, stroking the ornate cross like a talisman. By the time Flora returned she'd made a tray of hot drinks and was perched on a kitchen bar stool that all but disappeared under the folds of her caftan.

'So tell me,' Vera said while Flora started on the kitchen drawers, 'why exactly is your company called Shakers? It's a rather odd name, isn't it? Conjures up images of one's precious belongings being shaken about in the back of that little van of yours.' She laughed nervously, then went back to sipping her tea.

Flora smiled. Their "little van" was in fact a seven-ton pantechnicon, inside which Vera's radically reduced possessions would indeed rattle around if they weren't well strapped down.

'Are your family religious, perhaps?'

Flora shook her head. 'It's nothing like that. My dad had a weird sense of humour, is all. It's called Shakers as in "Movers and ...". See?'

Vera face was blank. 'Not sure I follow.'

'Movers and shakers – it's a saying for people who are on the up. My dad started the business from nothing. He thought of himself as a bit of a mover and a shaker, I guess. And then with the moving reference ...? Well, anyway. Shakers it was.'

Vera seemed disappointed with the explanation. She picked up a yellow printed leaflet and began to read. Flora sighed and went back to the packing. By rights the contents of Vera's house should have been ready to load

– she hadn't paid for any extras – but Flora didn't mind. She had been hoping for some news of Celeste, though. The letter Vera had mentioned hadn't turned up yet, and the old lady didn't seem very interested in discussing her globe-trotting great-niece.

'So tell me more about the people at the Maples,' Vera said suddenly. Flora noticed that her hand as she set down the cup was shaking slightly. Poor old thing. A move like this, all on your own … it was enough to make anyone anxious. Making her face bright and encouraging, Flora described some of the residents, and mentioned the various classes and activities they offered at the retirement village. She told Vera about Joy, leaving out Otto's horrid accident and Joy's current obsession with poor old Mr Felix, of course. Vera's face broke into a smile when Flora recounted their trip to the funicular railway and how terrified she'd been.

'You are a silly. That journey up the cliff only takes about two minutes.'

Flora grinned and shook her head in a gesture of self-deprecation. 'I know. Celeste would despair of me.'

She carried on painting a picture of the Maples as the residence *du jour* for Shropshire retirees. Which it was, really. Whatever Marshall said.

Speak of the devil.

'If you've quite finished, we could do with a hand out here.'

Marshall, looking grubby and dishevelled – not so far from his usual look, just slightly hotter – appeared in the doorway and raised his eyebrows at Flora. 'You'd be more use in the van than standing here drinking coffee.'

'Oh, my dear man,' protested Vera, 'carrying furniture is not a woman's job.'

Marshall gave Flora a meaningful look and stalked away.

Idiot. Flora patted Vera's hand and said, 'Don't mind

him, he's American,' which seemed to do the trick. Mollified, the lady of the house leaned back against the counter top and sipped her tea.

Outside, the van was already half loaded. Flora jumped up and quickly surveyed the strapping down and the loading order to make sure all was okay. Richie sat in the cab reading a newspaper, taking his job description just a bit too literally, perhaps. Flora made a mental note to have a word with him about the more general nature of his role at Shakers.

Before long they were on their way, with Vera following in an electric blue motability super-mini.

'She must have some dosh stashed away,' Richie said as the old lady overtook them on the Minsterly Road. 'No family to help her move?'

'Most of her family live in Canada,' Flora said. 'She could have gone with them but she was too attached to the church.'

Richie had turned the radio on before she'd even finished her sentence.

Flora slumped back in her seat with a sigh. Marshall winked at her in the mirror, then lay back on Vera's sofa and closed his eyes. She smiled and shook her head, then put her hands over her ears trying – and failing – to block out Richie singing along to 'Bat Out of Hell'.

***

Vera's arrival at the Maples was marred somewhat by a grim piece of news, delivered in person by the warden herself.

'There's been another accident,' Cynthia said. She'd been waiting for them by the topiary arch, pulling Flora aside the minute she stepped down from the van. 'Another pet. It's a terrible coincidence, after Otto's little mishap, but this time it's far worse.' She smiled at Richie and gave him a little wave, which Flora thought odd until she remembered that Cynthia was Richie's aunt. The warden turned back to Flora just as Vera pulled into the car park behind them.

The warden waved to her newest resident, her smile still firmly in place. 'Your friend is on the warpath,' she whispered to Flora. 'I think you should have a talk with her. She's starting to make the other residents anxious.' With this cryptic warning, the warden nodded to Richie and walked off in the direction of the main building. Richie jumped down from the cab and followed without a word. So much for getting him to help with the unloading.

The residential units were arranged in a quadrant around a patch of well-tended garden the residents all shared. Newly planted maples in every variety dotted the area, not much more than saplings at the moment, but in twenty years or so they would provide privacy, shade and a riot of colour. Not that any of the current residents would be here to see them, Flora thought sadly, but at least efforts had been made to soften the concrete and the boxy architecture.

There was access to the rear of the properties, but it was strictly for emergency vehicles. Flora had queried the logic of this – it meant each new resident had to have their belongings carried through the gardens and along the gravel paths, not much fun for anyone in the rain, and not very practical either. But the warden was adamant: what if a resident was taken ill while Shakers' van was blocking the access road? Flora was too desperate to secure the contract to argue, much to Marshall's disgust when they moved in their first resident.

Which had been Joy, of course, and here she was now, hurrying across the courtyard waving her arms frantically.

'Flora, thank God you're here. It's happened again.

You won't believe it. This time it was Merlin, poor little mite. Electrocuted, he was. Right there in his bed while Dolly was at her yoga class. Dead as a door nail.'

'Yoga?' Vera had joined them by the arch. 'Oh, that's not my thing at all.'

Joy looked Vera up and down – Flora could see her taking in the bright caftan and the heavy iconography. Joy raised her eyebrows then turned back to Flora.

'Who ...?' she began. Flora dived right in, pulling Vera forward eagerly.

'Joy, this is the lady I've been dying for you to meet.' Oops, wrong choice of word in the circumstances. 'Vera, meet Joy Martin, my absolute favourite person in the world. She's been here for almost six months now, so if anyone can show you the ropes, she can.' Oops. Another bad choice of word, considering Otto's recent mishap. 'Joy, meet Vera – Vera's moving in today so she'll need someone to take her under their wing.'

She linked arms with Joy and started walking her back towards her own unit, calling over her shoulder to Vera, 'The boys will be ready to unload now, why don't you start showing them where you want your things?'

But they'd only taken three steps across the garden when Joy shrugged her off. 'What on earth was that all about, Flora? You're acting like a demented person.'

Flora sighed. 'Look, Vera doesn't need to hear anything upsetting, okay? It might really spoil it for her. Can't you remember how you felt the first day you moved in here?'

Joy shrugged and carried on walking. 'Do you want to hear what happened to Merlin or not? I know you don't really like dogs much, but–'

'Joy! That's not fair. I do like dogs. I think Otto is a little treasure.' Flora fell into step beside her friend. She smelt of soap and lavender, and Flora inhaled the scent as they walked. It reminded her of something intangible, like the memory of something you've never had. She picked a leaf off a privet hedge as they passed.

'Go on then, what happened to Merlin?'

'Oh, what's the point? You'll just say the same as the warden. He was old, he shouldn't have been chewing on the TV cable …'

They reached Joy's unit and Flora waited for her to unlock the door.

'You're wheezing,' she said as they stepped inside. 'Are you taking your tablets?'

Joy pushed the door closed behind them, gently nudging a yapping Otto back into his basket. She gave her pooch a loving pat, then turned to glare at Flora. 'I'm fine. Stop nagging. It's Dolly you should be concerned about, not me. Otto was lucky – we got back in time to rescue him. But it looks like Mr Felix is branching out, trying a different modus operandi. We need to figure out how to stop him doing it again.'

'Joy, please will you stop it with all this Mr Felix nonsense. Look at you – your skin's flaring up, your asthma's getting worse, and I'm still not happy about you keeping it a secret from the warden like this, no matter what you say about Special Care. I'm worried about you. Really worried.'

'You're worried? Try being in my shoes.'

Joy headed for the kitchenette and filled up the kettle: her reflex when under duress. The sight of her friend's pronounced back hunch brought a lump to Flora's throat. She remembered Joy confiding that getting her hair done was an ordeal, even with the specially designed basins at the Maples' on-site salon. The hunch got in the way, she said, and she never failed to get a complete soaking. But it was important to look nice, important to keep on top of her weekly shampoo and set, one of the little rituals that gave her a sense of security, of normality.

'Eddie would hate to see me without my hair done,' Joy had said. And even though Eddie had been dead six months, she had meant it in earnest.

'Of course, it's all my fault,' said Joy. Her words floated out of the kitchenette, rising along with the volume of the boiling kettle. 'Poor Merlin. Maybe if Aubrey had got what he wanted with Otto he'd have left Merlin alone. But now … I just don't know what I'm going to do.'

'What,' said Flora, leaning against the wall by the fridge, 'are you rabbiting on about?'

The kettle reached boiling point and clicked off. Joy turned to face Flora. She had tears running down her cheeks.

'It's my fault, that's what. It's my just desserts. I'm a terrible, terrible person and I'm going to be punished for my sins.'

Flora couldn't believe her eyes. Joy never cried. This was the woman who had been so stoical when she moved from her three-bed bungalow that Flora hadn't been able to sleep for a week, so touched was she by the woman's strength. She'd been married for fifty-nine years. Fifty-nine years seeing the same person every day, in the same home, sharing breakfast, sleeping side by side. And then one day he was gone, and she had to sell up because she couldn't bear to see the garden he had tended so lovingly – all one and a half acres of it – go to rack and ruin. She had to leave all those memories behind and move to a one-room unit in Sleepy City, and yet all day the woman had run around making cups of tea and offering biscuits and enquiring after Stuart's wife who was expecting their first child any day.

She was amazing, and Flora cared for her like family. But now she was breaking her heart because her friend's dog had suffered a tragic accident? Well, you didn't need a psychology degree to see that this was repressed grief.

41

Flora put her arm around Joy's narrow shoulders. The older woman felt frail under her layers of clothing. Her faded blue eyes, usually so bright and mischievous, were screwed up tight and disappearing inside wrinkled eyelids. Tears spurted out over her cheeks. It just about broke Flora's heart to see her like this.

'That's okay, Joy. You let it all out. It's time you did, that's all. You've been so brave, but it does you no good to hold it all in. I know what it's like, believe me. Eddie wouldn't want you to put on a brave face every day. It's fine to let it out.'

'What are you blathering on about?' Joy pulled away and looked at Flora as if she were the crazy person. 'Eddie? What's he got to do with all this?'

'Well ... I,' stammered Flora, 'I just thought, you know, you being so upset ...'

'Oh, Flora, you are barking up the wrong tree this time. Barking! I'm sorry Merlin, wherever you are. It was all my fault, but I'm going to try and put it right, I promise.'

Alarmed, Flora made her voice as firm as she could. 'Listen, Joy, you're not making any sense and you're starting to really scare me now. If you don't calm down and tell me what the hell you're talking about I'm going straight to the warden to ask her for help.' She bit her lip. 'You don't want her thinking you're losing it, do you? What about the third floor?'

This had the desired effect, and although Flora felt bad for using Joy's fears against her, she was relieved when her friend gave herself a little shake and turned to pour out the tea.

'You should sit down, Flora,' Joy instructed. 'There's something you need to hear.'

Chapter 4

I t was the summer of nineteen forty-seven.'

Joy brought the tea into the lounge area on a plastic tray covered with a flower-patterned tea towel. She laid it on the low coffee table. 'I've never told anyone about this. Not even Eddie.'

'Why not?' Flora kicked off her flip-flops and tucked her feet up under her legs.

'You'll understand when you've heard it all. Flora, what I'm about to tell you must stay between us. You must promise not to tell another soul. Do you promise?' Flora gave her friend a solemn nod. 'Okay. It all happened long before I met Eddie. During the war I was sent to the Grange – it was a boarding school back then, girls only, and I stayed until I was fifteen. My parents thought the city far too dangerous, but I was too old to be evacuated through the usual channels.'

'Where were you from, originally?'

'Manchester. But I never went back. Not permanently. After I left school I got a place in secretarial college right here, and then I met Eddie of course ... I'm going off at a tangent, Flora. Could you just listen and not ask questions?'

Flora pulled a face. 'Sorry.'

'So anyway.' Joy sat in the armchair opposite, her back to the window, her face in shadow. 'Nineteen forty-seven – the war was over, but women, like our English teacher Miss Lester, they were less than happy to see all the men coming back and taking over again. That's what she used to say to us – they're coming back to take over and we don't need them. We've managed fine without them until now.'

'She was a feminist?'

'We didn't know a feminist from a funfair back then, not in the circles I mixed in. But yes, I suppose she was by today's standards. A vicious one, too. She created a club, a secret society, and invited a select few girls to join.'

Flora sat up and smiled. 'Sounds exciting. A bit like *Dead Poets Society*?'

'I've no idea what you're talking about, Flora, but yes, it was exciting. She was charismatic, very striking to look at, and incredibly intelligent. She taught us about the famous women in history. She brought them to life in her lessons – we were in awe of her, all of us.'

'What was it called? Your secret society.'

Joy turned her head to the side. Her hands twisted around and around in her lap, clutching at something, some kind of belt.

'It was called the Joan of Arc club.' Joy swallowed and cleared her throat. 'It was all so innocent at first, you see. Just a way to feel special. We were closeted, kept away from the real world. My parents were well off, successful, but they'd had me late in life and they weren't all that interested in children. And the other girls, their families were the same.'

Flora wanted to reach across the coffee table and take her friend's hands in hers. She held back, sensing that Joy needed the distance. 'You were impressionable,' she said softly.

'Yes, that's right. We were impressionable.' Joy was silent for a minute, then she shook her head and carried on, her voice now quite different, almost detached. 'There were four of us, only four, in the club. Me, Dizzy,

Frances and Melody. Dizzy's real name was Daisy, but there was nothing dizzy about her. She was the ringleader ... She was very affected, very full of herself, was Dizzy. We all were. I was the last to join, always the newbie. That's why they ... Well, anyway. The club met once a week with Miss Lester in her tutor room and we talked about literature and how women were portrayed in the classics. We made up our own stories, alternative histories – I enjoyed that part. But mostly we talked about men.'

'About men?' Flora prompted when Joy fell silent. 'You mean, about men you liked? Fancied?'

'Oh no. Not that. About how awful they were, how they repressed us.' She laughed bitterly. 'We were plotting their downfall. It was Miss Lester's great dream, you see. To reduce men to the level of servitude that women had suffered for centuries.'

'She sounds hard core. Poisonous, even.'

Joy leaned forward and looked into Flora's eyes. 'She was. But Dizzy and the girls, they were worse. They were the ones who found the Venus Tree.'

'What? What was that?'

'Biscuits! Goodness – we can't have tea without biscuits.' Joy dived into the kitchenette, tea cup in hand, with Flora on her heels.

'Well, what happened then? What about this tree?'

Joy was on her knees, shuffling cereal packets and unopened boxes of crackers around the cupboard. 'I can't find any. Sorry, Flora. We'll have to make do without.'

'Joy, stop procrastinating and tell me about the bloody tree.'

Her friend stood with a huff and leaned on the counter, a hand resting on her lower back. She sighed. 'We used to meet there, in the grounds of the Grange. It's not important. But I fell foul of them, the other members of the club. And then I had to pass a test, I had to prove myself worthy again.' She shook her head, her eyes magnified by unshed tears. 'I never gave in to peer pressure again my whole life, Flora. Not for anything. But back then I didn't know any different. I just wanted to belong.'

When Joy paused, Flora became aware of the almost unnatural silence that had descended on Joy's unit. She felt as though they were the only two people in the world, wrapped up in a pocket of time, slipping back sixty-five years to witness – what? Just what had Joy done that haunted her so, all these years later?

'Go on, Joy,' she whispered. 'What was the test?'

'There was a boy at the school. The only boy we knew. He wasn't a pupil, of course – he was the caretaker's son. His name was Aubrey, and he was my friend.'

'Your friend?'

Joy nodded, her white curls bouncing on her forehead. 'Yes, he was. And they hated it, they teased me about it, but Aubrey was so lonely, and so kind and gentle. I had eczema really bad back then, there weren't the treatments for it like there are now. Now I take these antihistamine thingies every day, but then I just had to put up with it. I was hideous, with my skin all raw and flaky. I hated myself, could barely look in a mirror.'

'I'm sure you weren't that bad.'

'Well, I thought I was. But Aubrey didn't seem to notice. Or care. The other girls teased me, even my friends. But he never did. Not once. He said when he grew up he'd become a doctor and find a cure for me.'

Flora smiled. 'That was sweet.'

'He was very sweet. But he was a boy, and boys were forbidden – they were the enemy. I didn't know what to do, so I kept our friendship secret as much as I could.'

'Were you, you know – in love?'

'No.' Joy laughed, but sadly. 'I didn't know what that meant back then. Fifteen-year-old girls were far less mature than they are these days.'

Flora raised her eyebrows, thinking that young girls in general were probably not as different sixty years ago as Joy, the innocent, believed. But she said nothing. She sipped her tea and leaned closer. 'So, what happened with this Aubrey?' She remembered Joy's words from earlier. 'You mentioned Aubrey when you were talking about Merlin, didn't you? You said if Aubrey had succeeded with Otto he'd have left Merlin alone.' Hearing his name, Otto gave a low woof from the other room. 'You think Aubrey is here? At the Maples?'

Joy nodded. 'He wants his revenge.' Her voice was barely a whisper.

'But how? I mean, how could a boy from your childhood be here? And revenge for what, Joy? What did you do?'

'I don't know how, but he must have found me and moved in under a false name.' Joy's face was lit up now, animated. 'But he can't fool me. I knew it was him the moment I saw him. There's still something of the caretaker's son about him, don't you think? You can't fake good breeding, especially in your seventies. It's his trousers, you see. They give him away completely.'

Flora shook her head, trying to bring the sane world back into focus. She heard a noise outside, a faint shuffling, but she ignored it and pressed on. 'Joy, you are not making sense. Who is this caretaker's son?'

Joy's smile was grim. 'Mr Felix, of course. And now he's trying to hurt me, just like I ...'

'Joy, are you okay, dear?'

They turned as one to the doorway of the kitchenette. Framed in yellow sunshine was the warden. She smiled and stepped across the threshold. 'Ah, there you are, Joy. I've been looking for you. We're about to start the line dancing class if you're coming. Oh, hello Flora. Vera all settled in, is she?'

'Hi Cynthia. I'm just on my way to see how they're getting on.' Flora patted Joy's hand. 'Do you want me to walk with you to your class?' She was hoping to carry on their conversation out of the warden's hearing.

Joy shook her head. 'I've got to change first. Can't do the ankle rock in these, can I?'

They all looked down at Joy's slippers: two brown balls of fluff with doggie ears and little, woeful-looking doggie eyes.

'No, probably not,' said the warden, heading for the door.

'I'll come back tomorrow,' whispered Flora. 'You can carry on with your story.'

Joy nodded, still gazing at her feet. Then she gripped Flora's arm with surprising strength. 'Please think about taking Otto for me, Flora. Just for a little while. You're the only person I can trust. Mr Felix might have failed once, but next time … who knows what will happen?'

***

Flora found the warden in the dining room, huddled over by the hotplates with Richie. It took two Hellos for their heads to move apart and for the warden to acknowledge Flora's presence. Richie didn't even do that. She'd finally got Vera sorted, after moving her bed for the third time – who would have thought there were so many positions for it in such a small room? – and she was annoyed to see Richie so obviously skiving: he must be confident of avoiding a reprimand when the warden was effectively their boss.

'We're heading back to base soon,' Flora said, weaving her way across the room. 'Marshall's looking for you. He needs a hand stacking the boxes.' Richie shrugged and slouched away. The warden turned to

Flora with a tight smile.

'Joy's enjoying her class. Well done for calming her down.'

Flora could hear the faint strains of country music coming from the communal area. 'That's okay. I'm not sure I was much use really. Do you have time for a quick word?'

The aroma of roasting meat drifted from the kitchens. The long tables in the dining room were already laid for dinner even though it was only three o'clock in the afternoon. Flora found the white linen and vase of flowers on every table reassuring – it was these little details that made the retirement village the kind of place she felt comfortable moving lovely old folks like Joy and Vera into. The Maples' contract had made up thirty per cent of Shakers' revenue this past six months. Flora was grateful for the work, and knew she had to go carefully with what she was about to say. She didn't want the warden to think she was overstepping the mark.

'We'll have to walk while we talk,' Cynthia said, striding off in the direction of her office without waiting for an answer. 'I'm expecting a rather urgent phone call.'

Flora hurried to keep up. 'It won't take long. It's about Joy, actually. I'm worried about her. She's in a bit of a state. After what happened to Otto, and now the other dog. She's–'

'What happened to Merlin was an accident,' the warden said over her shoulder. 'He'd been chewing on Dolly's TV cable. Apparently for some time. It was an accident waiting to happen.'

'Poor thing.'

'Well, he was ancient, of course. At least fifteen years old. Shock like that might not have killed a younger dog but he wasn't in the best of health.'

Was fifteen old for a dog? Flora had no idea, but then you could write her knowledge of dogs on the back of a postage stamp.

'It might have been our fault, in a roundabout way.' The warden stopped suddenly next to a set of double doors and puffed out her weathered cheeks. Her wiry grey hair stuck out at odd angles – Flora couldn't tell if it was curly or just badly cut. 'We certify every item of electrical equipment on the premises, but I thought under health and safety regulations it only applied to company-owned equipment. Maybe I should look into that. I wouldn't want it to be down to our negligence. We're already having child-safety catches fitted on every set of blinds on the complex.'

'Well, that's good.' Flora was a little taken aback at the warden's attitude. Wasn't the most important thing to take care of the owner's feelings? Dolly must be in a terrible state, especially if her own frayed cabling was partly to blame.

'Look,' she said, running to catch up again as the warden strode away, 'it wasn't really Merlin I wanted to talk about. Joy's really scared of something, and although I can't say exactly what, I'd like you to keep an extra eye on her, if you don't mind.'

'Who?' The warden reached her office and put her hand on the door handle. All the doors at this end of the main building were solid oak, impenetrable. A brass door plate read: *Cynthia Curtis, Warden & General Manager.*

'Joy. That's who I've been talking about.'

'You want me to keep an eye on her? Why?'

Flora sighed. How much should she share? Joy had sworn her to secrecy, but the warden wasn't going to take Flora's fears seriously without some information.

'The other day she got a bunch of daffodils left outside her door. She totally freaked out about them, said they'd been left there to scare her. Started going on about narcissuses and stuff.'

'Narcissi,' corrected the warden.

'What?'

'The plural of narcissus is narcissi.'

'Right. Anyway, also she had the shock of finding Otto all tangled up in her blinds, which was obviously very distressing. She's not well, Cynthia. And she has to watch out for stress, with her ...' Flora tailed off. She shouldn't be the one to tell the warden about Joy's asthma. Her friend had reassured her it was under control, but had sworn her to secrecy on this too.

The warden was looking at Flora oddly. 'Why does she need to watch out for stress?'

Flora forced a laugh. 'Oh, well, no more than any of us does, I suppose. But she gets herself in a state about things. And then there's all this third floor business, isn't there?'

Flora only mentioned it to try and change the subject, but the warden's face hardened and she tipped her head to the side. 'What? What about the third floor?'

Keep digging, Flora. 'Only the silly nonsense they all talk about, you must have heard them.'

'No. Do enlighten me.'

'Oh, all that "no one who moves up there lives longer than three months" stuff. They're scared of losing their independence is all, you know how these rumours start.'

Flora wondered, as the warden turned a vivid shade of pink, how this particular rumour had started. The Maples village had only been open for a year.

'*Have* you lost a lot of residents from the third floor?'

'We've said a sad farewell to three wonderful people in the entire time we've been operational,' snapped the warden. 'And as you can imagine, they were each very elderly and infirm. Otherwise, they would not have been receiving special care.'

Not that special perhaps, thought Flora, but this time she kept her thoughts to herself.

'And I think it's best for everyone concerned that we don't feed these wild rumours. It can't be good for the residents' peace of mind.'

'No, of course not.'

'And if you are finding it hard to distance yourself from your contract here by being friends with Mrs Martin, maybe that's something we need to deal with.'

Flora nodded, understanding the warden perfectly well. Keep your beaky nose out. Or else.

'Sorry. I just wanted to ask you to keep an eye on her, that's all.'

'Which is exactly what I'm paid to do.' The warden turned her back on Flora and opened her office door. 'As for the flowers,' she said, turning around again, her face back to its usual expression of rosy-cheeked benevolence, 'maybe Joy has a secret admirer. Isn't she rather close to the Captain? I'm sure it's nothing to get in a tizzy about.'

Flora stood looking at the blank oak door for a full minute after the warden had closed it. Resisting the urge to stick out her tongue like a five-year-old, she turned on her heel and stalked off towards the exit. She rounded a corner and walked directly into a woman carrying a stack of magazines. The magazines went flying, and the woman nearly joined them.

'Oh, my goodness. I'm so sorry.' Flora dropped to her knees to help pick them up. She recognised the woman as the Maples' main receptionist, Elizabeth.

'No, it was my fault entirely. I wasn't looking where I was going. In a little world of my own, I was.'

Flora smiled, her tension ebbing away. The woman's long blonde hair was loose and flyaway, held off her face with a silver Alice band that would have been cool on a teenager but looked incongruous on a woman who must be pushing fifty. She'd noticed Elizabeth around, noticed her leopard-skin tops and maxi-skirts, and she'd certainly noticed Stuart and Steve noticing her too.

Elizabeth was an attractive lady, with a breathy voice and a distracted air. Just crying out to be rescued, Steve had said admiringly. And he was at least twenty years her junior.

'Here,' said Flora, passing over the last of the magazines. 'Where are you off to with these?'

'The medical centre – someone donated them this morning. We keep having to replace them over there, people are always stealing them.'

Flora laughed, and Elizabeth smiled uncertainly.

'Well, sorry again. I need to be more careful when I'm in a bad mood.'

Elizabeth looked concerned. 'What happened? Are you okay?'

'I'm fine. Just had a run-in with … Never mind.' Flora stopped herself in time. For all she knew the warden and her chief receptionist might be the best of friends. 'I was worried about a friend, that's all. But I'm sure it will all be okay.'

'Good. Well, thanks for helping with these.'

Flora watched Elizabeth trip away along the corridor. 'Can I ask you a quick question?' she called out on impulse.

'Of course.' The other woman turned and smiled openly. 'What do you need to know?'

'You have a resident here, a Mr Felix. Would you happen to know his first name?' Flora held her breath. What was she doing? Surely she was out of line even asking personal questions about a resident?

Elizabeth didn't seem to think so. She thought about it for a moment, hoisting the magazines onto one sharp hip. 'I know who you mean, but I can't remember his first name. He likes to be called *Mr* Felix,' she added with a smile. 'I see quite a lot of him, he's always having parcels delivered to reception, a new one every week. Vitamins, they are. He's obsessed with his health. The warden, she wasn't too happy about it. Said she didn't want the other residents getting ideas.'

'Ideas?'

'About the health benefits of vitamins bought over the internet. She runs a pretty tight ship, you know. Likes all that kind of stuff to go through her.'

I can imagine, thought Flora. She'd have a fit if she found out about Joy's secret stash of daily medication.

'But you don't know his first name?'

Elizabeth shook her head. 'No, sorry. Why do you need to know?'

Flora gestured vaguely. 'I wanted to send him a … birthday card.' It was the first thing that popped into her head.

'Ah. That's nice. I'll make sure we get him one too.'

Flora said goodbye and watched the receptionist walk away. She shook her head and headed for the exit. Mr Felix was clearly just a harmless old man with nothing more than the state of his health on his mind. Joy had too much time on her hands, that was the real problem.

She pushed through the glass doors and smiled into the sunshine. The sight of Marshall leaning against the wall with his arms folded, glaring at her, was so unexpected she forgot for a moment what she was doing at the Maples in the first place.

'In your own time, Miss Lively.' Marshall turned and stalked away across the quadrant. Flora had no choice but to follow meekly at his heels.

***

At least her love life wasn't as bleak as her work life. Flora hadn't dated anyone for over a year – a long time for a woman in her prime, but not for someone recovering from the loss of both her parents. Things had picked recently though, for reasons Flora didn't analyse too deeply. So far she'd been out on four dates with three perfectly eligible guys; men were indeed like buses, only much harder to catch when they were trying to get away from you.

No such worries with Heston. She'd totally given up on the bad boy vibe this time and was excited to be dating a librarian who thought the sun shone out of her tiny behind. Flora didn't really have a type – her mum had always said she wasn't fussy enough – but if she did, Heston probably wouldn't be it. With neat blonde hair and smooth fair skin that clearly didn't see much sunshine, Heston was almost as slight as Flora. But he was handsome, with a fine mouth and a chiselled nose and chin, aristocratic-looking and very clever.

And he was a secret. Marshall had made fun of both guys Flora had dated, and he'd only met one of them – an accidental bumping-into situation which had left Flora unaccountably rattled and making excuses to end the date early. The other had been ridiculed merely for his name, job, and the car he drove.

God only knew the mileage Marshall would have with Heston the librarian and his Volkswagen Beetle complete with fresh daisy in the dashboard.

She left work early on Tuesday to get ready for her second date with Heston. Her bedroom at the bungalow was not the one she'd occupied as a child – her parents had moved here when she left for university – but it was the only room in their house she'd managed to make her own. In here she had her vintage tailor's dummy and the patchwork armchair she'd made at night school during that phase when she'd been heavily into upholstery. The red and blue quilt on the bed was from yet another phase, as was the decoupage bird of paradise tray which sat on her grandmother's old dressing table, now painted and distressed in a fair approximation of shabby chic.

'Why don't you study something practical?' her parents had asked her over and over: as a child she'd been almost aggressively creative, making complicated collages and odd structures out of cardboard and bits of wool, held together by Scotch tape and sheer determination. But Flora had been adamant psychology was the university route for her. She needed to understand what made people tick. From the moment she found out, aged fourteen and already at the stage of incomprehensible insecurity, that she'd been adopted as a baby, Flora had been on a mission. Not to find her birth parents – she had no intention of going down that route, Kitty and Peter Lively must have been relieved to discover – but to find a way to make sense of the world.

She'd made them proud with her 2:1 in psychology, but the gap year she'd taken to help out in the family business had turned into two years, then four, then six. Her dreams of working as a counsellor had receded even further from her reach, and now she had someone else's dream to take care of. Besides, she couldn't even figure out how to stop an old lady obsessing about bunches of flowers, secret societies and canine catastrophes. She'd have no chance with a set of real problems.

She pulled a delicate floral-patterned dress from her creaky wardrobe, smoothing out the creases where the fabric had been packed in too tightly. For work, Flora always wore the same uniform of jeans and T-shirt; cut-offs if the weather was fine. She never made a conscious decision to hide her tattoos – the one on her thigh was a lot easier to hide than the one on her shoulder – but this particular vintage find had elbow-length sleeves, which was probably just as well. She wondered what Heston would think if she changed her hair colour. It had been its natural chestnut brown for too long and she was getting the urge for something brighter, maybe a pillar-box red. Flora looked in the mirror and thought about her mum. What would she have made of Heston?

'Should I dye my hair again?' Flora whispered.

What she really meant was: Will it make me a bad person if I start to move on?

It was warm for April, the opposite of an Indian summer, and Flora enjoyed the short walk into town. She wore her favourite sparkly flip-flops with the tea dress and carried a light wool cardigan in case it grew cooler later. She fairly bounced along the pavement, looking forward to an evening of easy conversation and mild adoration. Oh yes, there were definite benefits to dating a man who liked you a little more than you liked him.

Heston was sitting outside on the pizzeria's terrace, shielding his eyes from the sun with one pale hand. He was wearing a white linen suit, and the effect it created, together with his pale hair and translucent skin, was that of a ghost watching the world go by, insubstantial as a gust of wind.

His embrace was reassuringly firm though, as was the expression in his eyes when he kissed her on the cheek.

They ordered garlic dough balls and a bottle of white wine and sat back to take in the last of the sun. Heston held her hand as though it was made of china, stoking it occasionally with his soft, smooth fingers.

'How have you been, sweetie?' he said.

And the great thing was: he really cared.

Flora told him all about Otto's near miss, then spilled her worries about Rockfords and their imminent move into Shakers' territory. Heston sighed heavily and dropped her hand back into her lap.

'I do sometimes wonder about that job of yours.' He gazed off down the street to where two teenage girls with multiple piercings were posing languidly on a bench. She heard his soft tut, then he shook his head and looked back at her. Flora shifted uneasily and smoothed her dress over her flat stomach. She'd kept the belly-button ring, even though her other teenage rebellion piercings –

nose, eyebrow, the usual places – had closed up years ago. What would someone as straight-laced as Heston make of that?

'I mean, it just doesn't really seem to suit you.'

She brushed off a momentary feeling of irritation: he wasn't the first to question a woman being in charge of a removals company, and he wouldn't be the last.

'What do you mean, exactly?' she said, keeping her voice level.

'It's just that you're so feminine, so delicate. I can't imagine you hulking great lumps of furniture around the place. Don't you sometimes wish for something a bit less physical?'

Flora laughed. 'It's nice that someone sees me as feminine – I'm not sure about delicate, though. And Marshall would say that I'm not physical enough! He's always going on at me to pull my weight.'

Heston's expression tightened. 'That manager of yours sounds like an idiot. I don't know why you put up with him.'

'I put up with him because I have to.' Flora sipped her wine, then looked out across the terrace. 'He was my dad's choice, not mine.'

'Didn't you say he was American? What's he doing over here anyway?'

'He's my Uncle Max's stepson.' She smiled at Heston's confused expression. 'Marshall was nine when Max met his mum. My uncle was only visiting, but he ended up living in the US for ten years. Marshall's mum is a serial marrier – I think she's on hubby number six now. He's very sensitive about it.'

'I'm not surprised.'

'Max is probably the closest he's got to an actual father – he stuck around the longest. Anyway, Marshall was between jobs, came over here to visit with Max and while he was here Mum got sick.' She bit her lip, aware of the tremble in her voice. Heston stroked her arm gently.

'It's still pretty raw.'

She nodded, but didn't trust herself to speak. Heston, sensitive as always, filled the silence by telling her about his day at the library.

'We've started a book group for our older readers,' he said. 'One of our members is from that retirement village of yours. Felix, I think his name is. Mr Felix. Nice old chap, comes in on his mobility scooter. Looks a bit the worse for wear.'

Flora was wrong-footed for a moment, hearing that name mentioned again, and in such incongruous surroundings. But then she smiled, picturing Mr Felix and his wispy ginger comb-over. He did look the worse for wear, it was true. Heston no doubt preferred his old people spick and span, shirt and tie for the men, twinset and pearls for the ladies. He'd love the Captain, with his manicured moustache and shining medals.

But thoughts of Mr Felix brought her mind back to Joy and the story of her secret society. Poor old Joy – grief could certainly do strange things with your memory.

'Flora? Are you still with me?'

She gave her head a little shake. 'Sorry. Yes, a book group. That sounds like a lot of fun.'

Their pizzas arrived, but Flora couldn't keep her mind off the Maples. Or rather, she couldn't stop thinking about Joy's story of the caretaker's son. What *had* they done to him that was so terrible? If only the warden hadn't come looking for her at that precise moment.

Heston put his fork down and looked at Flora's plate. 'Not hungry, sweetie?'

Flora was on the brink of telling him about Joy's crazy accusations, vow of silence or not, when her phone rang. She slipped it out of her bag and answered, glancing sheepishly at the other diners.

'Hello?'

'Flora? Is that you?'

'It's Joy,' she mouthed to Heston as she pushed back her chair and walked to the edge of the terrace. 'What's wrong?'

'I'm afraid I've had a bit of an accident.'

'Are you okay?'

'It was just a fall. I'm not too bad, but I've hurt my hip.'

'Have you seen the doctor?'

'Not really. The thing is, Otto needs you.'

Flora turned her back to Heston and all the pairs of eyes boring into her. 'Joy, you need to go to the medical centre right away. Can you walk?'

'Oh, I have been. I'm fine, really. But I need you to take Otto for a few days. I won't be able to look after him properly. I'm feeling very stressed about taking him for walks, making sure he's okay ... You don't mind, do you?'

'Well, no, of course not, but–'

'That's wonderful, thank you. I'll have everything ready for you. Can you come right away?'

Flora walked back to the table, a knot of anxiety forming in her stomach. Heston jumped up to pull out her chair, ever the gentleman.

'What's wrong? You look like you've seen a ghost.'

'It's worse than that. I've seen my future, and it's not pretty.'

Heston raised one eyebrow.

'I have just,' explained Flora with a heavy sigh, 'acquired a dog.'

'Pardon?'

'A pug called Otto. Joy's had a fall – she wants me to take him in for a couple of days. She's totally paranoid about his safety at the moment, so I have to go over to

Sleepy City right now and rescue him or I imagine there'll be an uprising the likes of which Shrewsbury has never seen before.'

'Even during the wars with the Welsh?' said Heston, smirking.

'Funny.' Flora picked up a slice of pizza and looked at it disconsolately. 'I don't even like dogs, especially. I'm more of a cat person myself.'

'Me too.'

They looked at each other in silence.

'Do you want a lift? We can stop off at the supermarket for dog food.'

'Thanks, Heston, but I think I'll walk. If my life is going to be taken over by a small animal I need to enjoy my last moments of freedom while I can.'

She kissed him on the cheek and waved goodbye.

She didn't much like dogs, Heston didn't like dogs, and Marshall was going to have a field day with this. Why did her life have to turn so complicated?

And why hadn't she just said no?

Chapter 5

'Why didn't you just say no?'

Marshall reclined in Flora's chair with his feet on the desk, laughing at her plight, while Otto sat in her arms panting and wheezing like an old steam engine.

'I couldn't,' whined Flora, sounding a little like Otto had at five o'clock that morning when he'd scratched at her bedroom door to be let in.

'Why?'

Flora could see Marshall was genuinely bemused. He would never put himself out this way, especially if it meant turning over his house to an unwanted canine guest.

'I couldn't say no because a poor old lady's peace of mind depended on it,' she snapped. 'It's what friends do.'

Marshall shrugged. The gesture was so typically Marshall, so laid back and all-American, it made her want to slap him. She took a calming breath. It wasn't Marshall's fault she was a total pushover. She just didn't like having it pointed out, was all. Especially by him.

'Well,' he said, standing up and stretching his arms back like an athlete, 'we've got other things to worry about today. So little Oscar there will just have to behave, won't he?'

'Otto,' said Flora, trying to keep the irritation out of her voice. 'And he is behaving.'

'Only because you haven't put him down all morning.'

It was true that Otto didn't seem to like being anywhere but in Flora's arms. From the moment she'd taken him from a triumphant Joy last night, the pug had clung to her like a baby. She'd rocked him to sleep, then laid him in a makeshift bed on Joy's spare dressing gown, hoping the smell would be enough to keep him there all night.

She'd only got four hours, and now the lack of sleep was starting to take its toll.

Flora hoisted the dog up onto her shoulder and patted his back. 'So what's to worry about now?'

Marshall threw a newspaper across the desk. 'Page eight. Take a look'

Flora turned the pages with her free hand. When she reached page eight she nearly dropped the damn dog on the floor.

'Jesus! A full page ad? What are they trying to do, shut us down completely?'

Marshall gave another trademark shrug and got up to stand beside Flora. They looked down at the paper together.

ROCKFORDS INTERNATIONAL REMOVALS

Top Quality Removals at Rock-Bottom Prices

You've tried the rest, now try the best!!!

We do the work so you get to shirk!

Try our packing service – 50% off for new customers

'Fifty per cent off! Surely they can't make any money with an offer like that?'

'Maybe that's not their prime objective.'

'What do you mean?'

Another shrug. 'Getting customers seems to be what this is about, not making money.'

'But those customers are *our* customers. They've got

no right to undercut us this way.' Flora put Otto on the floor and hopefully pushed his nose towards a dish of biscuits. 'What are we going to do?'

'There's nothing we can do, is there? We can't match that offer. Just haven't got the manpower.'

Flora's head jerked up sharply. She was sure she'd heard Marshall put just a bit too much emphasis on the word "man", but he was still looking at the newspaper. Don't be paranoid, she told herself. Apart from teasing her about Otto, Marshall had been almost friendly today. Maybe he too was sick of the sniping. Whatever the reason, Flora wanted to enjoy the calm and not rock the boat.

'Maybe it's time to think again about some other ideas for the business,' she said. 'You know, like my removals counselling service?'

Marshall groaned. He picked up the paper, screwed it into a ball, then threw it across the room. It landed in the wire waste bin with a thunk. Bullseye.

So much for not rocking the boat.

Richie chose that moment to clatter up the steps and burst into the office, smelling of diesel and outdoors. Flora looked at the clock on the wall.

'It's almost eleven, Richie.' She tried to keep her voice light. 'Where've you been?'

Marshall dipped his head. She wasn't going to get any support from him, then. This was the first she'd seen of Richie all morning. Tardy was an understatement.

Richie dropped the keys onto the table. 'Took the van for a wash, didn't I?'

'Yes, you did – yesterday, after we'd finished moving Vera into the Maples. What have you been doing *this* morning?'

Richie was looking at Marshall, but when Marshall refused to return his stare he turned to Flora and shrugged. 'Was delivering leaflets, wasn't I? Drumming up new business.'

'Really?' Flora was surprised, but pleased. This showed initiative – maybe Richie would turn out to be a good worker after all. He was Cynthia's nephew, and she had a good work ethic. A bit cold-hearted when it came to pets, perhaps, but clearly good at business. Maybe Marshall *had* made a good choice.

But then she had another thought.

What leaflets?

'Which leaflets were you delivering, Richie? The Shakers ones ran out last year, and no one' – she looked pointedly at Marshall – 'has gotten around to printing any more.'

The only sound in the room was Otto slurping water from a bowl.

'Well, anyway, better go sort out the packing crates,' said Richie.

'I'll come and help you. They're in a right mess.' Marshall jumped up.

Flora smelt a rat.

'Just hold it right there, you two,' she ordered. They stopped by the door, Marshall a foot taller than Richie but his body language just as tense. 'Would someone like to tell me what's going on here?'

Neither one of them would meet her eye.

'Richie? Where exactly were you delivering these mystery leaflets?'

'On the industrial estate.' The words were out of Richie's mouth before Marshall could nudge him silent. Flora looked at them both, confused. Then realisation dawned.

'Marshall Goodman. You are just the worst, the most sneaky, underhanded person I have ever met!'

'Oh, come on, Flora,' Marshall said, clearly deciding the best form of defence was attack. 'If I'd told you, you'd have said no way. We have to do something –

business is going real badly. If we don't branch out soon there'll be no business left.'

'But it's not for you to decide, is it? This is *my* business, not yours. I'm sick of this, Marshall.'

'And I'm sick of you sitting on your skinny ass all day doing nothing about it.'

'I'm not doing nothing!' Flora tried to keep the wail out of her voice. 'I've had loads of ideas and you veto every one.'

'Like you veto all mine,' he countered stubbornly.

'Guys?' They turned to face Richie, who backed away, hands raised as if in surrender. 'I'm, like, outta here. You two have issues.' Grabbing the keys off the table, he made for the door and paused at the top of the steps.

'By the way,' he said over his shoulder, 'your dog's gone. Little bleeder snuck out ages ago.'

***

By the time they located Otto – fast asleep under the wheels of the van, nearly giving Flora a heart attack ('What is it with all these suicidal dogs?' Marshall joked) – it was nearly lunchtime, and Marshall suggested they call a truce and walk into town for something to eat.

'My treat,' he said.

Flora allowed herself to be persuaded, placing Otto carefully in her tote bag with his little head poking over the side. Really, his constant panting must be the sign of some illness. Pets taking after their owners was one thing, but surely Otto couldn't have asthma too? She made a mental note to tell Joy to take him to the vet. Once she managed to persuade the old lady that her pooch wasn't in mortal danger and offloaded him, of course.

They walked side by side up the hill, Marshall keeping to the outside of the narrow pavement, nearest the road. Whenever they met a pedestrian coming the other way and had to move off the kerb to make room, Marshall's arm hovered at her back protectively. Did he think she was so feeble she'd just fall into the road without him there? She gritted her teeth and tried not to let her irritation show.

Marshall was oblivious. 'You know, Flora, I haven't got anything against the handyman thing–'

'Handy *person*. And it's not just about fixing things up. It's a whole removals counselling service. You know, helping them with the stress of moving. Putting up curtains and hanging pictures and stuff is only part of it – I'm talking about offering a service that takes care of everything. Mail redirection, new utilities, things like that, but also someone to talk to when it all gets too much. You *know* how they get. I really think it would help.'

'Right. It's just, would they be willing to pay for it? I know you want to put your degree to good use and all.' He tailed off. Flora could read his mind: Why don't you put your degree to good use and leave me to run the business? She set her face determinedly forward and fixed her eyes on the castle ahead. Marshall sighed. 'I just don't think it's got the same money-making potential as my idea, is all.'

Marshall's idea, as Flora had heard many times before, was to branch out into commercial storage. Shakers owned some lock-up units out Telford way, currently rented for a pittance to people who had too much furniture for their overcrowded homes. Marshall's brainwave was to kick these people out and offer secure storage to local companies, complete with archiving and retrieval.

'It's big business,' he told her the first time he brought it up. 'I've done a cash flow forecast – it could make a huge difference to us.'

Flora hadn't so much as glanced at the figures. She'd dismissed the idea straight off. Why? Because she liked dealing with people, she told him. That was Peter Lively's vision for Shakers and so it was also hers. She wasn't about to go all corporate and sell out. No matter how tight things were.

Maybe Marshall was justified in being pissed off with her – or just "pissed", as he would say – but her plan was equally viable. And had been dismissed just as categorically by him.

They were at an impasse, with Flora not about to make the first move. She decided to change the subject: Marshall wasn't the only one who could go on the attack.

'For someone who's so concerned with the bottom line, you don't seem too bothered about Rockfords and their imminent theft of all our customers.' She stepped to one side to let a woman with a pushchair pass and Marshall's hand went up to her back as if on elastic. 'And will you please just give it a rest with the whole gallant gent crap?'

They'd walked another couple of yards in silence before Marshall stopped dead in the middle of the pavement, a great immovable object in the stream of lunchtime shoppers.

'You know what, Flora?' His voice was so low she had to lean in and crane her neck to hear. 'You can go to hell.' And with that he struck off back down the hill, and Flora wouldn't have stood a chance of catching him up even if she'd wanted to.

Which she certainly did not.

Flora decided to take a detour of her own. She would go to the one place where she might get some sympathy, or at least where it was guaranteed to be quiet.

'Come on, Otto,' she said to the sleeping dog. 'Let's go visit your mummy.'

Flora planned to grab something to eat at the Maples, after Marshall had reneged so grumpily on his offer of lunch. She headed towards the main block, her nose sniffing out today's special. Otto sat in her bag, panting and snuffling as though he had just run a marathon.

But in the main building the comforting smell of home-cooked food was oddly absent. And it wasn't the only absence: when Flora reached the dining area she was amazed – and a little perturbed – to find it empty. The tables were set, each with clean napkins and shiny silver cutlery and the Maples' trademark vase of flowers in the centre, but the chairs around each table were still neatly arranged and untouched.

Flora's stomach turned over uneasily. You don't deprive the over sixties of their lunch routine and get off lightly. The residents of Sleepy City set their clocks by mealtimes.

She exited the dining room through the rear doors and made for the corridor which led to the warden's office. If anyone knew what was going on it would be Cynthia. But Flora stopped short in the central lobby, where a crowd had gathered at the foot of the stairs. As the retirement village had only been open a year and was still to reach capacity, Flora guessed its entire population was standing in the cramped lobby, along with most of the staff. A few muffled sobs reached her ears above a low hum of voices. All she could see were the backs of people's heads – a dazzling display of bald patches and comb-overs and perms rinsed in blue and silver.

Vera was leaning against the library door with a dazed expression on her face. Flora hurried over.

'What's going on?' She craned her neck to try and see. Damn being so short she needed stepladders to bolt her own front door. She considered dropping to the floor for a better view, but decided against it.

'I think he's dead.' Vera looked ready to faint.

'What?' Flora grabbed Vera's arm and led her to a nearby armchair. The old lady fanned herself with a copy of *Shropshire Life* while Otto was attached to his lead and stowed safely behind the magazine rack.

'What happened? Was it another accident?' Flora recoiled when Vera nodded. Not again! The Maples was becoming a dangerous place to keep a pet, and this would only feed into Joy's paranoia about Mr Felix and his supposed vendetta. She pushed a cone of water from the cooler into Vera's hand and went to investigate. Nudging through the outer layer of the crowd, she found Mr Felix leaning on a crutch holding a soil-stained trowel and looking, at most, only vaguely interested.

Taking this as reassurance that the calamity wasn't too great, Flora said, 'So which poor mutt's bought it this time?'

Mr Felix regarded her coolly. 'I hardly think that's an appropriate way to talk about the Captain, young lady.' He raised his eyebrows and turned away. His hands were filthy, as were the hems of his trousers. Flora took a second to process his words. The Captain? *An appropriate way to talk about the Captain?*

With a mounting sense of dread, Flora pushed her way to the front of the crowd. At the foot of the stairs were two medics dressed in Maples-issue white uniforms with bright red insignias on their backs. They were working in tandem, one holding the Captain's head while the other pumped his chest. From Flora's vantage point one thing was clear: the Captain wasn't breathing.

***

'Oh, my God.'

Flora was barely aware she'd spoken. That the Captain wasn't responding to the medics' ministrations was horribly obvious, and Flora fought the urge to jump in and try to help. But what could she do? She knew nothing about first aid, was squeamish over a paper cut.

She took a step back. The voices of the medics continued, low and authoritative, encouraging, holding her attention hypnotically. In her peripheral vision, Flora could see one of the Captain's medals a couple of feet away from his flung-out hand. She recognised its shape, the distinctive silver wings. It should have been pinned carefully to his proud chest, not discarded on the polished tile floor while the brave man who had received it lay staring blankly into nowhere. He wasn't asleep. He wasn't unconscious.

He wasn't really there at all.

Instinctively Flora looked up, as if following his lead. High above, three U-shaped balconies curved around the lobby's walls. The ceiling beyond was a wide glass roof lantern, flooding the balconies with natural light. Flora had moved two residents into rooms on the first floor. Semi-care, they were called, with more on-tap services than the self-contained units around the quadrant outside the main building. The second floor contained a variety of multi-purpose rooms and offices, along with the guest accommodation for visiting relatives. Above that, the Special Care rooms. The third floor.

Where the Captain had been moved a couple of months ago.

Someone took her hand – an old lady called May, or possibly Mavis – and they stood side by side in silence. Flora's ears were ringing, a low hum that signalled her desire to escape this reality, slip sideways into a different one. It had been exactly the same the day her mother announced she had cancer; the same again when she'd gotten news of her father's heart attack. Ringing. Blocking out the real world. If only such a thing were possible.

The scent of flowers on the nearby lobby table was overpowering. Flora dropped her companion's hand and took another step back. She could sense by the slowing down of their movements, by a subtle shift in the air, that the medics had run out of options. The backs of their necks, red from effort, held a grim stiffness. The murmuring of the waiting crowd grew louder.

Flora forced back a sob. A sudden queasiness made her head spin; she reached out blindly to steady herself against the wall. Not dead. Surely not. Not the Captain. She'd spoken to him only the other day; he'd been picking a flower in the gardens for his buttonhole, had given her a rakish grin and doffed an imaginary cap as she passed. She looked up at the balconies above, and then down again to where the Captain now lay.

Had he fallen?

She looked up again. Not from there, surely. His position was wrong. Without knowing how she knew, Flora was sure of that much. Besides, there was no evidence of a violent impact. Her mind shrank away from imagining what such evidence might have looked like, and she shivered involuntarily at the thought. Of course, he might not have fallen at all – he could have collapsed right there next to the table with the flowers and leaflets. She shivered again. It shouldn't have been so shocking to come across death in a retirement village. She needed to get a grip, quell the rising nausea and sense of panic that threatened to overwhelm her. She forced herself to stare at the leaflets in front of her. The text blurred together and swam in and out of focus. *Line dancing. Pilates. Bobby's Bingo.*

The line dancing notice made her think of Joy, and she looked around for her friend, the panic rising again. But then she remembered: Joy had had a fall of her own. She would be devastated when she heard about this.

The medics were standing now, and one of them

72

produced a scratchy-looking grey blanket and handed it to his colleague. Flora couldn't bear to watch. She spun away. The warden was standing right behind her.

Too shocked to speak, Flora simply stared at the older woman, her eyes a question mark.

'He fell,' said the warden quietly. 'Down the stairs.'

Flora waited a beat, then turned back to look at the stairs, trying and failing to avoid seeing once again what lay right in the centre of their wide first step. The Captain was covered now, which seemed worse somehow than seeing his staring eyes and his carefully combed hair and useless curled up fingers. She forced her gaze beyond where the medics were lifting him onto a green fold-up stretcher and considered the stairs. It helped to have something else to think about.

'But how?' She hadn't been addressing the warden directly, but Cynthia took it upon herself to answer.

'He tripped. Right at the top there. He started down, but he wasn't using the handrail. He tripped,' she said again. A faint tut escaped her lips.

'You saw it happen?'

The warden nodded. 'Nobody else was here. There was nothing I could do. The medics were on the scene in seconds. But ...'

They watched the medics lift the Captain off the ground in one smooth, practised movement. The crowd of onlookers parted, carving a path from the foot of the stairs to the back exit, a direct route to the medical centre. And then what? thought Flora. What would happen to him now?

'Move back, please. Move back.' The taller medic, walking backwards, nodded to the warden, who gave herself a sudden shake as if waking from a dream.

'Come on now.' Suddenly she was officious, back in charge. 'Everyone should go to their rooms until someone comes and gets you.' Like they were children.

'Lunch will be served in half an hour. Everything is under control.'

The residents obeyed meekly, not one of them grumbling about lunch. Their faces were white, their expressions flown open. Death must be held at bay, not seen close up and personal.

The staff scurried away, all wearing the same resigned expression. As the warden started to move with them, Flora touched her lightly on the back. 'What happened?' she said again, trying to keep her voice steady. She meant, how did it happen? How could it happen, especially to someone so dear and dignified as the Captain? But the warden clearly wasn't one for subtext. She shook her head and told Flora again that he had fallen down the flight of stairs from the first floor.

'Was he ill? Did he trip?'

But Flora was talking to the warden's retreating back.

Alone in the lobby now, she looked across to where she'd left Vera and Otto. The easy chair was empty, with Otto peering out from behind as if waiting to see if the coast was clear. Something shiny on the tiled floor caught her eye. She bent and picked up the Captain's medal, blinking back her tears. Its wings glinted in the sun from the roof lantern high above. She could picture him so clearly, standing in the garden with his pink rose, his moustache neatly combed, his medals polished and pinned just so.

Did he comb that moustache every morning? When he dressed today in his suit and tie and pinned his medals proudly to his chest, there was no way he could have known he would end up lying under a Maples-issue blanket before the day was out.

Clutching the medal so tightly it bit into her flesh, Flora sank to the floor by Otto's side and rested her head on her knees. She wrapped her arms around her legs and rocked gently. She thought about the morning her mum had gotten ready for that first, devastating appointment with the doctor. How could Kitty Lively have known when she put on her make-up that by the time her husband came home from work her mascara would be washed away by tears, her lipstick chewed off a hundred times over?

It was the not knowing that did it. The getting on with the most mundane of tasks without the faintest clue of what was around the corner. Flora pressed her face into her hands and let the tears fall. She cried for the Captain, and for her mum and dad. But underneath it all, she cried for herself.

Chapter 6

So, let me get this straight. You're saying that the Captain didn't fall down the stairs at all. You're saying he was pushed. And naturally it was all Mr Felix's fault. The guy you don't like because his trousers are too long.'

Flora was beyond tired. Forty-eight hours after the Captain's death and she was still feeling totally flattened by the news. She hadn't had a good night's sleep in three days due to Otto's midnight wanderings, and she was not in the mood to indulge her friend's fantasies for a second longer.

But Joy nodded vigorously, failing to notice Flora's abrasive tone. 'Yes, exactly. Except for the trousers bit. I thought I'd explained it to you, Flora. Mr Felix is really Aubrey, the caretaker's son. Don't you remember?'

'Of course I do.' Flora groaned. Remember? Joy's ridiculous stories were indelibly inked on her brain. 'But I still don't believe it. Mr Felix is nothing but a harmless old man. And he's pretty ancient himself, in case you haven't noticed. Not to mention disabled. No, I'm not saying that all pensioners are past it, you don't have to look at me like that. I just can't see him being capable of any of the things you're accusing him of. Otto, Merlin, the Captain ... If you want my honest opinion, you're being really unfair.'

'You don't believe me,' Joy said sullenly.

Flora knew she needed to tread carefully. Her friend's

arms and neck were showing signs of a serious flare-up and her breathing was almost as laboured as Otto's. After everything she'd been through in the last six months, the Captain's death might easily prove to be the last straw. Mentally as well as physically. She looked at the bare windows and thought again about Otto tangled in the blinds. Right now he was probably being spoilt rotten by Vera, who'd offered to take him for walk while Flora visited with Joy. Flora decided to cut her friend some slack. She'd been through a lot. It was time to talk it through with her properly, let Joy figure out for herself that her theories were way off target.

'Okay, let's say, just for argument's sake, that you're right.'

Joy's eyes lit up and she leaned forward conspiratorially. 'Go on.'

'What do you think happened on the day of the accident? You think Mr Felix had a tussle with the Captain at the top of the main stairs for all to see? Then slipped out into the garden to dig up some weeds, creeping back after the act to remove himself from suspicion?'

'What do you mean?'

'I saw him in the lobby, Joy. He'd been gardening, it was obvious.'

'Probably burying the evidence.'

Flora tutted impatiently. 'Look, even if it *was* Mr Felix, who you think is really Aubrey, and who has held a grudge against you for sixty-odd years and tracked you down to right here, right now, and is hell bent on revenge for something you did to him years ago – something you still haven't told me about, by the way – why on earth would he want to hurt the Captain?'

It was all ridiculous, of course. But Flora still couldn't get her head around how it *had* happened. The Captain had been the very antithesis of clumsy or unsteady, as sure-footed as a mountain goat. And he was a rule follower. The Maples rule was to hold the handrails or use the lift. There were safety signs all over the main building, the warden was obsessive about safety.

And the Captain had been obsessive about following the rules.

But maybe he'd been ill. Or he'd fainted. He *was* very old, after all.

Joy grimaced, still considering Flora's question. 'Actually I was hoping you'd ask me that. I know exactly why he did it. It's because the Captain and I were, you know—'

'Really?' Flora's eyes grew wide with astonishment. 'You and the Captain were ... together?'

'No!' Joy slapped Flora hard on the hand. 'Keep your dirty thoughts to yourself, young lady. My poor Eddie's not been gone five minutes, we're two weeks away from our wedding anniversary! Anyway, I'm hardly likely to be getting up to that kind of thing at my age. And the Captain was almost ninety. Show some respect.'

'Sorry,' Flora said meekly. But she thought, *Why not?* Flora hoped she herself would be getting up to that kind of thing at ninety. God knows she wasn't getting up to much of it at twenty-nine.

'We were friends. We played chess together and listened to the Friday play. The Captain had a fine mind, an enquiring mind, and he was a very spiritual person. Lately he'd been talking a lot about some kind of charity – he really was the most ... Sorry.'

Flora passed Joy a tissue then looked away, giving her friend a chance to regain her composure. She reached into the pocket of her jeans and pulled out the Captain's medal. Silently, she handed it to Joy.

'I found it,' she explained. 'There was no one around for me to give it back to. I thought ... I think he would have wanted you to have it.'

Joy took the medal and held it to her cheek for a second. Then she jumped up from the sofa and rushed off to the kitchenette. A moment later Flora heard the tap go on, the click of the kettle. She moved to stand in the doorway and watched her friend with a puzzled expression. Something about the way Joy was moving bothered her. And then she had it.

'Joy Martin! You told me you'd had a fall. There's nothing wrong with you, is there? Look at you, you're walking fine!'

In the kitchenette, Joy froze, then staggered a little and held out her hands as if to steady herself on the counter. Flora shook her head.

'No way, I'm not falling for that. The whole thing was made up just to get me to look after Otto, wasn't it? I thought you were quiet when I came to get him, but I just figured you felt bad about dragging me halfway across town so late. I can't believe you would manipulate me like that.'

'You were too stubborn to just take the poor mite and keep him safe. I had to do something.'

'Joy, if I truly thought he was in danger I'd have taken him in a flash. But he wasn't. He still isn't. What happened was–'

'An accident. Yes. That's what you all think. But I know different.'

Flora put her hands on her hips and threw out a challenging glare. 'How? And I'm going to need more than a tale of some schoolgirl club if you want me to believe you. I need hard evidence, Joy. This has gone far enough.'

'I've got all the evidence you need right here.' Joy bent for a second, reaching inside the cupboard beneath the sink, then she stood triumphantly, clutching a bunch of drooping daffodils and a white envelope.

'More flowers. Very nice. And the evidence you

mentioned?'

'This is it. Don't you remember I got flowers just after Otto's accident?'

'Yes. I remember you grinding them into the path with your shoe.'

'Exactly. And yesterday, the day after the Captain's … well, these were on my doorstep.' Joy pulled Flora over to the sofa and thrust the flowers into the waste bin by her side. 'This time there was a card as well.'

Flora held out her hand for the envelope. It held an illustrated postcard, the type you could buy from any art shop, showing a scantily-clad woman standing on a giant seashell.

'Classy,' Flora said. She turned the card over and read: *Sorry for your loss.*

'What do you make of that?' Joy sat back with her hands laced together. She seemed to think she'd presented Flora with some kind of fait accompli.

'Someone feels sad for your loss?' Flora shrugged. 'I'm clearly not seeing what you're seeing.'

'How well do you know your Roman mythology, Flora?'

'Just the usual. Apollo, Zeus and the rest.'

'They're Greek. Venus was a Roman goddess.'

'Oh.' Another shrug. 'So?'

'So this is a picture of Venus. Do you remember the name of our tree? The special place we used to meet in the grounds of the school?'

Flora shook her head. But she was lying. She remembered perfectly well.

'We called it the Venus Tree. Something Aubrey knows only too well. And the daffodils, they're also known as narcissus, aren't they?'

'Joy, I'm sure all this means something to you, but–'

'In *Greek* mythology, Narcissus was a man who fell in love with his own reflection. Venus the goddess of love, falling in love with your own reflection, can't you see the connection?'

'Well, I suppose, but there's a–'

'There's more.'

Flora slumped back into the squashy sofa. She'd had a feeling there might be.

'You've probably never heard of the epithet meaning "lucky Venus" have you? Or the statue of Venus by the same name? In the Vatican?'

A shake of her head was all Flora could manage.

Joy pulled herself up onto her feet and planted a hand on each thigh. 'Venus Felix, Flora! And I'm guessing that Aubrey isn't as ignorant as you, which is exactly why he took that name. Don't you see?'

Frankly, Flora didn't see at all, but the one thing she could see with crystal clear vision was that Joy had it all figured out.

Which was pretty scary, however you looked at it.

***

Flora made some coffee for herself and strong tea for Joy, using the time to try and organise her thoughts. Her friend was overwrought, seeing conspiracies everywhere she looked, finding hidden meanings in innocent messages. She was perched on the arm of her easy chair now, her hand fluttering up to her chest every few minutes to steady her breathing. She'd already had two puffs of her inhaler, and Flora knew for a fact that Joy restricted its use to occasions when she was having real difficulties breathing. She stirred milk into her coffee and watched from the kitchenette.

This couldn't go on. Never mind this supposed caretaker's son – if Joy didn't calm down soon she'd be a danger to herself. The thing to do was talk it through calmly and try to get to the bottom of what was really eating away at her. If she could get it off her chest, maybe she would start to see her theories for the crazy ideas they clearly were.

Guilt could be so eroding. Something Flora knew only too well.

She took the tray into the lounge and laid it on the table. The flowers, crushed in on themselves inside the small waste bin, gave off an unpleasant smell. Flora pushed the bin away with her foot.

'Joy, I want you to tell me straight – are you still taking your medication?'

'Yes! Of course I am. I take it every day, just like the doctor told me.'

'Your skin is getting worse, and so is your breathing. You must have noticed.'

Joy held out her hands, palms up. 'I don't know what to tell you, Flora. I take the tablets, but you're right, it does seem to be getting worse. Maybe this latest batch isn't working so well. They do look a bit different.'

'Different how?'

'Just, I don't know, maybe bigger? And they taste a bit funny.'

Flora laughed. 'Aren't you supposed to just swallow them, not eat them?'

'Anyway, it's nothing to do with the tablets. It's all this stress and worry. You know it's bad for my asthma.'

'Well, exactly!' Flora shook her head in exasperation. 'Which is why I keep trying to talk some sense into you. You've got to stop getting all worked up about Mr Felix and see things clearly.' She pointed to the Venus postcard which Joy had propped up on the dresser. 'It's just a card, Joy, and a bunch of flowers. Maybe Mr Felix did send them – maybe he *likes* you.'

Joy shuddered at this. She picked up her tea and sipped it. Flora decided to push her luck a bit further.

'If you really think Mr Felix is trying to hurt you in some way, what I don't understand is why? Yes, I know you think he's the boy from your past–'

'Aubrey. And it *is* him. I don't just think it.'

'Fine, but what exactly did you do to him? Why on earth would he want revenge against you of all people?'

Joy's lips thinned into a defiant line. She put down her cup and walked over to the window, resting her hands on the sill.

'Besides,' Flora said, 'you're forgetting one important fact.'

'What?' Joy didn't turn around.

'What happened to the Captain had to be an accident. The warden saw it happen, she told me herself. He tripped. He wasn't using the handrail. So there's no way he could have been pushed.'

Joy seemed to deflate even further. Flora got up and patted her friend on the shoulder. She looked out at the gardens and saw Mr Felix chugging along the path on his mobility scooter, stopping every few seconds to pick up litter with an extendable grabber. He shoved the offending items into a black bin bag and then moved on grimly, his face set with disapproval. His faded red hair had come away from its comb-over and was flapping in the breeze like the flag of old age.

That man, thought Flora, couldn't hurt a fly.

She turned back to Joy. 'I'm sorry to have to be the one to point this out, but didn't you say yourself that everyone who moves up to the third floor is dead within three months? Although I'm sure you were exaggerating, the fact remains that the Captain must have been ill. Even if he didn't tell you.'

Flora looked at Joy's face, trying to read her expression. 'He fell, Joy. It was a horrible accident. Nothing more.'

Joy made a humphing sound and mumbled, 'Proves my theory about the third floor though, doesn't it?'

'And if you don't want to end up there yourself,

83

you'd better get over to the doctor and come clean about your asthma,' Flora said, taking the opportunity to ram her point home.

Joy turned on Flora, her face a picture of fury. 'Stop going on about my asthma! This isn't in my imagination. This isn't some problem that can be fixed with a bit of counselling and a new course of tablets. You have to start taking this seriously before it gets any worse.'

'Then give me a better reason to take it seriously than once upon a time there was a girls' club and a boy you teased,' cried Flora, matching Joy's uppity tone. 'Just give me one good reason why this Aubrey person should have it in for you so bad, then I might start believing you.'

'I killed his dog, okay?' Joy thrust her chin forward. 'I killed his precious Jack, his only friend and companion. That's why he's coming after me, and that's why he tried to kill Otto.' She whirled around and flung herself back on the sofa. 'It's all my fault. Otto, Merlin, and now the Captain. But he won't stop there, Flora. You mark my words. He won't stop until he's made me suffer every inch as much as he did.'

Flora, shocked into silence, instinctively reached for the tissues by the dresser. But right at that moment a piercing scream cut through the air, leaving a strange, vibrating silence behind it.

Joy looked up, her eyes puffy, her expression one of pure terror. As they raced through the door and out into the quadrant, Flora knew one thing absolutely: Whatever the truth of Joy's accusations, this was one genuinely frightened lady.

In front of the main block, Flora and Joy found Vera sitting on the ground surrounded by residents and clutching what looked like a pile of pale brown fur close to her chest.

'No,' whispered Flora. 'Not again.'

'What's that? Not Otto! Not my Otto.' Joy threw herself down at Vera's side and began to wail. Flora hung back, not sure what instinct made her search for Mr Felix, just wanting to know in that moment exactly where he was.

He was nowhere to be seen. Well, of course he wasn't. He'd passed through the gardens ages ago on his self-imposed rubbish collecting duties. She could hear Vera shouting over the top of Joy's sobs that Otto was okay, he was going to be okay, and she let out a relieved sigh. A near miss, was all. Another near miss. But as she moved forward to join her friend, Flora stopped short. There, off to one side and looking decidedly sorry for himself, was Mr Felix. His mobility scooter lay on its side, only a couple of feet away from the edge of Vera's caftan. Flora took it all in: the baleful look on the old man's face; the skid marks on the pavement under the scooter's front wheel; the warden throwing a blanket over Joy's shoulders while casting a disgusted glare in Mr Felix's direction.

It didn't take Columbo to figure this one out. But Flora was starting to wish the raincoat-clad, cigar-smoking detective would make an appearance for real. Because somehow she'd found herself right in the middle of this mess, and even now Joy was looking at her meaningfully, her eyes carrying a clear message: *See? Now do you believe me?*

I'm starting to, thought Flora. I'm not really sure I have any choice.

Chapter 7

To the north of Shrewsbury, tucked away in the middle of almost nowhere, the village of Whixall had offered the perfect escape for Max Lively and his collection of bedraggled animals when retirement beckoned. Not for him the communal comfort of a retirement village; after a lifetime of being sociable, Flora's uncle preferred his own company. To him, loneliness was an alien concept. A former councillor and multiple business owner, Max had, he told Flora, had enough of people to last a lifetime. Or what was left of his lifetime, anyway.

Flora took the train to Wem, then sat on a low wall to wait for Max to come and pick her up. There was no point phoning – he would either be on his way already or out in the fields. She looked at the sky suspiciously before pulling out her raincoat. Around here, you never could tell.

Before long she heard the familiar grinding racket of Max's ancient Land Rover. He swung into the car park and waved through the open window.

'Flora,' he bellowed, 'how the devil are you?'

She ran across the tarmac and climbed up into the car, hauling the passenger door shut behind her. It closed, then dropped open again, hanging from one hinge only. 'For goodness sake, Max! When are you going to get this door fixed? It's been like this since Christmas.'

Max Lively laughed and ruffled her hair affectionately. He strolled around to Flora's side and gave the door an almighty kick, popping it back into place and putting a dent in the side for good measure.

'Great,' grumbled Flora, surreptitiously readjusting her spiky fringe. 'Now I'll probably have to climb out your side.'

Max patted her knee as he threw the gears into reverse. 'It's nice to see you too, grumpy. And you're still too skinny. Didn't I tell you to start eating more?'

Flora clung on to the sides of her seat as the car limped out of the town and headed down a winding country lane. The hedges were so high she couldn't see the view, but she knew that in a few months, when the tractors came out to cut them back, she'd be able to see all the way across to North Wales from here. It was a beautiful part of the world: not picturesque in the traditional sense, but honest and wild and peaceful.

'I eat plenty,' she told her uncle. 'But I also work hard. Not that it seems to make much difference.'

'Business not going too well?'

'We're in a recession, in case you hadn't noticed. The housing market's as flat as a pancake – things are real difficult.'

'*Really* difficult, Flora,' Max corrected. 'You've been spending too much time with that American.'

'And that's another thing. Marshall is driving me insane.' She swallowed and looked out of the window. This was what she'd been steeling herself to say, the main point of her visit, but how her uncle would take it was a complete unknown.

'Uncle Max, I think it would be better if Marshall resigned as manager and moved on.'

They drove in silence for a couple of miles. Flora could see Max was taken aback: he'd make a terrible poker player with that little tic in his cheek. No wonder he'd retired to the country. Max Lively had worked harder than anyone she'd ever known – with the exception of her father, perhaps. He'd travelled the world, survived two painful marriage break-ups, and the stress had finally taken its toll. When Max had a mild stroke only a month after his brother died, he had sold up and bought a smallholding in deepest Whixall within weeks. Gone were the loose-fitting suits that had made his tall, spare frame seem even larger, replaced by country-issue padded checked shirts and jeans caked in mud. The blonde-grey hair was no longer slicked back with that sweet-smelling oil he had used since she was a child. Now it flew wildly about his head, responding to every breeze or gust. His hands were so deeply ingrained with dirt they looked like a child had been at them with a permanent marker. He smelt of earth, and clothes dried on a radiator, and something else she didn't want to even think about naming.

Flora often wondered if he was happier now, but theirs wasn't the kind of relationship where she could ask. Personal questions only came one way – at her.

Like now, for instance. 'I thought you and Marshall got on fine. I've often thought the two of you ...'

'What?' Flora stopped chewing her nail and regarded him warily. 'The two of us what?'

'Nothing.'

'Anyway, don't try and change the subject. Besides, Marshall's not the only problem. I know Dad wanted the business to pass to me, but there was no way he could have known I'd inherit Shakers so soon. I'm not sure I'm up to it, Uncle Max. I'm not sure I can–'

'Nonsense! You're doing a fine job, Flora. And I'm always here, you know that. I've always been involved with the business in some form or other – I'm always here if you need advice.'

'I know. And I appreciate that. But I inherited more

than just a removal company – I inherited Dad's choice of manager too. And I just don't think I can work with him. We're too … different.'

'Or maybe you're too similar.'

Flora grimaced. 'No. It's definitely not that.'

Max steered with one hand and rubbed his bristly chin with the other. 'I promised Marshall's mum I'd look out for him. I gave her my word.'

'And you have,' Flora said, throwing up her hands. 'Dad gave him the job on your recommendation and he's been great, really he has. But he's not *my* choice, Max. Besides,' she mumbled, 'I'm not sure we can afford him much longer.'

'He was a rock when your mum was sick,' Max said, turning around a sharp bend and throwing her to the side. 'I'm surprised you've forgotten that. Without Marshall taking over, Shakers would have gone down the pan quicker than you can say the vultures are circling.'

'But the vultures *are* circling, and Marshall's one of them. He keeps going on about "diversifying". He's got this scheme of his all worked out, and if he has his way Dad's company will be unrecognizable in a few years. Anyway, his mum is married to someone else now, in case you hadn't noticed. Why you still feel indebted to her is beyond me.'

'Home!' The Land Rover swung into a gravel driveway, scattering at least ten chickens and two grumpy-looking ducks. And a pig.

'What is that pig doing just wandering about?' said Flora, climbing over the gear stick and manoeuvring her way out on Max's side.

'Oh, that's Nelson,' he said, as though that explained everything perfectly. 'Time for tea. Come on, madam.' He tramped away along the muddy path that led to his dilapidated farmhouse, leaving Flora surrounded by inquisitive chickens.

'Great,' she sighed. Another intractable man to deal with. Another annoying old person to tax her patience. She really had to make some changes in her life soon, before she ended up old before her time. Maybe another date with Heston was needed. Or maybe she should do something wild like go clothes shopping and buy a whole new power-dressing wardrobe; maybe then the men in her life would take her seriously. Marshall was always saying she dressed like a child. That couldn't help matters, could it?

She grabbed her tote bag out of the footwell and picked her way after Max, trying to avoid the piles of white chicken poo that lined her way like spotlights.

And wellies. She really should buy wellies.

***

'So, what did he say?'

Date number three with Heston: a Rat Pack tribute at the Theatre Severn. Not exactly Flora's idea of kicking up her heels, but she hadn't the heart to tell him. They were standing in the foyer, waiting to go in – Heston had ordered drinks for the interval; Flora was already counting the minutes. She'd told him about her trip to the outback, and how she'd pleaded with her uncle for help in getting shot of Marshall. Heston was more amused than sympathetic.

'He said no.' Flora sighed and watched their reflection in the foyer mirror that tracked their progress into the auditorium. 'Said it was up to Marshall and he wouldn't interfere.'

'Fair enough, I guess.'

'Not really! It's Max's fault Marshall's here at all.'

'Why don't you just sack him? You're the one in charge.' A note of boredom had crept into Heston's voice. Flora bit her lip and didn't answer. She'd already gone on and on about it during their pre-show supper, and Heston had listened attentively, never once interrupting, not judging. Not even when Flora confessed to getting quite tipsy and knocking over an entire bottle of red wine.

She'd been sitting at Max's pitted kitchen table, her elbows propping up her drooping head, staring glumly at her third – or possibly her fourth – glass of wine, while Max got another bottle from the cupboard under the sink. He called it his wine cellar, which hadn't even raised a smile.

'Sometimes it feels like a poisoned chalice,' she'd said when Max placed the fresh bottle on the table by her side. 'Sometimes I wish Dad had never left me the business. I wish he'd left it to you instead. You and Marshall could run it together. Happy families.'

'You don't mean that, Flora.' Max was also two sheets to the wind, but he could hold his drink a damn site better than his niece. 'You'd have been mortified if that was the case. Shakers is your inheritance. But he would have known I'd stay close and look after you.'

'Which you demonstrably are not doing,' Flora countered, slurring so badly it took Max a full minute to decipher her words.

'Ah, Flora,' he'd said, but nothing more. And then Flora had gone off on a rant, flailing her arms to make her point, finally knocking the bottle of red from the table without even having the chance to sample its delights.

'Just as well,' Heston said when she told him. But he was smiling. And he laughed when she added that her uncle hadn't cleaned up the contents of the bottle very well, and that when they'd surfaced the next morning Nelson the pig was sitting boggle-eyed by the Aga, his tongue a telling shade of purple.

Heston sighed now as they inched forward in the

queue. 'Your uncle had the right idea getting away from the city. What I wouldn't do for my own slice of rural bliss.'

Flora did a double-take. 'Really? That's your idea of bliss? Spending your days knee-deep in shit and mud and having to dig up your dinner every night? Or wring its neck, depending what's on the menu.'

Heston laughed his dry, stretched laugh. 'You are funny, Flora. I doubt your uncle would eat his own hens if he keeps them for their eggs.'

'You don't know my uncle,' she said darkly. 'It would depend entirely on his mood.'

She was joking, of course. Max wouldn't hurt a red mite on one of his chickens' backs. Which was why his house and garden – if you could call four acres a garden – were overrun with livestock. She'd counted five pigs in addition to Nelson, three sheep, a donkey, a ratty sheepdog with numerous puppies and a forlorn-looking cow. The chickens were hard to count, but she figured on about twenty.

And the eggs! Max said he knew where to look for them, but his chickens had no discipline. They would lay in any old place: in bushes, right in the middle of the patio, on top of Max's rusty tractor – even inside his Land Rover, as Flora had discovered on the way back to the station the next morning.

She considered Heston as he chattered on about leaving the rat race and going eco. She really would never have guessed. Heston, with his tailored suits and button-down shirts in various pastel shades, with his polished shoes and polished accent, was the last person you'd put in the "frustrated farmer" category.

Just went to show, you never could tell.

***

Flora dragged Otto along the river bank, refusing to

make eye contact.

'No,' she told him when he pulled in the direction of some ducks.

'Absolutely not,' she said sternly when he sniffed a discarded chip wrapper.

Otto had disgraced himself the night before, and Flora had not forgiven him. Nor would she be likely to forgive him any time soon, she had told him over breakfast, if he kept trying to lick her face. What was it with dogs and faces? It was just so gross.

Heston had lapped up the Rat Pack tribute and they left the theatre hand in hand, singing 'Fly Me to the Moon' far too loudly all the way back to Flora's house. Flora put on her *Young at Heart* DVD and soon they were snuggled up on her sofa watching Frank Sinatra moon soulfully over Doris Day.

The movie was just coming to an end, and Flora was wondering if the mood was right for Heston to dive in for their first kiss, when Otto decided to jump on the sofa, lift his leg, and direct a yellow arc of pee at Heston's lap.

'Oh, my Lord, what is that?'

The problem is, thought Flora now as she tugged Otto's lead just a little harder than necessary, what kind of man actually says 'Oh, my Lord' when a dog pees on his leg? Shouldn't his response have been a bit stronger than that?

She sighed and slipped past the barrier into the Maples car park. Otto pulled on the lead eagerly.

'Okay, keep your wig on.'

A tall man dressed entirely in black emerged suddenly from the topiary arch and nearly stepped on poor Otto, who bared his teeth and emitted a low growl.

'Otto!' Flora sent the man an apologetic glance while trying to stop the dog attacking his ankles. The man's face was half hidden behind a neat ginger beard, but

Flora registered sunken cheeks and a pallid complexion before realising that Otto's lead was about to become entangled with the man's legs. This mutt was an accident-magnet on four paws.

'Sorry,' she said automatically, dropping to her knees to pull the dog out of danger.

'You should look where you're going,' the man said. Flora laughed, thinking he was joking. Another glance at his face told her he was deadly serious.

'Oh, right. Well, sorry. Otto, no!'

Not again. What was it with men and Otto's need to pee? Did he have something against lamp posts? She tugged the lead and managed to avoid a full-on disaster, hurrying away with the strange man's eyes still upon her.

She found Joy in her unit looking through her old photo albums. The minute Otto was through the door he leapt onto Joy's lap and began turning excited circles.

'He misses you,' Flora said, stating the obvious.

Joy shook her head. 'You shouldn't have brought him here again. Look what happened last time.'

'I have to work, Joy. He makes a mess when I leave him on his own. He's been chewing the piano legs again.'

'The poor little mite.' Joy gave the pooch a gentle cuddle.

'I thought he could visit with you for the morning. Marshall's going to go ape if I turn up with him every day. You know, Otto's *really* missing you. Been pining for you every second. I haven't been able to do a thing with him. He's off his food, he's barely drinking ...'

They regarded Otto, who sat happily in Joy's arms, panting and looking the absolute picture of health.

'And that's not all. He's hardly sleeping, and he's been acting really weird.'

Well, peeing all over a librarian was hardly normal behaviour, was it?

'Are you sure he's not just cramping your style and

94

now you want shot of him?' said Joy with laser-like perception.

Flora put on a hurt face. 'Can I remind you that I never wanted him in the first place, but I took him in out of the kindness of my heart after you *lied* and pretended you'd had a fall? Anyway, you're looking after him for the rest of the morning whether you like it or not. But first, we need to have a serious talk.'

Joy and Otto turned their faces up to Flora: one with bug eyes and a dopey expression, the other panting and wagging its stubby tail.

They made a lovely pair.

'Right,' said Flora, settling herself down in the armchair opposite, 'I need to know everything. And I mean everything. If you want me to take you seriously, you're going to have to start at the beginning and leave nothing out. Warts and all, Joy. I'm ready.'

Chapter 8

The Grange was a beautiful old building. It had been some kind of manor house before they turned it into a boarding school. I think there was something like twenty acres of grounds, and we were pretty much free to explore them as we liked. Parts were out of bounds, of course, but that didn't stop us.'

Joy took a sip of the sugary tea Flora had made. Her voice was quiet, her expression blank. Otto was asleep in his basket, making the most of being back home.

Flora listened, letting Joy tell her story in her own way. She'd said to start at the beginning, but a weight sat on her chest. Joy's words still rebounded in her head: *I killed his dog, okay? I killed his only friend and companion.* Half of her wanted to know the truth, but the other half didn't want to be hearing any of this at all. This sweet old lady, infuriating at times but stoical and mischievous and gentle – surely she wasn't capable of hurting a dog?

When Joy got to the part about the Joan of Arc club, and how the girls were whipped up into a state of man-hating by their embittered teacher, Flora relaxed a little. She'd heard all this before: she got a buzz out of the rebellious teacher and her loyal troupe. But then Joy started talking about the caretaker's son and Flora pricked up her ears.

'He was such a sweet boy, Aubrey. Ginger hair and freckles, quite the innocent, and not into typical boy

96

things like fishing or football. Aubrey loved books, although he said him and his dad didn't own any, so I would sneak him stories out of the library. And we talked. He told me that his mum had left his dad and run off with an American soldier. He said his dad was a lot older than his mum, some kind of scientist, but that he had a breakdown and was really ill and he had bad moods.'

Flora nodded. 'He was probably depressed. It must have been hard on him, and on Aubrey.'

'It was. That the only job his dad could get was in a girls' school can't have helped much. But Aubrey lived in a kind of fantasy world, I think. He didn't attend any lessons, although his dad had been offered a tutor for him. He escaped into his stories, and I was his only friend at the Grange.' Joy paused and swallowed. 'Me, and Jack.'

'Jack was his dog?' Flora's heart was beating so loudly it was the only sound she could hear above Joy's voice.

'A golden retriever. Beautiful beast he was. The kind of face on a dog that always looks like it's smiling.' Joy stopped again. Flora sipped her coffee, waiting.

'So you and Aubrey were friends?' she prompted after three full minutes had passed.

'Yes.' Joy jumped a little, roused from her thoughts. 'Although of course I had to keep it a secret from the others. Dizzy was the worst of them – Frances and Melody just went along with whatever she said. They were like the sun to me, Flora.' She looked up, her eyes pleading. 'You have to understand. All I wanted to do was belong.'

'I do understand, Joy. I promise I do.' Flora smiled reassuringly. 'Go on. What happened next? Was it something to do with the club?'

Joy nodded slowly. 'There were all sorts of loyalty

tests that Dizzy thought up. Melody said Dizzy made her drink a pint of whisky, but I'm not sure that was true. And Frances had to steal the head teacher's umbrella right out of her study. She did it, too. She was crazy, was Frances. Anything for a dare.' Joy smiled briefly, before becoming grim again. 'But my test was much, much worse.'

Flora said nothing. Joy's breathing was becoming laboured; her right hand scratched at her neck. She let out a shuddering sigh and carried on.

'There was a tree in the grounds where we used to meet. We were the Joan of Arc club, we prized strong women above all else, so Dizzy christened it the Venus Tree. Venus, she said, was the ultimate woman – Goddess of love, beauty, sex and fertility. Men were considered weaker because they couldn't produce children.'

'They do kind of have something to do with it.'

'Well, obviously.' Joy rolled her eyes. 'Miss Lester loved Greek and Roman mythology, said the roots of all fiction could be found in the ancient myths and legends. So we learned all about Venus, and her son, Cupid. The baby with the arrow, Miss Lester called him. Concerned only with love, whereas women were strong and had more than just love to occupy them.'

'So, this tree?' said Flora, fearing Joy was going off at a tangent.

'The Venus Tree was this amazing oak in the centre of the woods. Ancient, it was. Huge. We weren't supposed to go in the woods – there were old mine shafts and it was dangerous.'

'But you did.'

'Of course. As soon as Dizzy saw this tree she made it the unofficial home of the Joan of Arc club. She said she could see the body of Venus in the tree's bark, that the branches were her arms reaching out to us.' Joy coughed, made a brushing motion with her hands. 'All nonsense, of course. But we were very impressionable, and Miss Lester had filled our heads with tales of revolt and revolution. The whole Joan of Arc thing was based around it.'

'I had wondered about that. It doesn't seem a very patriotic name for a club, considering what was happening in England at the time.'

'Miss Lester told us how diabolically Joan of Arc – or Jeanette, as she was really called – had been treated by the English. It was more to do with her being a woman than a great general, she said. A man who fought so hard would have been an enemy, of course, but he wouldn't have been so feared. So reviled. They couldn't cope with the fact that she was a woman, a girl, and yet was stronger and more powerful than any man.'

'Or that her armies killed thousands of English soldiers, presumably.'

'Well, that too. But Miss Lester only saw things through her own personal lens.'

Don't we all, thought Flora. She said, 'So your Miss Lester saw men as the enemy.'

Joy nodded. 'You have to appreciate this, Flora, to understand what happened next.'

Flora said she did. She sipped her cooling coffee and told Joy to carry on with her story.

'We built a kind of tree house in the lower branches of the Venus Tree – some of them were so thick you could sit two people side by side across the width. We snuck rugs out of the school, and we made a rope ladder so it was easier to climb up. There was an old wooden swing hanging off one of the branches so we knew we weren't the first girls to use the tree. Dizzy would sit up there and tell us stories about pupils who'd come before us and all the wonderful adventures they'd had. She made it all up of course, but she told a great story. Very atmospheric. I had some wonderful times in that tree. It helped me forget everything else. My mum and dad. The horrible eczema and the itching and the pain, and the teasing from the other girls up at the school. The thought of not belonging anymore was too much to bear.'

Now we're getting to it, thought Flora. 'She sounds like one of those magnetic types. Someone who can get other people to do anything.'

'She was.'

'What was it she wanted you to do?'

Joy took a shaky breath, ragged on the exhale. 'Aubrey was always asking if he could come to the tree with me. He wanted to listen to Dizzy's stories too. So I did a terrible thing – I showed him where it was. And one day he turned up during one of our meetings. I didn't even know he was there until we were about to go back to lessons. Frances lowered the ladder and climbed down first – she must have nearly stepped on his head. I think he'd fallen asleep, otherwise he'd surely have realised we were about to come down. Anyway, before we knew anything about it, Frances was screaming and Dizzy was sliding down the ladder and there was Aubrey, running away across the grass, Jack bounding behind him.

'There was no mistaking who it was. There weren't any other boys – or dogs – at the Grange. Dizzy and the girls guessed right away that I'd shown him our special place, and I was in so much trouble.' Joy's eyes clouded over. 'They didn't talk to me for weeks. Even Miss Lester noticed. It was horrible.'

Flora reached for a tissue from the box on the dresser and handed it over.

'It must seem silly to you, an old lady crying over what a few spiteful girls did years and years ago,' sniffed Joy, wiping her eyes.

'No, it doesn't. Kids can be hurtful, girls especially

so.' Why, she could tell Joy plenty of stories about her own school days. Once Flora's school mates found out she was adopted they had teased her mercilessly. One girl even made up an entire family, claiming to know for a fact that they were Flora's real parents, and that they had abandoned her because they were rich and clever and she was the runt of the family, too small and useless to fit in.

Oh no, Flora didn't need to be told about spiteful schoolgirls.

'So, anyway,' Joy said, sitting back and squaring her shoulders as if for battle, 'it came to a head three weeks before the end of term. We were all going home that summer, the war was well and truly over and our families wanted us back. I thought I would just die if no one talked to me, I was desperate to be accepted again. So when Dizzy came up with her plan, I felt I had no choice but to go along with it.'

Joy was far away now, in another place and time. When she spoke again, her voice was almost childlike. 'Dizzy said I had to invite Aubrey to come along to the Venus Tree. She said to tell him he could come and listen to her stories with us. He'd be pleased, I told her. He was a nice boy, not like the men Miss Lester talked about. Dizzy just grinned at me. They would make him a nice surprise, she said. There was a mine shaft near the tree, we'd known about it since the day we made our den, and we would all work together to pull the wooden boards off the top. Then we'd cover it with branches and leaves, and mark it so only we would know where it was.

'I went and found Aubrey. He was in the vegetable garden with his dad. He came when I called him and his dad smiled. He was happy that day – his dad was in a good mood. He asked if Jack could come. I said yes, if he liked. I didn't tell him anything else. He followed me into the woods and out into the clearing. I made sure we approached the tree from the right direction. The others were there already, Frances and Melody leaning against the trunk, Dizzy sitting on the wooden swing. She had this bright blonde hair, I can remember it so clearly. The sun was behind her and her hair was almost glowing. She looked like Venus herself. Aubrey couldn't take his eyes off her. He couldn't believe he was actually being allowed to join in. I wasn't thinking, not really. I suppose I knew what was about to happen but I'd blocked it from my mind. I was doing what Dizzy told me. It was like a joke, just like the whisky and the umbrella. A test I had to pass. So I did what I'd been told to do. As we reached the hole I stopped and bent to tie my lace. Just like we'd planned. Aubrey and Jack walked on.'

Joy stopped. Flora was hardly breathing.

'And then?' Flora whispered. 'What happened then?'

Joy looked away, her face twisted with remorse. 'They fell in, of course. Dizzy never failed in anything she did. Her plan worked perfectly. The dog went in first, he'd been pulling ahead on his lead. And then Aubrey went in straight after him.

'I heard the dog yelp – it was like nothing I'd ever heard before. Aubrey must have landed on top of it. Hopefully it died instantly.'

Flora noticed how Joy had moved from *him* to *it*, trying to depersonalise the dog, distance herself. She couldn't say she blamed her. But there was still more she needed to know. Although Joy was clearly wrung out, Flora couldn't let it go just yet.

'What happened to Aubrey, Joy? Did you help get him out of the shaft?'

He couldn't have died, not if Joy believed Aubrey and Mr Felix were one and the same. That was something, at least.

'That was the worst of it, perhaps,' Joy said, not meeting Flora's eyes.

'What do you mean?'

'I don't know.' Joy turned her face to the light, her powdery cheeks streaked with tears. 'I never saw him again. Nobody did. We ran, Flora. Frances, Melody and me. Even Dizzy ran. We ran away from the Venus Tree and we never went back. Even though we could hear him calling and crying all the way back to the school. We never went back.'

***

Flora walked across town, heading for Shakers, trying to process her thoughts. Try as she might, she could not get them straight in her head. Images competed for attention: Otto pulling on his lead as she walked along the riverside; Mr Felix sitting on the ground beside his overturned scooter; a teenage Joy, climbing up a rope ladder to hero-worship an enigmatic girl, desperate for approval, no matter what. And the caretaker's son, walking across a clearing, his faithful dog forging ahead, pulling like Otto, and then plunging down through sticks and leaves, down to the depths of an abandoned mine shaft, dragging its owner behind it. What a horrendous way to go. To be crushed by the one you loved the most.

Another image, hauntingly poignant: a young boy, frightened and alone, sitting at the bottom of the shaft with his dead dog. No one answering his calls.

But he had gotten out, Joy was sure of that. She'd told Flora that the caretaker had left the school the next day. And there was no search, no fuss at all. So someone must have heard his cries and pulled him out. Him and his beloved pet.

'Did you get into trouble?' Flora had asked, but Joy shook her head.

'So Aubrey didn't tell on you? He didn't tell them

what you did?'

'Oh, I'm sure he told them exactly what we did. His dad's job extended to groundsman, he knew where the mine shafts were and there was plenty of evidence we'd been using that tree as a den. No, I've thought about this for years and my best guess is that Aubrey told his dad and his dad told the headmistress everything, and she refused to believe it. Or refused to act upon it, which is more likely. So Aubrey and his dad left. What choice did they have?'

Flora slipped into an alley off Dogpole and headed for the castle, taking a short cut to avoid the late morning shoppers and tourists that crowded Shrewsbury's main thoroughfares. As a child she'd known these streets so well she could navigate them in her sleep. She'd prided herself on finding the quickest ways from A to B – a skill that turned her into her dad's favourite navigator when she started helping out at Shakers as a teenager. The town had changed so much since Flora's childhood; these days she often challenged herself to find her way around with only her nose and her memory to guide her. The narrow side street she entered now had once been lined with metal dustbins and littered with fag ends, but the boom had seen cute boutiques open alongside cupcake shops and a tiny gift emporium. Now it was deserted again, the shop fronts blank-faced and sorry for themselves, the bustle of shoppers a distant echo.

Her sandals clicked on the cobbles. The lane narrowed even more and took a right turn up the hill. She picked up her pace, enjoying the slight burn in her thighs. Why should she worry about learning to drive? Walking was much healthier, not to mention good for stress.

A movement in her peripheral vision caught her attention and she swung around just in time to see the sleeve of a dark blue jacket disappear into a narrow doorway behind her. She paused for a second, then pressed on, her heart hammering unevenly. Silly to be spooked. Something else to blame Joy for. She focused on the top of the lane, on a red door that got nearer with every step. At the top she would turn right, then skip across another alley and emerge on Castle Gate. From there it was a mere hop down to Shakers.

But when she reached the top she was dismayed to find that her legendary bearings had deserted her. Instead of the expected alley, mapped in her mind so clearly, there was another narrow street running perpendicular to the one she'd just marched up. She couldn't see any way to cross it directly, and from here couldn't get a view of the orientating crenellations of the castle to guide her. On impulse, she turned right anyway. This way took her further uphill – she would head up until she reached the top, which had to be near the castle, and from there could easily find her way down again. When you're lost, head for high ground, was what her dad had told her whenever he took her walking as a teenager.

This street was one she almost certainly hadn't been up before. Flora observed the various buildings she passed, telling herself how interesting it was to be somewhere new in the town she knew so well. But in truth, the silence was bothering her. Or more specifically, the footsteps she kept imagining she could hear in the silence behind her.

There was no one there. She turned now for the tenth time, but again the cobbled street was empty. Or had she seen a flash of blue again? Just back there, next to that broken wooden gate with the lion's head knocker. No. She shook her head firmly and pursed her lips, bending her head into the hike up the hill, determined not to look back again.

Something touched her legs. She was wearing her cut-off shorts and a light cotton T-shirt, the fabric starting to stick to her back already. When a warm sensation swept across her calves she let out a cry and jumped to the side, flattening her palms against the rough wall behind her.

A cat. The moggy meowed and stuck its tail high in the air.

'Well, thanks a lot,' Flora told it, panting. 'You scared the shit out of me.'

The cat gave her a haughty stare, then showed her its rear. Flora laughed. She'd been stalked by a cat. Nothing to be so jumpy about.

She reached the top of the lane and saw an archway to her left. Why, she knew exactly where she was – this led around the back of the Regimental Museum and brought her out at the foot of the castle. She emerged into sunlight and the relief of a crowded street, turned right and headed down towards the station. There was a new shop down here she loved, selling vintage quilts and patchwork cushions and beautiful, intricate designs on fabric, from wall hangings to tea cosies. A framed collage of a hare caught her eye, and Flora stopped to admire it. Someone pushed past, jostling her against the plate glass, and as Flora refocused she noticed a figure across the street behind her. His face was hidden by a dark blue hood. It was impossible to tell whether or not he was looking at her, but somehow she knew he was. She whirled around, her line of vision broken every few seconds by the shoppers piling past. The moment she turned the figure hunched and moved away with the crowd. Within seconds he was gone.

'Excuse me.' A young woman with an impossibly wide buggy stood to Flora's left, giving her a hard stare. Her words were polite but her look said, 'Get out of the way, idiot.' Flora apologised and walked on, dazed. Was someone following her? Maybe she hadn't been imagining the footsteps back in the alley. She shivered involuntarily. Whatever she had or hadn't imagined, that person in the hoodie had been real. And she could swear they had been watching her. But why?

She reached the busy road that led to the railway arches and breathed a sigh of relief. Although she hated to admit it, she was almost looking forward to seeing Marshall. If Flora was to be any help to Joy at all, she needed to get this Mr Felix business into perspective. Marshall would reassure her that it was nothing but the guilty mind of an old lady seeing revenge where there was none, tormenting herself with her memories.

Well, he'd probably just say it was all bullshit, but that amounted to the same thing.

Flora turned into the entrance to the arches, flinching as a train shot over the tracks ahead. She felt a drop of rain on her face and quickened her step. She headed for Shakers, keeping close to the buildings as the rain started to fall more heavily. She heard a noise behind her and turned, still jumpy. Her foot went sideways in a pothole, pain searing up her ankle as she started to fall. But before she hit the ground her forward motion was halted by a pair of strong hands, gripping her arms above the elbows.

Flora screamed. She couldn't help it, her nerves were frayed to shreds. But almost as soon as the girlish sound had escaped her lips she realised that the hands gripping her upper arms had already let go. She brushed herself down, mumbling an apology. She could feel the colour rising in her cheeks. The man in front of her wore a smart grey suit, tailored to fit perfectly. His green eyes regarded her with obvious concern.

'I'm so sorry,' he said. His voice was like chocolate.

'It's cool,' Flora replied, flicking her fringe off her forehead. 'No probs.'

Had she just said "no probs"? And "cool"? Oh boy.

This guy was going to think she was a total idiot. An idiot trying to imitate a teenager.

'It was my fault anyway,' she added, lowering her voice which had suddenly turned unaccountably high-pitched. 'I wasn't looking where I was going.'

'No. I noticed.'

Flora stole another look at the stranger. Out of Marshall's mouth that statement would have been loaded with sarcasm, but out of this guy's it seemed completely without guile.

'I thought I was being followed,' she found herself saying. 'I was a bit spooked.'

'That's terrible. Are you okay?' Genuine concern clouded his eyes. He looked behind her as if he might see the culprit hovering there. From the way his shoulders strained against the expensive fabric of his suit, Flora had no doubt he'd be able to sort out her hooded stalker in no time.

If only this guy had turned up a bit earlier.

A sticky reminder of her fraught trail through Shrewsbury's back streets lingered in the shape of sweat marks on the armpits of her T-shirt. She probably stank too, after panicking and practically running up the hill like that. Plus her hair was plastered to her head now, although they were reasonably sheltered from the diminishing rain under the canopy where they stood. Facing each other. Not talking.

Seconds passed, and Flora found herself torn. For some unaccountable reason she wanted to prolong this odd meeting. She wanted to ask him what he was doing here – where exactly had he come from, anyway? And she couldn't help but like the way his eyes held hers, crinkling at the corners in concern. He smelt fantastic, some kind of musky aftershave or cologne. If only he'd come across her looking normal and unflustered, not sweaty and staring over her own shoulder like a paranoid simpleton.

'Are you lost?' he said, breaking the silence. 'Did you come down here by mistake?'

'No.' She smiled. In a minute he'd be offering to escort her home.

And maybe he'll get down on one knee and propose. Get over yourself, Lively! Flora gave herself an internal scolding. What was she doing, standing around in the car park with a total stranger? And … oh, just great. There was Marshall, leaning against the window, staring down at them. Craning his head to get a good look.

'I'd better go,' Flora said reluctantly.

'Oh. Okay. Do you need a lift anywhere?'

She smiled. 'No, I work just here.'

'Just where?'

'There.' Flora pointed to the faded sign above the entrance to Shakers. She noticed that the 'r' was so faded it was almost invisible. "Shakes" the sign read. He probably thought it was some kind of fast food outlet. Or worse.

'You work there?' Was it just her imagination or did the handsome stranger recoil slightly? Flora couldn't tell if his emphasis had been on the word *work* or *there*, but she was right about him not being impressed.

'I own it,' she said, trying to win back some credibility. 'It's a removal company. Shakers.'

The guy in the suit was nodding. His eyes had clouded over again, and she could have sworn he looked a little sad. Maybe he was disappointed she didn't need rescuing after all.

Fat chance. More likely he was yet another guy frightened off by a woman who owned her own business.

Aware of Marshall's eyes boring down from above, Flora said a hasty goodbye and ran the last few steps. She pulled the metal door shut behind her and stood for a moment, her back pressed against it. Her heart was pounding again.

'Are you okay?'

When she reached the office Marshall was reclining with an air of entirely fake and unconvincing calm. He threw the question at her without meeting her eyes. He knew she'd seen him spying.

'I'm fine. Why?' She threw her tote bag under the desk and flopped into her chair.

'You look a bit flushed.'

'And you saw me outside talking to a stranger,' added Flora. No point beating about the bush.

'A stranger?' He looked up and tilted his head. 'You didn't recognise him? I mean, you don't know him?'

Flora shrugged. 'I just bumped into him.' She forced a laugh. 'Literally. I was walking back through town and I … It doesn't matter now.'

'What?'

'Nothing.' She was too tired to get into it. Marshall had that air of tenseness about him that always set her on edge. There was something eating him, she could tell.

'Can't help noticing you're kinda late, Flora.'

She picked up the message pad and pretended to read it. All the messages were at least three days old. 'I went to drop Otto off at the Maples. You moan whenever I bring him into work.'

'Bit risky, isn't it? Leaving him there.'

'What do you mean?'

'You know my theory about that place. Dogs trying to hang themselves, throwing themselves under mobility scooters, chewing on electrical cabling. All those pooches are plain losing the will.'

She looked around her desk but there was nothing to hand she could throw. Nothing that would do enough damage, anyway. Instead she sent him daggers with her eyes. He had the good sense to let it drop.

'Well, I'd better go grab a sandwich. You want anything?'

She shook her head. Marshall hauled himself up but stopped in the doorway. He leaned his elbow against the frame and rubbed the back of his neck. Flora switched on her computer. She looked at Marshall and raised her eyebrows.

'Something bothering you?'

'No. Just … no. Nothing.'

She watched him struggle for the right words. What was going on with him?

'So, this guy,' he said, lifting his other arm and lacing his fingers behind his head. His T-shirt hoisted up, exposing a half inch of tanned skin above the waistline of his jeans. Flora dropped her eyes to the keyboard.

'What guy?'

'The one in the car park.'

'Uh huh.'

'What did he say to you?'

She shrugged. 'Nothing.'

'Didn't look like nothing.'

'Well, it was. Like I said, I bumped into him. He made sure I was okay, then he went. Why are you so interested?'

'I'm not. Just looking out for you.'

Sure you are. She kept her mouth shut tight, not trusting herself to speak. The next time she looked up, Marshall had gone.

Good riddance.

The phone rang and Flora grabbed it, eager for a diversion. It was a customer, but one with bad news.

'Okay. I understand.' She replaced the receiver and put her head in her hands. Another cancellation. That was the third this month. The first two had used the excuse that they weren't moving after all, but at least this customer had the decency to tell her the truth. He'd found a better deal elsewhere, he said. An offer he couldn't refuse.

And Flora knew exactly where that offer had come from. Bloody Rockfords. How she'd like to get David Rockford in a room and tell him what she thought of him and his empire-expanding, tramp all over the little guy, business enterprise.

She picked up her pen and threw it across the room, where it landed with a clatter against the side of the bin.

'Bad shot,' said Richie.

Flora's head flipped up. 'Where did you come from?' He was like a ninja sometimes, this boy.

'Just hanging around downstairs. Is there anything else you need today? I could do with finishing early, my aunt's got some stuff for me to do over at the village.'

Flora was torn between finding a reason to make him stay and actually do some work for his money, and simultaneously wanting him to go away so she could be alone to think. Mind you, if she let him off early it might curry her a bit of favour with Cynthia.

'Okay,' she said finally, 'you might as well get off now.'

Richie gave a half-wave and bounded down the stairs. Oh, to have that much energy, thought Flora. It was only lunchtime and already she was feeling completely wrung out. She stared out of the smeared window, out across the car park and the soot-blackened brick of the railway arches; over the tops of the shabby buildings and mismatched roofs that made up this part of town. A sense of suffocation swelled up inside her chest. Thanks a lot Dad, she thought, looking up at her father's photo on the noticeboard. You sure did me a whole world of favours when you left me this place to look after. But then she looked away, tears prickling her eyes. 'I miss you so much,' she whispered. 'Wherever you and mum are, I hope you're happy.'

Chapter 9

'What the hell is that?'

'Nothing. Just my new bag.'

'Funny bag. Just make damn sure you keep it out from under my feet.'

Flora smirked and peeped inside the oversized fabric tote on her lap. She put her finger to her lips and Otto gazed back, panting. She'd stayed up two nights sewing his new carry-home. It even had a plastic lining for little accidents, and pockets for food and toys and his water bottle. Her mum would have been proud of her needlework. Joy would probably think she was crazy.

Friday morning and they were on their way to the Maples to clear out the Captain's room. Marshall was up front with Flora and Steve because Richie had called in sick. Word on the grapevine was they were getting the room ready for someone else, but Flora hadn't bothered asking the warden who. She knew what Cynthia's reaction would be to a question like that.

Otto shuffled around on her lap and gave a little bark. Flora cleared her throat to disguise it. Marshall rolled his eyes.

'Sure must cramp your style, carrying that thing around with you all day. Bet your boyfriend doesn't like it much.'

She threw him a sarcastic smile. M nothing about Heston – she was pretty su fishing, trying to needle her. Still, he was his observation: Heston hadn't been in touch since the peeing debacle on Monday night. She hadn't phoned, thinking it was best to give him time to cool down. Regain his sense of dignity. She kind of figured that the way she'd found the whole incident hysterically funny hadn't endeared her to him much. It was funny, though. Who would have thought such a small dog could produce so much pee!

'What are you so happy about?' Marshall said.

'Oh, being here with you, of course. You're such a ray of sunshine in my life.'

'There's no need for sarcasm, you know. You're bright enough to make your point without it. Or so I've heard,' he mumbled, making a right turn too sharply and causing Steve to almost fall into Flora's lap. Otto gave a yelp in protest.

'Marshall!' She shoved Steve's hands away as he tried to push himself back upright. 'You're an even worse driver than Richie.'

'Well, at least I can drive,' he countered with a wink.

Flora opened her mouth for another retort, but Steve cut her off.

'Could you two just give it a rest with the Flora and Marshall show? Please? It's really getting old.' He picked up his phone and started tapping at it furiously. Flora caught Marshall's eye and raised an eyebrow.

'What's with him?' she mouthed.

Marshall shrugged and smiled. She grinned back. The Flora and Marshall show indeed. What a nerve!

***

It was as bad as Flora had expected. Actually, it was worse. There it was laid out before her: the life of a dignified, dear old man, cut off with no warning and no time to prepare.

His bed was made, military-style, with hospital

corners and an inch-perfect turnover on the top sheet. On his bedside table was an alarm clock, now wound down and set forever to six fifteen; a carafe of water with tumbler lid; a photograph, square to the wall, of a woman in forties' dress, her face smiling shyly in perpetuity. His dressing gown was hung on the back of the door, pulled neatly into shape, belt-ends tucked into pockets so they wouldn't dangle. An empty medal case sat on an ancient but spotless dressing table, alongside a small notebook, Parker pen, and a smart brown leather wallet. The room smelt of shoe polish and hair cream. It was as though the Captain had literally just stepped out for some air.

Even Marshall seemed affected. He was standing by the window with one hand resting on a wing-backed chair, his mouth thin-lipped as if holding back some emotion.

'Where's Steve?' Flora asked from the doorway.

'Gone to get the van ready.'

'Couldn't stand it, huh?'

'His granddad died a month ago. It's just too close for him.'

Flora nodded and stepped into the room. She did a slow turn, ending back where she'd started, her eyes on Marshall.

'It's just so sad. A sad end to a brave and dignified life.' She pointed to a row of medals, mounted and framed on the wall. 'Those were the ones he didn't even wear. You know, Joy doesn't think it very likely that he just fell. He wasn't ... well, he wasn't infirm.'

Marshall sighed but he didn't jump in the way she expected him to. 'He was her friend, Flora. And she's old too – she doesn't want it to be true. But he was up here, in Special Care or whatever they call it. If he'd been capable of looking after himself he'd still be out there with the others.'

Flora looked around sceptically.

'It wasn't all that special though, was it? He walked out of here and only minutes later fell straight down a flight of stairs. I don't call that care, special or otherwise.'

'They can't watch them twenty-four hours a day. Besides, that's what the lift's for.' Marshall picked up a book, looked at it blankly, then set it down. He sighed again and shook his head. 'Come on, we need to get started. This isn't gonna get any easier, no matter how long we stand here.'

'That's it, Marshall. That's what doesn't make any sense.' Something had been bothering her ever since she'd stood in the lobby and watched them carry the Captain away, and Marshall's words had suddenly brought it back. She put Otto down in the corner behind the door and crossed the room.

'If he was feeling ill, like faint or dizzy or something, he'd have taken the lift, right? So why get out of the lift at the first floor and walk the rest of the way down? Why would he do that? Besides, he hated the lift. He was a guy who liked to keep himself fit, never mind his age, and also he really liked his routines. He would have walked all the way down the stairs, or gone all the way down in the lift. Anything else doesn't make sense.'

Marshall was looking at her with a puzzled expression. 'Actually, it makes perfect sense to me. The walk down all those stairs was too much for him and by the time he got to the last set he was faint. Or maybe he did the first thing, got the lift part way then took a constitutional for the last flight. What difference does it make?'

'I don't know.'

Marshall was right, of course. But something still niggled at her, and being here now, surrounded by all the evidence of his careful, ordered life, it was hard not to keep coming back to the insistent question of how, exactly, it had happened.

'Where are you going with this, Flora?' Marshall's voice was low, gentle. It was the voice he'd used after her mum died, when she had thought she would break with the weight of it all. She looked around for somewhere to sit, but the only place was the Captain's bed and that was totally out of the question. She leaned against the dressing table instead, looking at the notepad but not daring to touch it.

'You know what I think?'

No, thought Flora. But I'm pretty sure you're going to tell me.

'What?'

'I'm thinking it's hard for you, me being Shakers' manager and all, because it's like you're in charge but not really in charge – it's like there are two bosses and that's never gonna work.'

Flora stared at him, open-mouthed. 'You think?'

'I'm not talking about your ability to run the business. Just that ...'

'What?'

He shook his head. 'Nothing. This isn't the time or the place, right? Come on, let's get packing. Did you bring the boxes up?'

Flora gestured to the dog sleeping on her cotton bag in the corner. 'Kinda had my hands full.'

'I'll go get them. Will you be okay to get started on your own?'

Flora nodded mutely. He hadn't berated her for forgetting the boxes. He must be feeling really sorry for her.

'I'll be back in a minute. You start wherever you can.' Marshall gave her a look she couldn't interpret, then left.

His absence seemed to pull any remaining strength from Flora's legs, and she sank to the floor with her back against the dressing table and closed her eyes.

Start wherever you can, Marshall had said.

How about fifteen years ago? she thought.

**

They worked in companionable silence, Flora tackling the wardrobe and Marshall doing the cupboard and bedside table drawers, and the paperwork, of which there was little.

After half an hour, Flora sat back on her heels and flicked her fringe out of her eyes. 'You know,' she said, trying to keep her voice light, 'Joy doesn't think it was an accident at all.'

Marshall suppressed a groan. 'You don't say.'

Flora was glad she couldn't see his face – the rolling of the eyes thing would put her off her stride, and she really, *really* wanted to get this off her chest.

The irony that the person who irritated her the most was also the most level-headed person she knew was not lost on Flora.

Quietly, with as little extraneous detail as possible, Flora told him Joy's story. By the time she'd finished, Marshall was on his knees packing up the last box.

'And she's never shared this with anybody?' he said, incredulous. 'Not even her husband?'

'Especially not her husband. She said Eddie had such a high opinion of her it would have been a crime to tell him.'

Flora had finished the wardrobe ten minutes ago; she was sitting on the bed, which didn't feel like such an imposition now it had been stripped. While she told her story, she'd almost felt as if the Captain was in the room with them, listening, understanding. If only he was – then he could tell them what really happened that day on the stairs and put them all out of their misery.

But then again, maybe not. A ghost at the Maples

would just about finish Joy off.

'Surely she can see now, as an adult, that it wasn't her fault?' Marshall stood up and stretched. 'I mean, it was a stupid kids' prank that went horribly wrong. Who hasn't been involved in something like that?'

Flora looked up at him doubtfully. 'Well, *I* haven't. Are you saying that tricking a boy into a mine shaft and accidentally killing his dog is, like, an everyday type of thing?'

Marshall laughed. 'You're so literal, Flora. I'm saying it's her guilty mind making her imagine all this stuff. And if she'd told someone about it sooner, they might have been able to make her see that.'

Flora nodded. Of course that's what she'd thought all along. It was also exactly what she had wanted him to say. But ...

'I just don't buy all these accidents. Merlin fine, poor soul, but Otto's nearly met his maker twice in the space of two weeks. Two near misses for Joy's dog and one old man dead, who also happened to be a close friend. Don't you think that's bad luck? Even for an old folk's home.'

'Well, you know what I think about the dogs,' said Marshall with a smile.

'It's not the time for your suicidal pet theory, Marshall. This is serious.'

A snuffling in the corner caught their attention and they looked across the room to see Otto poking his turned-up nose out of her blanket.

'I still don't know why you agreed to take that mutt on. It's kinda ugly.'

'Rubbish! Otto's so cute. Anyway, Joy has a way of getting what she wants. I couldn't resist.'

'I'll have to ask her what her secret is.'

Their eyes locked for the briefest of moments. Flora broke the connection, reaching over to cuddle Otto to her chest.

She watched Marshall's back as he used the parcel tape dispenser to wrap up the last of the boxes securely. They had worked well together. Without anyone else around, and without anything to spark off an argument, they'd slipped right back into the companionable routine they'd had when Flora was just the boss's daughter helping out in the family business. Surely there was something she could do to bring him back on side, to stop all the sniping?

Maybe she should agree to his idea for the storage business. She didn't want to, and he knew she didn't want to, so if she did say yes it would be a big enough gesture to restore the equilibrium. He could head up that side of the business and she could carry on with the removals. In fact, the more she thought about it, the better it sounded.

'Hey,' she said, idly stroking Otto's round little head.

Marshall hoisted two boxes off the floor. 'What?'

'I've been thinking about your commercial storage thing–'

'Not now, Flora,' he said quickly. 'Let's not talk about that, okay?'

'But I was only going to say–'

'I don't want to talk about it.' Now he was angry. How did he get from happy and friendly to angry so fast? Sometimes Flora got dizzy just watching his emotions change.

'Well,' she said slowly, 'that's fine. But all I was going to say was–'

'Jesus wept!'

Before she could finish her sentence, Marshall stormed past her and was halfway down the corridor. Flora put Otto on the floor and raced after him. She reached the flight of stairs just as he got to the bottom, and she grabbed on to the handrail to lean over and call out.

A wave of vertigo hit her and she reeled back, her head spinning.

Boy, it was high up here.

Flora returned to the balcony and edged forward carefully. Marshall had reached the ground floor already and was striding towards the exit, carrying those two enormous boxes as if they were full of feathers. She sighed. For a big guy, he was pretty touchy.

She pushed away from the handrail and then stopped. She'd been holding on to a chrome rail that ran along the stairs all the way to the bottom. The flights to the upper floors ran to the left of the U-shaped balconies, while the first floor staircase – grand and shallow-stepped – took centre stage below. Flora looked up and down the corridors that led off from the top of the stairs back to the rooms. The handrail snaked off along the walls like a silvery rope, guiding the way. Here, at the very top of the steps, the rail came out in a kind of S shape each side, obviously designed for residents to hold on to while negotiating the descent. The lift was at the other end of the corridor, a two-person affair with mirrored walls and Braille bumps on the buttons.

Flora began to walk down the stairs, holding on to the handrail all the way. When she reached the first floor she followed the rail to the top of the main stairs and stopped. This was where the Captain would have stood. Whether he'd taken the lift or the stairs this far, this was the point where his hands would have gripped the rail, exactly the way he knew he was supposed to.

He might have been nearly ninety but he wasn't stupid. He'd lived through two world wars, won medals, survived goodness-knows-what dangers. The guy didn't have a death wish. And if he'd been about to walk down these stairs right here, then right here is where he would have descended. Holding on all the way.

She looked down. True enough, the bobbly carpet

was already starting to wear along the edges on both sides. The middle, about a metre or so wide, was unmarked and unworn. Ergo, rarely used. Apart from the handful of staff fit enough to run up and down the centre of this extra wide staircase, every single person who used it was sensible enough – wary enough – to step gingerly down the outer edges holding on to the handrail for dear life.

Flora walked slowly back up to the Captain's room. Her finger trailed along the rail all the way. Even if he'd suffered a heart attack, right there at the top of the stairs, he would have fallen where he stood. The steps were shallow and wide. Would he have tumbled all the way to the bottom? Maybe. But it didn't seem very likely.

She stepped into his room and sat on the bed. The Captain, his essence, was gone now. It was bland again, ready for the next addition to the third floor. But Flora spoke out loud, hoping he could hear her wherever he might be now.

'Did you really trip and fall?' she said softly. 'I just can't see it. Not down those stairs, not ending up where you did.'

'What did you say?'

Flora started, her hand flying up to her chest. In the doorway stood the warden, her eyes wary.

'Cynthia,' Flora said with a sigh. 'You made me jump.'

The warden smiled thinly. 'Talking to yourself?'

'Something like that.'

Otto began to bark, rolling around on his special bag, tugging at the lining with bared teeth.

The warden's voice was ice. 'That dog again. I thought Joy asked you to keep it at home.'

'She did. I mean, I am. Except–'

'While you're being paid to be here, this is your place

of work, Flora. And I don't think it's appropriate to bring a dog to work with you.'

Flora bristled. Cynthia Curtis, efficient warden though she was, should take a dose of her own advice and keep her nose out. But before she could think of a suitable comeback, Marshall appeared, bursting into the room like a whirlwind and picking up another two boxes.

'That's what I said,' he told the warden, laughing. 'Check out the special dog carrier she's made for it. Too much time on her hands if you ask me.'

Flora took a moment to adjust to yet another of Marshall's mood changes. Mercurial wasn't the word.

'One more trip and we're out of here,' he told the warden. 'Dog and all. Flora, could you give me a hand with these? This is supposed to be a two-man job.'

Gritting her teeth, Flora faced him down. 'A two-*person* job is what I think you mean. And I am helping. Look, this is me helping.'

She made to pick up the last box, but Cynthia stopped her with an alarmed shriek.

'You can't leave that dog in here alone. What if it escapes?'

The warden had a point. Otto was beyond accident prone. 'Maybe you could keep an eye on him?' Flora said, but the expression on the warden's face told her that was highly unlikely.

Marshall sighed impatiently. 'Put it in the bag, why don't you. Just bring it with you.'

'I can carry a box as well.' Flora knelt down and hoisted the canvas tote onto her shoulder, then grabbed the box containing the Captain's papers. 'Whoops.'

The cardboard box, taped badly underneath, collapsed in her grip and spilled its contents on the regulation brown carpet. A thick manila folder caught Flora on the shin; sheets of paper, yellowed with age, fluttered down on top of it.

With an exasperated huff, Marshall set his load down and bent to re-stack the box. Flora picked up an envelope with an official-looking stamp on the front. She turned it over.

'This is sealed with some kind of wax. Must be important.' She looked up at the warden. 'Maybe it's his will.'

'I don't think so.' The warden was glaring at Flora as if she'd intentionally violated the old man's personal belongings. 'I think you've done enough damage for one day, don't you? I'll clear up this mess. Just take your dog and go.'

Flora pulled a face at Marshall, who shrugged and got to his feet. 'If you're sure you don't mind,' he said, putting on his best all-American drawl. But the warden, clearly immune to his charm, ignored him.

'What's eating her?' Flora said when they were out of earshot.

'No idea, kiddo. But it can't be easy, losing a resident.'

'Well, no. But in her line of work she has to expect it occasionally.'

'She freaked out when they told her there might be a postmortem.'

'What?' Flora stopped dead. They were on the first floor now, not two steps away from where she'd pondered the Captain's accident only ten minutes ago. 'What did you say?'

'Liz told me. You know, the receptionist.'

'Elizabeth?'

'Yeah. She said the police told them it was a possibility because there was only one witness.'

'Who was the warden.'

'Right.'

'When?'

124

'I dunno. Soon, I guess. His family will want to bury him, won't they?'

'He didn't have any family,' Flora said distractedly. 'I meant, when did Elizabeth tell you this?'

And why were you hanging around reception talking to an attractive older lady?

Calling her "Liz", no less.

'Earlier, when we were picking up the key to the room. She said the warden had totally freaked.' Marshall shrugged again as if it was no big deal. He always got self-conscious when he was gossiping. 'Said it was unnecessary and a waste of taxpayers' money. That kind of thing.'

'Really?' Flora couldn't get her head around it. 'Did you think there'd be a postmortem?'

'Sure. Why not? They need to know how he died, don't they?'

'But everyone thinks it was an accident. He tripped.'

They started down the stairs together, Marshall holding his load to one side so he could check his footing.

'Not you, though,' he said when they reached the bottom. 'Or Joy.'

Flora took a step to the left. Marshall couldn't know he was standing on the exact spot where the Captain had died. She looked up into his hazel eyes.

'What?'

'You said just now that everyone thinks it was an accident. Everyone except you and your friend, right? Well, now it looks as though you're gonna find out for sure.'

Chapter 10

I *know UR here I can C YR lorry. Meet U in grdn in 5.*
Flora read the text again and looked at the time.
That she'd managed to persuade Marshall to take Otto
back to the van was a miracle – she just hoped he'd give
her the ten minutes he'd promised. She'd already been
waiting well over five minutes.

'Hello,' a voice hissed behind her ear.

Flora jumped, then glared at her friend. 'What the hell
did you do that for?'

Joy lowered herself onto the bench by Flora's side.
'Didn't want anyone to see us talking. Word on the
street is the warden's upset with you. She's put up a
notice in the communal area warning residents not to
talk about private Maples' business with outsiders.'

'Outsiders? What is this, some kind of sect? And what
the bloody hell are you wearing?'

'There's no need for language, Flora. My skin's a bit
sensitive, that's all.'

Flora took in her friend's odd attire. She was dressed
in some kind of caftan, with long sleeves and a skirt that
floated all the way to the ground. A floppy straw hat
was pulled low over her eyes and around her neck she'd
looped a floral chiffon scarf.

'Are you in disguise?' Flora said, incredulous.

Joy just winked and tapped her nose. 'Loose tongues.'

Whatever that meant. Flora flipped the top off her
water bottle and pointed to the caftan. 'Are they Vera's

clothes?'

'I have some information for you.' Joy lowered her voice to a whisper. 'To help with your investigation.'

'What investigation?'

'You said you were going to help me find out what really happened to the Captain. And you said you were going to prove Aubrey is the caretaker's son.'

Flora shook her head, outraged. 'I did not! I said I was going to try and find out more about the Captain's death, but only because I want to prove to you that it had nothing to do with Mr Felix. Ditto this Aubrey business – I said I was going to prove Mr Felix *isn't* Aubrey, not the other way around.'

'Well, you won't be able prove that because he is, so it's the same difference.'

While Flora was trying to decipher this sentence, Joy peered around the gardens. 'There's been a development,' she hissed.

'Terrific.'

'The Captain had a visitor the day before he was murdered.'

Flora, about to take another sip from her bottle, sprayed water across her lap. 'Joy! You can't go around saying he's been murdered. Think of the other residents, they'll be really upset.'

'They're already upset, Flora. They're frightened and confused, even more so now these rumours are circulating.'

'What rumours?'

'This man I was just telling you about. He's been seen around the complex before – he's quite odd-looking so he sort of stands out. No one knows who he is, or why he visits, but he was seen leaving the Captain's room the day before he died.'

The air was humid and Flora could feel her T-shirt sticking to her back where it pressed against the slats of the wooden bench. She had the beginnings of a headache and an itchy, unsettled feeling she couldn't name. She pressed a button on her phone and looked again at the time.

'Have you mentioned this to the warden?'

Joy nodded. 'She doesn't know who he is either.'

This gave Flora pause. While the units around the quadrant had open access, visitors to the main building were supposed to report to reception.

'There's more,' said Joy.

Flora swallowed. Of course there was.

'Do you remember Ida?'

Flora did. 'The lady who passed away at Christmas?'

'It was Boxing Day, actually. She'd been on the third floor for a month. I didn't know her too well, but it was very sad, especially happening just after Christmas.'

'Wasn't there a bit of a scandal about it at the time?' Flora scanned her memory. 'Didn't she leave all her money to charity, to some kind of animal rescue place?'

'Something like that. Anyway, it turns out that only two days before Ida died – on Christmas Eve no less – she was visited by this same man.'

'What man?'

'The man in black.'

Flora shook her head. 'You've lost me.'

'The man!' cried Joy. Her hat fell off and she grabbed at it and plonked it back on. 'The one I was just telling you about, who visited the Captain last Tuesday.' She laid a hand on her chest, which was heaving under the layers of chiffon.

'Your asthma's still getting worse,' said Flora, her tone resigned. 'And don't think I didn't get a look at your scalp just then. You have to see the Maples' doctor.'

'I'm taking my tablets, it's fine. And don't change the subject,' Joy said between breathy coughs. Flora sighed and looked away. Who'd be friends with anyone over seventy? They were completely intractable.

She watched a bold squirrel dart out from behind one of the newly planted maples. She wondered if her parents would have become stubborn and difficult in old age. She would never have let them end up in a place like this, of course. Not that there was anything intrinsically wrong with it, but most of the residents had no family and that had to tell you something. They'd run out of options. Sleepy City was the last-chance saloon.

'Okay,' said Flora once Joy had got her breath back. 'About this man. How do you know the man who visited the Captain and the one who visited Ida are one and the same?'

'Ha, that's easy. I told you he's really odd-looking. Tall, at least six foot six, and he dresses entirely in black–'

'Yes,' Flora interrupted, 'I got that part.'

'And he's got this bright red beard but almost no hair on his head. No one knows who he is or what he's doing, it's all very mysterious.'

Flora stared at her open-mouthed. 'But *I've* seen him. I saw him right here. I bumped into him walking through the archway just the other day.' She laughed, feeling the tension ebb away. 'Hardly mysterious, but I will admit he looks quite strange.'

'You can't have seen him. Not wandering around in broad daylight.'

'Well, I did.'

'*This* man has these sunken cheeks, looks like an extra from a horror movie,' said Joy, not looking happy at all. 'It can't be the same one you saw.'

'Yep. The very same.' Flora pulled a sucking face. 'Hollow cheeks. And really strong cologne, if I remember rightly. Not the expensive kind, though. Have *you* seen him, Joy?'

Her friend shook her head, but by the expression on her face Flora knew she was right about the cologne.

'When?' Joy demanded. 'When did you see him?'

Flora thought about it for a moment. 'It was Tuesday. The day you told me what happened to Aubrey's dog.'

'Tuesday,' mused Joy. 'Exactly a week after his visit to the Captain.'

'Do you know for sure he went to see the Captain? Maybe he visits someone else on the third floor. Maybe he comes once a week to see them.'

Joy shook her head dismissively. 'If he came every week, don't you think we'd know who he is? No, he definitely came to see the Captain – he was seen leaving his room just before lunch.'

'And Ida? He definitely visited her too?'

When Joy nodded, Flora had an idea. 'Maybe he's like a vicar or something. Come to think of it, he had that sombre thing going on. He certainly wasn't very smiley.'

'Then why wouldn't the warden know about him?'

Flora had no answer to that one. She said, 'So is poor old Mr Felix finally off the hook? It's all about this man in black now, is it?'

Joy tapped her nose again. A crow squawked behind them and Flora jumped. 'I know more than you think, Flora.' She looked over her shoulder, then dropped her voice to a whisper. 'Mr Felix and the man in black are in it together.'

Flora had to bite her lip to stop herself from laughing. 'In it together. Like … accomplices?'

'That's right.'

For a moment, Flora could see the girl Joy had been at fifteen, climbing trees and making up stories in the grounds of a posh boarding school. Did we ever really outgrow our childhood selves? Was this Joy, sixty-five years older, really so different from the teenager who'd yearned for approval and enjoyed stirring up a bit of drama?

'You know what,' said Flora, shuffling to the edge of the bench and stretching out her calves, 'I'm going to go and find your Mr Felix right now and just ask him. This has gone far enough.'

Joy gasped. 'You can't just march up to him and ask him outright. What are you going to say?'

'I don't know yet. I'll figure it out when I find him. But we can't go on like this, Joy. Look at you. Look at your face, your skin. Listen to your breathing. If your tablets are still doing what they're supposed to be doing it must be the stress making you ill. Can't you see how unhealthy it is, all this creeping around and living in the past? And I don't think it's okay for you lot in here to be going around scaring each other with tales of strange men in black and talking about murder. The third floor rumours were bad enough.'

But Joy wasn't paying attention. 'You can't go and talk to him anyway,' she said. An unspoken 'So there' hung in the air.

'Why not?'

'Because he's not here. I saw him go out half an hour ago. He goes to his book group on a Friday afternoon.'

'Do you know where it is?'

'I suppose it's good you've seen the man in black for yourself,' Joy said, ignoring Flora's question. 'At least now we have a witness on the outside too.'

A witness? Flora was about to protest when Joy stood up. 'I need to go,' she said, and then she crept back along the gravel path towards the main building without even saying goodbye.

Flora closed her eyes briefly. She heard shuffling in the hydrangea behind her and half-turned, expecting to see the squirrel again. There was nothing there. She stood and turned full circle. The prickling sensation returned to the damp patch on her back. Was someone watching her?

'Hello?' she said. Her voice sounded shaky. She said hello again, more firmly this time. No one answered.

'Get a hold of yourself, Lively.' She wiped her hand across her forehead and gave her shoulders a little shake. Then she jogged out of the gardens, telling herself she was only jogging because Marshall would already be annoyed at waiting so long. She glanced at Joy's unit as she passed the hedging on the other side of the quadrant, and was surprised to see the warden letting herself out of the door. Why was Cynthia in Joy's unit without her? Flora watched until the warden had disappeared around the corner of the building, then she ran forward and peered in Joy's window. Her friend definitely wasn't home. She shrugged. Probably just doing a security check or something. It stood to reason she would have keys to all the units on the complex.

She thought about the warden's frosty attitude earlier, and her sharpness the day she'd talked to her about Joy. Cynthia sure was a prickly character, primarily concerned about how the retirement village looked to "outsiders". What if there *was* something about the Captain's death that she was hiding? Something that might make her look bad. Maybe he'd slipped on some spilled water, or a sticking up bit of carpet, and she was trying to cover it up. Flora thought back to that horrible day and surveyed the scene in her mind. She was sure she'd have noticed anything like that, and the warden herself said the medics had been with the Captain in minutes. Not long enough for her to have carried out some kind of cover up.

Flora reached the car park and stood in the shade of the topiary arch, lost in her memory. She could see it clearly, see the layout of the stairs from above and below. The warden had been the only person to actually see the Captain fall, she'd said so herself. But for the warden to have seen the Captain start his descent from the point Flora identified today, she would have had to have been standing right in the middle of the bottom of the stairs. Close enough to run up if someone tripped, surely? Perhaps not close enough to catch them, but close enough to break their fall.

For the warden's explanation to make sense, she would have had to have been standing too far away to reach him in time. Except the lobby wasn't that large. Which could only mean one of two things: either the warden had watched the Captain fall and done nothing, or she was lying and she hadn't seen it at all.

And if that was the case, anything could have happened. He could have dropped dead at the foot of the stairs as he was about to climb them; he could have tripped over something at the top of the stairs; he could even have fallen from one of the balconies. Or, he could have been pushed.

Flora shook the thought away. Just because the warden's story didn't make sense to her didn't mean the Captain's death was suspicious. The postmortem might reveal he'd had a heart attack or a stroke – it was impossible to second-guess it. Besides, Cynthia seemed like a woman of character; she'd been genuinely concerned about the Captain. Look how annoyed she'd been when Flora dropped the Captain's personal papers on the floor earlier. She might be overprotective, and a little heartless where pets were concerned, but it didn't make her a liar.

'Flora bloody Lively, stop daydreaming and get in this freaking van. I'm going to strangle your dog in a minute, and this time it won't be an accident!'

'Sorry,' she said as she climbed up into the cab and was greeted by an excited Otto in typical face-licking style. 'It was Joy, she had something to tell me.'

'Whatever. Buckle up.'

She did as she was told. 'Marshall, would you mind dropping me straight home? I've got a bit of a headache.'

'You live a ten-minute walk away, Flora. If you were going straight home why did I have to wait around for you?'

'Because, Mr Grumpy, I didn't know I was going to have a headache, did I? Come on, it's only round the corner.'

'My point exactly.' When they stopped at the traffic lights he said, 'Are you sure you're not just trying to get out of coming to the storage facility?'

'It's not that.' She felt bad about leaving him to unload the Captain's stuff alone, but Marshall was more than capable of dealing with it. The headache wasn't a total lie, but it wasn't the whole truth either.

Marshall drove on. He asked Flora if she'd seen the warden again.

'I saw her but not to talk to. Why?'

'Wondered if she knows what's up with Richie. His message just said he wasn't coming in, no detail.'

Flora pulled a face. 'She didn't mention him at all, did she? Even earlier when we were in the Captain's room. Which is odd, isn't it? If he's ill.'

'Maybe he's – what do you call it over here? Tipping the lead?'

'Swinging the lead.' Flora laughed. 'You've been "over here" for nearly two years, Marshall. When are you going to start acting like a native? I'm sure it's all an affectation.'

'Will this do ya?' he drawled, putting on an exaggerated Texan accent as they pulled up at the end of Flora's street. She laughed again and shook her head. He wasn't even from Texas.

'Can't you get a bit closer,' she teased, knowing full well it was tricky to drive up the narrow road and get the van out again.

'This is close enough,' he said, leaning against his window. 'So you're finishing for the day, are you?'

'Well, I am the boss.'

'You're lazy,' he said mock-seriously.

'I am not. I have a dog to look after and a mystery to solve.'

'The mystery of the suicidal dogs?'

'The mystery of how a sweet old man fell to his death,' Flora corrected.

Marshall dropped his eyes. 'Right. Sorry. But you're not really taking Joy's story seriously, are you?' He turned the key and killed the engine. 'You don't actually think that old guy with the ankle flappers is behind all this?'

Flora picked up a wriggling Otto and popped him back in his carrier. 'Honestly? I just don't know. It all sounds like you said – her guilty mind playing tricks on her. But she's genuinely scared, Marshall, and it's making her ill. I'm going to do whatever I can to reassure her.'

Flora passed the oversized canvas bag across the cab so she could climb out of the van. She came around to the driver's side and held up her arms.

'You're getting too involved, Flora.'

She thought: Tell me something I don't know.

'You're blocking traffic,' she told him, even though the street was clearly empty. 'Better get a wriggle on.'

'Flora Lively investigates,' Marshall said, starting up the engine. 'The mystery at the Maples.'

She pursed her lips in mock disapproval.

'Maybe we should turn Shakers into a detective agency. Beats a handyman service any day.'

Flora shielded her eyes from the sun and squinted up at him. 'Are you trying to be funny? Because this is actually quite serious.'

'Well, good luck with it all.' She could hear the laughter in his voice. 'See you Monday. If you can drag yourself away from your investigation.' He backed out expertly, then drove away with a triple beep of the horn.

Cheek! She shook her head and strode past the rows of identical nineteen seventies bungalows. Her next-door-but-one neighbour was reorganising his garden gnomes, a regular weekly activity. He raised his arm in greeting and Flora called hello, but not before the familiar feeling of being a square peg in a round hole reared its head. There was no way she was ever going to fit in here: Sunnybank Rise was meant for retired couples and gentle middle-aged folk who enjoyed gardening and collecting figurines. Not twenty-nine-year-old single girls who wanted to play their music loud, have garden parties and hot dates, and fill their homes with funky vintage rummage-sale finds.

Not that the hot dates were proving much of a problem. Heston still hadn't called, and Flora was loath to make the first move. But if the afternoon's activities went to plan, she might be able to find out where she stood with her favourite librarian *and* reassure Joy in one masterstroke of detective work. She smiled and slipped down the overgrown path to her mum and dad's front door, lifting Otto out of the bag so she could root around for her key. Otto peered up at her adoringly and tried to lick her on the chin.

'Listen,' said Flora, wiping her face with her sleeve, 'if you and I are going to get along there is one rule you must obey. No licking of my face. At all. And no peeing on handsome men. That's an absolute no-no too.'

***

Shrewsbury's main library was right at the top of Castle Hill, a fifteenth-century Tudor building that once housed the town's school. Flora loved the nooks and crannies offered by the haphazard layout: the deep window seats with their view of the web of lanes and side streets; the echoing stone steps that led from floor to floor. At the main reception she asked for Heston but was told he was on his break. She also found out that the book group was indeed meeting in the Old School Room and would finish in around ten minutes. Flora clattered up the stairs, pleased with her detective work. She'd wanted to talk to Mr Felix, and he was right here in the library with the group Heston had told her about. She could spend some time in the Darwin Room while she waited and look out for them both. Two birds, one stone – she was efficiency personified.

She grabbed a book from the local history section and settled in a vacant window seat, tucking her feet up under her legs. In the street below, a woman was carrying a tiny Chihuahua on her arm like a handbag. Two weeks ago, Flora would have thought she was crazy – crazy and affected and very eccentric. Now she just thought it was sweet. She was actually starting to like having a canine companion. Maybe with a little friend waiting at home every night, panting and trying not to look guilty for chewing her mum's best oak-framed armchair, she wouldn't feel so lonely.

She tried to focus on the book in her hand. Charles Darwin, it said, had been a pupil at Shrewsbury school, in this very building, but not a very distinguished one by all accounts. Her attention wandered again. She breathed contentedly, taking in the muted silence. In here people still believed in whispered conversations, not like most modern libraries. The computers were in a different room; the children's section was far below. Up here, readers took their peace and quiet seriously. The ancient arched windows, set in places with thick, uneven stained glass, threw brightly coloured rays of sunlight across the dusty bookshelves. Her stomach took on that heavy, pulling sensation, like she needed to go to the bathroom, but also a kind of excitement.

She dropped her eyes back to the page as someone began to limp down the aisle towards her. He didn't get very far, she could see his feet turn towards a shelf on her right. His shoes were almost hidden under too-long trousers and next to his left foot was the rubber end of a crutch. Flora looked up. There, only four or five feet away from her, stood Mr Felix. He was already engrossed in a book with a green jacket, leaning over and resting it on top of a precarious-looking trolley loaded with large-print romances. Her greeting died on her lips when she saw what the old man was doing. In one hand he held a bitten-down pencil, and as Flora watched, Mr Felix, his eyes narrowed in concentration, made a note in the book's margin. She moved her head slowly from side to side. Heston would have a fit. Defacing library property, he called it. In his eyes there were few worse sins.

She craned her neck to try and see which shelf he was standing in front of. As far as she could tell it was all medical titles. He cut a surprising figure as a rule-breaker. Why not just take the book to the photocopier instead of writing in it? With his head lowered, Flora could see his pink scalp clearly. She remembered his attitude of mild boredom the morning of the Captain's death, and pictured again his face the day he'd almost run Otto over. Annoyed, rather than mortified. Was there something shifty about him? Something other than merely worn around the edges and perhaps a little bitter? Flora stared, trying to see what Joy saw, trying to imagine how much he might have changed in sixty-odd years. It was impossible to tell.

Flora turned her attention to the book Mr Felix was scribbling in. It had to be something really fascinating to be keeping him so absorbed. Maybe he was sick, trying to research information on a cure. What had Elizabeth said about all the parcels he received? Ordering vitamins over the internet. Sounded like he had a real interest in medical stuff. To get a better view, she dropped to her knees and crept forward, feigning an interest in the parenting section. If the Maples' resident noticed she was even there, he gave no sign. Flora peered across the top of the trolley. On the front of the book was a picture of a plant. She still couldn't see what it was called. She shuffled along a little more, keeping her face averted in case he looked up suddenly. *How to Tame Your Testing Toddler*, she read. *Tantrums From Hell and How to Avoid Them*. Flora shuddered. It wasn't exactly a great advert for motherhood.

Figuring she was close enough now, Flora grabbed a book blindly off the nearest shelf for cover, then shifted her body around, hoping for a quick look at the title of Mr Felix's medical text before he noticed her. But she'd misjudged the distance completely and was now far closer than she'd realised. As she turned, her shoulder smashed right into the trolley, knocking it – and the old man – flying.

Chapter 11

O h, my goodness!' Flora cried, jumping to her feet. 'I'm so sorry!'

Mr Felix was lying on the thin carpet, staring up at her balefully. The lower half of his body was entirely covered in books, while the trolley itself had mercifully fallen on its side between them. His single crutch had also been flung to the side; Flora retrieved it for him and laid it next to his hand. The old man looked so frail, she was sure he must have broken something. If the heavy wooden trolley had hit him ... Well, it didn't bear thinking about.

'Let me move this lot so I can help you up. I can't believe it, I'm so sorry.' She scooped a pile of romances to one side and offered Mr Felix her hand. He didn't take it. While Flora scrambled to release him, he continued to glare at her. But then his expression cleared.

'Aren't you the girl who works for that removal firm? Shaky's or something?'

Flora didn't bother correcting him, on the name or her position within it. She just nodded and smiled disarmingly, offering him her hand again. This time he allowed her to help him up.

'What happened?' he said. Flora frowned.

'They really shouldn't leave these overloaded trolleys cluttering up the aisles, should they?' She shook her head and pursed her lips. 'It was an accident waiting to happen.'

The old man nodded warily. Perhaps he was wondering if she'd seen what he was doing to that book. Flora cast her eyes about, hoping for a glimpse of it. But there was no way to distinguish one single book from the mess of paperbacks and hardbacks cluttering the floor by their feet.

Mr Felix was watching her carefully. His eyes dropped to the book Flora still held in her hand. It was the one she'd grabbed when she'd snuck up on him, and as she followed his gaze she was horrified to find herself gripping a thin paperback called *Herbal Cures for STDs*.

'Take it from me, there aren't any effective ones,' Mr Felix said, grinning.

Flora opened her eyes wide. 'And how, may I ask, would you know?' She smiled. Thank goodness he was having a joke with her. If he realised she'd been spying on him it would be mortifying. Not to mention difficult to explain without getting Joy into trouble.

'I know all about herbal medicine. Herbs generally. I brew up a mean cup of herbal tea. You should try it sometime.'

Flora shoved the offending item back on a shelf. The wrong shelf, of course. Heston had told her about the Dewey decimal system, but right now Flora couldn't give a stuff. Thank goodness Heston hadn't seen her holding that book.

'I'd better tidy this lot up,' she said. Mr Felix helped her right the trolley and together they began to re-stack the books. Flora flung them back haphazardly, while her companion took his time. She pretended not to notice when he carefully slipped a particular title back onto its shelf, but she did make a note of its location: 635. She filed it away for future reference, then turned her attention back to Mr Felix.

Now was her opportunity to ask about Joy. She just

had to find the right way to get into it.

'How are you settling in at the Maples?' she said, making her voice nonchalant.

'Fine,' he replied.

Hmm. Might need a more direct approach. So much for Marshall's idea of her as some kind of investigator. So far she'd alerted the subject to her presence by showering him in Mills & Boon novels and was now struggling to think of a single clever question.

Flora Lively investigates indeed!

'What made you choose to move there?' she said, inspiration striking.

He replaced another book then stood back to consider. In the fall his comb-over had come loose and now it hung comically down the wrong side of his head. Flora tried not to look at it.

'It seemed like an okay place to retire to,' he said, leaning heavily on the crutch. 'Although the food isn't as good as they promised. They don't cook *everything* on site, you know. Some of the meals are brought in.'

Flora tutted. 'Shocking. And did you know anyone else who lives there? Before you came, I mean?'

He shook his head. 'No. But that doesn't bother me. Always liked my own company.'

'But did you recognise anyone once you moved into your unit? Anyone from your past?'

The silence made her look up from the trolley. Mr Felix was staring at her, and his expression was no longer friendly. 'Why are you asking me all these questions? Oh, I get it.'

Whatever he got made him pretty mad. Flora shrank away as his eyes darkened.

'You and that woman with the dog – you and her are thick as thieves, aren't you? And don't think I haven't noticed she's been spreading rumours about me. It's always the same with people like her, people with money. They think they can look down on me, just because I'm renting my unit with my pension, which I've worked damn hard for, mind. Well, you can tell her that I don't care what she says about me behind my back. I didn't try and knock her stupid dog over on purpose, it ran out in front of me, and I've never done anything to upset anyone in that place. I just keep myself to myself.'

Flora was backing even further away, still on her knees, holding out her hands in a calming gesture. But he was winding himself up, creating his own momentum, and she was horrified to see tears forming in the corners of his pale eyes. He waved a book at her menacingly, his hand shaking. *The Billionaire's Secret Cove* it was called, with a cover depicting an impossibly beautiful woman gazing up adoringly at a remote-looking man. Mr Felix advanced, almost tripping over the couple of books that still lay on the floor, berating her and waving his unlikely weapon.

'Were you spying on me?' he cried, raising his voice to a high-pitched wobble on "spying".

'No, not at all. I was just–'

'Trying to spoil the little bit of peace I get, making out I'm some kind of criminal. I love dogs, you know, I'd never hurt one. I don't know why they've all turned against me, I don't know why.'

He was openly weeping now, and Flora was beside herself with guilt. How could she have gone against her own instincts like that and let Joy convince her this poor old man was anything other than harmless?

'I'm so sorry,' she said, nearly crying herself. She tried to reach out and pat his arm but he squealed and shrank away from her touch.

'Flora?'

Oh no. A bad situation just about to get so much worse. There was no mistaking the cultured tones of Heston's voice. Slightly too high-pitched for a man, but smooth and assured. Flora closed her eyes briefly, still holding out a conciliatory hand to Mr Felix, before turning to face Heston's shocked countenance.

'What on earth is going on?' Heston looked like he might keel over himself as he took in the scattered books, the haphazardly filled trolley, and the old man crying amidst it all.

'Nothing to worry about,' Flora said briskly, forcing a bright smile. 'Just a bit of a mishap. We'll get it straightened out in no time at all.' What a nightmare. The last time her so-called boyfriend had seen her he'd gotten covered in dog pee; now he'd found her at the centre of a rumpus in his precious library with a crippled old man crying and accusing her of spying on him. Flora began to shove the rest of the books onto shelves, more to avoid meeting Heston's eyes than out of any real desire to help.

'Leave it, Flora,' Heston said. His voice was cool. 'You're messing up the Dewey decimal system.'

Sod the bloody Dewey decimal system. What about your girlfriend – don't you care that she might be hurt? Or embarrassed? Or both? Her shoulder was in fact throbbing quite badly from where she'd shoved into the heavy trolley, and her pride was in serious need of attention too. Worse, an old man was genuinely upset and her stupid meddling had been the cause of it. Flora stared hard at the floor and wished she could simply disappear.

'Flora?'

When she finally stood up she was gratified to see a small amount of concern in Heston's eyes.

'Can you tell me what's going on?'

Flora opened her mouth, but she could already see she wasn't going to get a chance to speak. Mr Felix, finally realising Heston was a member of staff, started filling him in in graphic detail. Flora had no choice but to stand by and listen while the old man embellished her role in the trolley fiasco, accusing her of everything bar stamping on his hands while he lay prone on the ground. She rolled her eyes towards the ceiling – he might be harmless but he was a tell-tale alright. She decided to keep her silence regarding his own particular crime of writing in library stock. It would only sound churlish if she brought it up now, and she didn't think Heston could cope with any more shocks.

With a final, despairing glance over his shoulder, Heston led the Maples' resident away, promising a cup of tea and a complimentary DVD rental to compensate for his troubles. Flora slid down the nearest shelf and parked her rear on the floor, trying to steady her breathing. Mortifying. Absolutely one of the most embarrassing moments of her life.

After a few shaky breaths she pushed herself back to her feet and headed for the library's exit. At the main counter she borrowed some paper and wrote Heston a note, saying she was sorry and asking him to call so she could explain. Then she raced outside, desperate to put some distance between her and the scene of her crime.

All that "Did you recognise anyone at the Maples?" nonsense. Her cheeks burned just thinking about it. Well, at least she had gotten an answer to that question: there was no way Mr Felix was Aubrey. Either he was an amazing actor or he'd had no idea what Flora was talking about.

What he did seem aware of, painfully so, was that Joy had it in for him. Flora stepped out into the late afternoon sunshine and vowed that she was not going to get involved in Joy's crazy theories anymore. It would all right itself in the end. The Captain's death would no doubt be explained by the postmortem, and this man in black would turn out to be someone's son or long-lost cousin. Eventually life at the Maples Retirement Village would return to normal and go on as before. Peacefully. Where the only thing to fear was being moved to the third floor and losing your independence.

Leaning against the foot of the Charles Darwin statue, Flora took a moment to drink in a bit of peace of her own. What a day. Otto was waiting for her at home, and Flora needed to stop off at the supermarket and pick up more dog food and treats for the weekend. Plus a bottle of wine and a ready meal for herself. A nice quiet weekend, with nothing more onerous than a bit of light housework and perhaps some time spent thinking about the Rockfords situation. At least Joy's capers had kept Flora's mind off that particular problem for a while, but she wondered whether it was wilful procrastination. Rockfords weren't going away, and Flora needed to come up with a strategy to deal with it fast. Otherwise she'd be at Marshall's mercy – not a prospect she relished.

Preoccupied, Flora didn't see the man walk past her, crossing the square and heading in the direction of the offices in School Gardens. What she noticed was the smell he left behind. She wrinkled her nose. It was familiar, but not in a good way. Cheap cologne. Musk, mixed with the cloying scent of over-ripe fruit. Yuk! But then a flash of black caught her eye, and she turned in time to see a distinctive form stop, glance around briefly, then slip under an arch and out of sight.

Those hollow cheeks were noticeable even from this distance. And there was no mistaking that bright red beard and bald pate – he looked like a man who had his head on upside down. Tall, wearing black …

Don't do it, Flora, said a voice in her head. Just let it be. If you really think there was something odd about the Captain's death go to the police and tell them. Let them deal with it. What can you do, anyway? You couldn't even make a proper job of questioning a harmless old man.

But what if there was a link, innocent though it might be? The visits to the Captain and Ida … If Flora could discover what the link was, surely that would be enough to satisfy Joy? And if Joy would give up on this caretaker's son business, finally see that there were no mysterious happenings at the Maples whatsoever, she would get back her peace of mind and be well again. Her asthma would improve, her skin would clear up, and she'd stop terrorising the other residents. Really, thought Flora as she pushed away from the statue and started across the square, she had no choice. She had to finish what she'd started. It was time to clear up this nonsense once and for all.

***

'What do you mean you followed him? Wasn't that really risky?'

'I guess. But I'm glad I did. I found out who he is, and what his connection with the Captain was.'

'Wow, Flora. That's awesome! I totally under-estimated you. You're much more capable than I ever gave you credit for.'

Flora smiled to herself. Otto had stopped to investigate a lamppost; Flora allowed her mind to wander again.

'I've been wrong about lots of things, haven't I?' Marshall is wearing one of his fraying fraternity sweaters and pale blue jeans. His face is contrite.

The problem with imaginary conversations, thought Flora as she tugged at Otto's lead, was that they always left you feeling unsatisfied. Even if such a conversation did take place, it would be bound to degenerate into a snippy row. Anyway, she should be focusing on the real reason for this Saturday morning meeting, which certainly wasn't to discuss Flora's discovery about Joy's mystery man in black. Yet another Saturday without any removals booked in had triggered crisis talks. Uncle Max was getting the train into Shrewsbury and meeting her and Marshall at ten o'clock. Flora pulled her mobile phone out of her bag and noted the time: quarter to. She was going to be early, which meant she could get Otto settled in the makeshift crate she'd set up, thus avoiding another lecture from Marshall about bringing pets into work. Max wouldn't mind, of course. In fact, he'd be amazed. Flora's mum and dad had often joked that she couldn't take care of herself properly, let alone a pet. They'd never bought her so much as a goldfish. She bent and picked Otto up as they approached the railway arches, giving the panting pooch a cuddle.

'Look at me, Mum,' she whispered. 'Looks like I'm finally growing up.'

Flora rounded the corner, but what she saw outside Shakers stopped her in her tracks. Marshall was standing by a bright red sports car, hands in pockets, looking typically rumpled and dishevelled. Flora's eyes widened when she saw who Marshall was talking to. Leaning proprietarily on the car's bonnet was the handsome stranger Flora had seen in this very car park only four days ago. As if to contrast even more dramatically with Marshall, today he sported a dark grey suit over a cool cotton shirt, open at the neck to reveal just the tiniest glimpse of dark hair. His green eyes were trained on Marshall intently, while his posture remained relaxed.

Flora swallowed and began to step slowly backwards, seeking the shelter of the nearest doorway.

What was he doing here? She ran her free hand through her hair and looked down at her dog-hair-covered T-shirt in alarm. Had he come to see her again? Not likely. Flora laughed at herself. 'What am I like?' she said to Otto, who responded with a quick woof. Flora put her finger to her lips. 'Shh, I don't want them to see us.'

Of course he wasn't here in search of her. His appearance was so polished, so immaculately groomed, he looked completely out of place outside Shakers' yard. She peeped out to see what they were doing. Just talking. Uncle Max could arrive at any minute – she couldn't let him catch her hiding in the doorway of the kebab shop. She'd just have to brazen it out and face the guy, even if she did look a fright.

Just as she was about to launch herself out into the yard, Marshall stuck out his hand and the stranger, after the briefest pause, gave it one firm shake. Then he jumped into his car and drove away, mercifully not catching sight of Flora who hid her face behind splayed fingers. She waited until his car had disappeared under the bridge, then stepped out of her hiding place. Marshall was still standing in the car park looking pensive. When he saw Flora approaching he gave himself a barely perceptible shake and plastered on a grin.

'You're early. Dog wet the bed again?'

'Funny. Is Uncle Max here yet?'

'Nope.'

Flora started towards Shakers' entrance, with Marshall trailing behind.

'Who was that guy?' she asked, gratified to find she sounded only mildly interested.

'No one.'

'No one? I saw you shaking his hand.'

Marshall shrugged and walked past her, pulling up the shutters with a deafening clatter. About to press him further, Flora was cut off by a familiar voice at her shoulder.

'Not bickering again, I hope? You two lovelies should learn to play nicely.'

She threw her arms round her uncle, accidentally letting go of Otto's lead as she did so.

'Now what on earth,' said Max when Flora had retrieved the pooch, 'is that dog doing here?'

'Long story. You don't mind, do you? I'm kind of looking after him for a while. For a friend. But he's no trouble.'

'Mind? Of course I don't mind.' Max beamed, his teeth white against his weathered skin. 'I think it's a wonderful idea for you to have a pet. Hey, if you decide you want one of your own, I've got some collie pups going.'

'Well, this is real lovely, but if it's all the same to you guys I'd like to get on with our meeting.' Marshall stood by the open door, practically glaring at them. Flora raised her eyebrows to Max, who grinned.

'Come on then, boy. Let's get this show on the road.'

***

'The thing with business is, it's all about knowing when to change and when to stick with what you have.'

Flora couldn't stop the huff that escaped from her mouth.

'You don't agree, Flora?' Max's eyes were creased at the edges, and in the creases Flora could see lines of grime. She couldn't help but marvel at the change in him – he had thrown himself into the good life one hundred per cent. This was his first visit in months to the town where he'd lived for nearly seventy years, and he'd not bothered dressing up for it, that was for sure.

She smoothed her hands across her knees, regretting her own choice of smart linen skirt in lieu of her usual jeans. She'd wanted to create the right impression, but apparently neither Marshall nor Max had had the same idea.

'I do agree, but Marshall's only saying that because he thinks it's time to change. He's got this idea – has he told you his idea? Of course he has. It's not right, Max. Dad wouldn't have wanted it. Not without a fight, anyway.'

'I've never proposed anything that would be disrespectful to your father, Flora, and I resent the implication that I would.'

'See what I have to put up with?' Flora turned despairing eyes to her uncle. 'Now he's gone all pompous on me, all hard-done-by, but I'm telling you, he's been pushing this commercial storage idea for months.'

'Well, let's hear him out, why don't we?' Max was sitting in Flora's chair, his grubby hands laced across a bulging stomach. Flora and Marshall had arranged their seats opposite, and the resemblance to naughty school children reporting to their head teacher was already starting to grate on Flora's nerves.

'Fine,' she grumbled. 'Go on then.'

'And Flora, I don't know anything about this idea of Marshall's, although I do know he's had some thoughts about the business. That's what we're here for, right? To discuss them.'

'Hm.' She couldn't trust herself to say any more.

Marshall leaned back in his chair so far Flora thought he might fall off. Hoped he would, more like. 'Flora's right, Max. I was keen on branching out into commercial storage. But now I'm not convinced it's the way to go.'

Flora's head shot around so fast she cricked her neck. 'What? That's news to me!'

He shrugged. Infuriated, Flora jumped up and turned her back on the two men. She grabbed a packet of coffee and switched on the machine. 'So what's caused this change of heart?' she said through gritted teeth.

Marshall took his time answering, and Flora wondered what silent communication was going on behind her back.

'I'm just not sure it's the right area for us to move

into now. Six months ago, maybe. But the opportunities are closing up fast.'

'Oh, right. I get it.' Flora swung around to face him. 'I see exactly where you're going with this. You had an idea that could have saved Shakers, but I blocked you all the way. Now that idea is redundant, and it's all my fault for not going with it. So Shakers is stuffed and you can sit back and say "I told you so" but take no responsibility. Brilliant, Marshall. You must be really proud of yourself.'

'Flora, what are you saying?' Max was on his feet now, hauling his huge frame up to lean over the cluttered desk. 'You can't honestly believe Marshall has anything other than the best interests of this business in mind, whatever ideas he comes up with?'

'No. Yes. Oh, I don't bloody know.' She was trying to rip the top off the packet of coffee but it was sealed too tight and the little tag had already come away in her hand. 'Damn this bloody thing!' She threw the packet onto the worktop and picked up another.

Marshall leaned even further back in his chair and held out his hands, palms up. *See what I have to put up with*, was the clear message. Flora could see through him completely. He'd engineered this whole situation to make her look bad. Give him a week and he'd be harking on about the storage scheme again, or something else equally far away from Peter Lively's vision.

'Max,' she said, struggling to keep her voice level, 'Shakers is not doing great. You've seen the accounts, bookings are down and we've hardly had to use Steve at all this month. Stuart's already moved on, and we can barely afford to keep the new driver. What do *you* think we should do?'

She turned back to the coffee machine and yanked at the fresh packet. The top came off in one smooth movement. Hallelujah!

'I know your dad's original idea was to focus on domestic removals, the personal service that Shakers has always done so well.'

Flora couldn't resist a jubilant smile in Marshall's direction.

'But, like Marshall said, in business you have to know when to change and when to stick with what you know. What's happening with Rockfords? Any news on their new branch in Shrewsbury?'

Marshall rocked forward and planted his feet on the floor. 'They've pulled out of the lease for the offices in Battlefield. Don't know what that means for us, exactly.' His tone was casual, but the atmosphere in the office changed immediately.

'What?' Flora nearly dropped the jug of water on the floor. 'When did you hear this?'

'Just now.'

Max sat down heavily, his brow creasing. He waited for Marshall to carry on, but Flora was too impatient to wait.

'What do you mean, just now? Like, you got a text or something?'

'No.'

'Well, what then?' She came to stand beside her uncle and laid a hand on his shoulder. For some reason she needed the support.

Marshall took a deep breath. 'I found out just before this meeting. I was ... chatting with the younger son of the Rockford clan.'

'He phoned you? Out of the blue? What for?'

Looking up into Flora's eyes, Marshall said, 'No. He dropped by. I talked to him in person.'

'You ... In person?'

No. It couldn't be.

'The man you were talking to outside was David Rockford?' Flora's cheeks began to burn. 'Are you sure?'

Marshall threw her an odd look. 'Of course I'm sure.'

'What was he doing here, son?'

'I think he was sizing us up, to be honest,' Marshall told Max. 'We got chatting outside. He's okay. Kind of friendly.'

'Well, he would come across as friendly, wouldn't he?' Flora cut in. 'Sizing us up, trying to take away our customers, dropping round here all the time, undercutting us at every opportunity.'

Acting so kind and concerned that day when she'd been spooked by the guy in the hoodie. Gazing at her with those deep green eyes.

Furious at herself for being so easily taken in, Flora turned her anger on an easier target. 'I can't believe you would consort with the enemy like that, Marshall. He's probably much cleverer than you realise, I bet he was pumping you for information. Did he mention me?' she added, then could have bitten off her tongue when she saw Marshall's amused expression.

'No, he didn't mention you. Why would he?'

'No reason.'

'And I wasn't consorting with anyone.'

'Of course you weren't,' Max said, reaching over the desk to give Marshall's hand a reassuring pat. 'And Flora, I think you'll find our Marshall is more than a match for that Rockford boy, eh?'

Marshall grinned and nodded. Dropping to her knees to check on a sleeping Otto, Flora made a gagging motion under the cover of the desk. What a love-in. No wonder she hadn't managed to convince Max he should give Marshall his marching orders. The question was, if she decided to do it herself would Max back her up?

Not likely.

When she stood again Marshall was eyeing her with interest. 'Have you and David Rockford met before?' he said, smirking.

'What? Of course not. I had no idea who he was.'

'Well, that's not what I asked. But you said earlier he was round here "all the time". Are you sure you haven't bumped into him yourself at some point?'

Flora glared at him. An image of Marshall's face pressed against the office window sprang into her mind. He knew perfectly well they'd met before. The swine.

'I have no idea what you're talking about. And stop trying to deflect attention away from yourself, you're the one who's been–'

'Consorting. With the enemy, right. But maybe you were thinking about a different kind of consorting?'

'Children, please.' Max was smiling, but his expression was strained. 'This isn't getting us anywhere. Now, if Marshall says Rockfords might not be taking up those premises it's a cause for celebration. My vote is that we dig in a while longer and see how things go. What do you think? We can meet up again in, say, three months and see where we're at. Okay?'

Flora nodded mutely; Marshall reached over the desk and shook Max's hand.

Like he shook David Rockford's hand.

Just what had they been discussing? Flora wanted to know so badly it was like an ache in her gut, but there was no way Marshall was about to share it with her. And she had no intention of exposing herself to any more teasing, either.

The coffee machine started to announce itself ready for action. 'I'll have one of those,' her uncle said. 'Marshall?'

'Gotta go, I'm afraid. Great seeing you, Max. Catch up soon, yeah?'

Flora looked away while they hugged. She ignored Marshall's 'See you later, Flora' and busied herself making the coffee. Two sugars and as milky as possible for Max. He took his coffee the same way as her dad.

They took their mugs down into the warehouse and sat by the open shutters with their feet on packing crates, enjoying the sunshine.

'You and Marshall. Not going too well?'

The understatement cut through Flora's annoyance and she started to laugh.

'No, not really. You noticed, huh?'

Max nodded sagely. He opened his mouth to speak, but Flora cut him off.

'Let's talk about something else. Like you said, let's just leave things as they are for a while. See how it goes.'

Her uncle's face was a picture of relief. While he sipped his coffee, Flora filled him in on the latest from the Maples, finally telling him her theory that the Captain's death may not have happened exactly the way the warden told it.

'That's a serious allegation, Flora. If you really believe she's lying shouldn't you go to the police?'

'They'd laugh at me. I've got no proof, no evidence. Although …' Flora told Max about the strange man in black who'd visited the Captain the day before his death. 'I found out who he is – he's a solicitor with offices by Castle Gate. Chances are he was the Captain's solicitor, and that's why he was visiting. But I'm no closer to finding out what really happened to the Captain. Or to proving to Joy that it's nothing to do with Mr Felix.' The memory of knocking the old man over in the library made Flora wince. 'I have a feeling about this Mr Vasco, though. I just can't put my finger on what it is. Max? What's wrong?'

Flora laid her hand on her uncle's arm. Max Lively looked like he'd just swallowed something completely disgusting.

'That solicitor, what did you say he was called?'

'Vasco. It was written on the nameplate of his office and I saw him inside, talking on the phone. W Vasco and

Co., Solicitor. Wills, trust and probate. That's what gave me the idea that he might be visiting the Captain to help him write his will. Why?'

'Vasco,' Max repeated. He shook his head. 'Billy Vasco. It must be him – there can't be many solicitors in Shrewsbury with a name like that. Unless it's his son – how old is your man in black?'

'Fifty.' Flora shrugged, she wasn't great at guessing ages. 'Maybe mid fifties.'

'The very same, then. Well, I don't believe it. You'd have thought he'd have been disbarred by now. Billy Vasco still operating, and in his old stomping ground no less. Well, nothing should surprise me anymore, I suppose.'

'So you know him? You know this Mr Vasco?'

'It was years ago.' Max sipped his coffee thoughtfully. 'When I was working for the council. It caused quite a stir, mainly because it involved a fellow councillor – can't remember his name now. Robert? Phil?'

'Uncle Max, I don't have a clue what you're talking about. Could you, like, start at the beginning?'

Max smiled and shifted to the side so Flora could perch on the crate by his feet. A swallow flew up to the edge of the doors, hovered for the shortest moment, then turned abruptly and flew away. Flora tipped her face to the sun and listened.

'I don't remember all the details, to be honest. Just that one of the bigwigs on the council got involved in something bad. Nightclubs, it was, if memory serves. Something to do with a dodgy licence. Anyway, this Billy Vasco of yours, he made it all go away. Sharp, he was. Odd-looking fella, big bushy beard and ginger hair.'

'He's still got the beard, but not the hair.'

'Ha! No, I don't suppose he would after all these years. Well, he was a hotshot back then, and like I said, he made it all go away for Phil. Or was it John? John …

157

what was *his* name?'

'Max? Tangent. Coming back to the story?'

'Sorry. We all figured Vasco must have had someone in his pocket. The councillor had to step down of course, but at least he avoided prison.'

Flora slipped her foot out of her flip-flop and rotated her ankle. 'And how does that make Mr Vasco such a bad egg? Sounds like he was just doing his job. Seedy though it was, obviously.'

'There was a sting in the tail for the councillor. Word was, Vasco blackmailed him. For years. Fleeced him good and proper, used what he knew to earn himself a nice little sideline. And I had it on good authority it wasn't the first time.'

'That's terrible! What, and this was common knowledge? How did he get any clients in the first place?'

'He was good, for one thing. Really clever, especially about financials. Knew all the red tape and the ins and outs of the legal system. Wills, probate, embezzlement, tax avoidance, he was your man. And it wasn't common knowledge at all – you're forgetting that your old uncle was pretty high up in the county council. I had my ear to the ground, that's all. Like I said, it was quite a scandal. And it wasn't the only one he was involved in, either.'

Flora tucked her legs up and rubbed them. She had goosebumps on her calves.

'What happened to him?' she said, but Max had put down his mug and was staring at her, his expression grave.

'Flora, I don't want you mixed up in anything that's got Vasco's name on it. You say you followed him?' Flora nodded. 'Why? What on earth are you getting mixed up in now?'

'I wanted to find out who he was. He was the last person to visit the Captain before he died.'

Max didn't say anything for a while. He got up and stood by the shutter, looking out at the empty yard. Flora took in the greasy patches on his collar and felt a stab of sadness deep in her belly.

'Flora, I want you to promise me something.'

She looked up, shielding her eyes. 'What?'

'Promise me you won't go near Vasco again. He's bad news, and whatever he's up to, you don't want any part of it.'

The day she'd bumped into Mr Vasco was the same day she'd been followed. Or not followed – the guy in the hoodie might have been totally innocent. And of course the two things couldn't be connected, but thinking of those footsteps on the cobbles behind her and the reflection of the faceless figure in the shop window caused her goosebumps to turn into a shiver.

And then the memory of the guy with the green eyes, so concerned and caring when she confessed to being spooked, caused a completely different kind of shiver. David Rockford – yuk! And she'd been so gooey over him. Marshall had stitched her up, not telling her straight away who he was. Not sending him packing. She wouldn't forget that in a hurry, no way. She didn't need any handsome strangers to protect her, she knew exactly what she was doing. And Max's words had just given her an idea.

'Flora?'

'What?'

'Will you promise?'

She nodded. 'Okay, Uncle Max. I won't go near him again.'

It was just as well he couldn't see her right hand, or the way her fingers were firmly crossed behind her back.

Chapter 12

The ringing of the phone woke Flora early on Monday morning. Groaning, she rolled out of bed and pulled her ragged old dressing gown around her shoulders, tying the belt in a daze. She looked at her alarm clock, which she hadn't bothered setting on her day off. It was seven thirty.

Otto was snoozing in the middle of the duvet, his paws still fighting away an imaginary foe. Flora tutted disgustedly.

'Oh, you just have a lie in, why don't you? It's not like you kept me awake all night or anything. Don't let a little thing like the phone wake you up, will you?'

She grumbled her way through the lounge and out into the hall. Her mum and dad had been old school when it came to telephones, and the only one in the entire bungalow was situated on the wall by the front door. The part-glass front door, which meant if anyone walked past the drive right now they'd catch an eyeful of Flora in ratty PJ bottoms and gaping dressing gown with her hair sticking up like a flat-top. She tried to flatten her hair with one hand while reaching for the phone. Which stopped ringing the very second she touched it.

'Just great. Perfect, in fact.' Not even bothering to dial 1471, Flora traipsed back through the bungalow on autopilot. Otto was stretching out on the bed, rolling from side to side, his face a picture of bliss.

'Shove over. It's not officially morning yet. Don't get

any ideas.'

But no sooner had Flora snuggled down, her pillow cool under her cheek, than the ringing started up again. This time she made it in thirty seconds flat.

'Flora?'

'Joy. What's up?'

Flora couldn't help the silent groan that escaped her lips. Seven thirty on the morning of her day off meant it had better be some problem of mammoth proportions.

'They're moving me, Flora. On Saturday.'

'Moving you where?' Surely this wasn't the time to be asking for a quote from Shakers, although if Joy really had decided to leave the Maples Flora would offer to do the removal for free.

In fact, she'd be glad to see her friend out of there. Maybe then they'd all get a bit of peace.

Joy's voice was muffled, as though she was trying to cover her mouth and talk at the same time.

'I can't hear you. Say that again?'

'They're moving me to the third floor. The warden found my medication. She knows all about the asthma and she says I can't stay in my unit anymore. This is it, Flora. This will be the end of me. I don't know what to do.'

Flora rubbed her eyes and thought for a minute. Time to be super tactful.

'Joy, maybe this isn't such a bad thing. You've been so ill lately – your medication doesn't seem to be working at all. You knew you couldn't hide it forever.'

'Someone must have tipped them off,' Joy whispered. 'Cynthia turned up at six o'clock this morning and demanded to know what meds I had on the premises. Apparently residents have to get approval for medication now, they're cracking down on health and safety or something. We're only allowed a week at a time.'

Flora sighed. She could see where this was going.

'How could anyone have tipped her off, Joy? No one knows about your condition except you and me.'

'Not so. Aubrey knows. I had it as a teenager. He knows all about it.' The old lady laughed breathlessly. 'I flushed the tablets down the toilet so she wouldn't find them. Unfortunately I forgot to get rid of the packet.'

Flora shook her head in despair. Otto's wet nose pressed into Flora's palm. He probably needed to pee. She knelt down to stoke him. Poor Joy, there all alone with her favourite companion in exile. 'What can I do? Do you need more medication?'

'No, the warden's marching me off to the centre's doctor at nine. I need you to come over and talk to her. Will you do that for me? Will you tell her that I'm fine, that I don't need to be moved up to Special Care? It's only asthma, for goodness sake. It's not like I'm really sick.'

Flora ended the call with a promise to visit later that morning. She let Otto out into the garden, then emptied a tin of dog food into a bowl. Joy's fears about the third floor were totally unfounded, but her psychological state was now in even greater peril. Still, she baulked at the idea of talking to Cynthia. Why would the warden listen to Flora? She hadn't seemed especially keen on her meddling last time they'd spoken. But a promise was a promise. And while she was there, it would be an ideal opportunity to ask about the Captain's visitors. Mr Vasco would be on record if he were there on official business. No matter what Max had warned, Flora was determined to find out what the shady solicitor was doing at the Maples. She owed it to Joy to prove once and for all that there was nothing to worry about on the third floor – now more than ever.

And she figured Mr Vasco was as good a place as any to start.

'No. Absolutely not. I'm sorry, but I've got the entire complex to think about, not just your friend. I can't risk having another death on the premises. Joy is seriously ill – you do realise she has chronic asthma?'

Flora kept her head down and fixed her eyes on the warden's sturdy shoes. There was no way she was admitting to knowing about it for the last six months. Cynthia would have a fit.

'Anyway, your fears are unfounded. She'll be perfectly safe up there. We provide the very best of care here, and I resent the insinuation that our residents are anything but well looked after.'

The warden was sitting on her desk, not behind it, looking down on Flora, who felt like a naughty school girl asking for permission to be excused from PE. They were in the office behind the main reception with the door half open; Elizabeth could be heard typing outside, her long nails clacking furiously against the keyboard.

On her way over, Flora had tried to get the Vasco connection straight in her head. Ida was bothering her – the other unfortunate Maples' resident who died just after Christmas. Joy had said the same man visited Ida on Christmas Eve. And Ida had died only days later, just like the Captain.

A solicitor visits a resident of a retirement village – and if Flora's instinct was right, the visit was most likely linked somehow to the writing of their will – and the next day, or day after, the resident is dead. Deaths in old folks' homes aren't usually suspicious, of course. In some cases they are almost to be expected. But it was too much of a coincidence to mean nothing. If Vasco didn't have such a shady past it could be written off as pure bad luck, but Flora wasn't convinced. She wondered if the Captain and Ida were connected in some way – what if the person who benefited most from their deaths was in league with Mr Vasco? Maybe he even faked their wills, getting them to sign all their money over to him, then engineering their deaths in some way, too impatient to wait for nature to take its course.

She knew this was ridiculous. For one thing, as their solicitor Vasco surely wouldn't be able to claim the money for himself. That would press so many alarm bells he wouldn't get away with it for a minute. And from what Max had said, he'd be far too clever for that. Also, hadn't Ida left her entire estate to charity?

The whole situation was too unsettling to be ignored. If she could just dig around a little, find out what she could about the solicitor – prove to herself that there was nothing untoward going on – she might be able to set Joy's mind at rest about the third floor.

'Well of course, it's not her physical safety I'm concerned about,' she said, smiling up at the warden disarmingly. 'Joy's incredibly stressed about this sudden move – she was on the phone to me before breakfast this morning, worrying herself sick about it. Whatever the rights or wrongs of her fears, Cynthia, you've got to consider her mental health as well. Independence is so important to people like Joy. Take it away and she'll just get worse.'

Cynthia tutted. 'Independence is an illusion in a place like this. Besides, we do consider mental health. We have groupwork and counselling sessions – there's an Adapting to Special Care programme Joy will be put on straight away. They meet once a week in the yoga room. It's very positive.'

Flora tried to imagine Joy taking part in a groupwork session. Sharing her feelings. Circle time. She pulled a face, then tried to cover it up by biting a nail. Cynthia wasn't watching, she was staring out of the window towards the medical centre.

'Reports for you to sign.' Elizabeth appeared at Flora's shoulder, holding a sheaf of papers. The warden held out her hands distractedly, then dropped the papers on her desk.

'You've got no idea what it's like here at the moment,' she said. It was hard to tell who exactly she was talking to. Elizabeth looked at Flora, who shrugged. 'We've had the police sniffing around, asking questions about the Captain, quizzing us about our COSHH procedures.'

'Control of substances hazardous to health,' Elizabeth explained in answer to Flora's raised eyebrow. 'Drugs and stuff.'

'Ah.' Flora pursed her lips. 'Joy said something about you searching her unit. She said you'd been tipped off.'

'And just as well we did. Do you know she actually tried to flush her medication down the toilet? That's not the behaviour of a well person. Maybe you're right,' the warden mused. 'Maybe we should get Joy assessed by the centre's psychiatrist.'

Not good. 'I don't think that's necessary. She's under stress, and she's worried about … well, lots of things. But there's nothing wrong with her mind.' Great, thought Flora. Joy sent me here to improve things, not make them worse.

'Well, that's all fine then. She'll be much happier when she settles into Special Care, you'll see. She hasn't got any actual family now, has she?'

Flora shook her head.

'Well, we'll look after her. Money doesn't seem to be a problem, which is good. I'm sure Joy can afford to live up on the third floor for a long time to come.'

About three months, if the rumours were true. Flora blanched at the thought.

'At least she has you to help keep her spirits up,' Elizabeth said to Flora.

The warden shook her head. 'Oh, you won't be able to see so much of her now I'm afraid.'

Flora looked up, alarmed. 'Why not?'

'Visits to the third floor are monitored. Guests have to be signed in, or have a special pass. We have to protect our most vulnerable residents. I'm sure you understand.'

Like you protected the Captain, Flora didn't say.

'How do I get a pass?'

'I issue the passes, and guests who are on the approved list can be signed in with permission.' The warden's expression hardened, and the look she gave Flora was loaded with meaning. No passes or permissions for nosey parkers who asked difficult questions and made a nuisance of themselves. Flora swallowed. The problem was, she wasn't quite done with the questions yet.

'Speaking of visitors, there was a man who came to see the Captain the day before he died. He's a solicitor called Mr Vasco. Would he have been issued with a pass?'

A door slammed somewhere down the hall. The warden's expression was blank, impossible to read, but Flora was sure she saw her fingers curl more tightly around the edge of the desk.

'I'll check, hold on a mo.' Elizabeth headed back out to reception, her skirt swishing against Flora's arm. 'What did you say his name was?'

'Vasco.'

This time Flora watched Cynthia's face closely. 'Do you know him?' she asked. 'Is he some kind of official Maples legal representative?'

The warden seemed to have turned to stone. Not a single muscle moved, not even a flicker of her eye. The clock on the wall behind her head ticked hopefully. Flora started to feel uncomfortable.

Finally the warden smiled. 'Vasker? Never heard that name before. I'm afraid legal advice is outside our remit here at the Maples. We have medical staff, as you know, and all sorts of other facilities for our residents. But they have to arrange some things for themselves.'

Flora didn't bother correcting her. Elizabeth called out from reception.

'No one by that name in the book for April at all. Are you sure you've got the right person?'

'Pretty sure.' Flora pushed herself up from the low chair and stood in the doorway. 'Are there any visitors signed in to see the Captain the day before he died.'

'Oh, I don't think I can tell you that, Flora.' Elizabeth looked pained, but her eyes were trained beyond Flora's head.

'No, you can't.' The warden's voice was clipped. When she next spoke she was standing right behind her. 'Well, if there's nothing else?'

Her dubious welcome fast running out, Flora scrambled around for an idea.

'Speaking of the Captain, do you happen to know when his funeral is?' Her first thought was that if the executors had set a date it would confirm that the postmortem was over and done with. Elizabeth answered immediately.

'Actually, it's on Wednesday. I saw it in the paper.'

Flora wasn't the only one to register surprise.

'Really?' the warden said. 'Which paper?'

'The Star, I think. It was in the obituaries – I always read them, don't you?' Cynthia shook her head from side to side very slowly. 'Well, his name just caught my eye, it's so unusual. Did you know it, Flora? Solomon Wares. It's his funeral on Wednesday afternoon with the reading of the will straight after. Bless his heart, I mean who'll be going to the funeral, anyway? It's only a cremation. He had no family, and hardly any friends left.'

'Joy was his friend,' Flora said softly.

Elizabeth bit her lip. 'Well, maybe she should go along. Perhaps he left her something.'

It was certainly a possibility. But finding out the main beneficiary of that will would at least give Flora a name, and the best case scenario was that the person named had nothing to do with Vasco, or Ida, and all Flora's wild theories were plain wrong. Then she could finally convince Joy there really was nothing suspicious about the Captain's death and they could put the whole thing to bed once and for all.

'I think Joy's too ill to go,' she said. 'And I don't think it would be good for her anyway. Too stressful.' Flora smiled ruefully at the receptionist. 'Poor old Captain. I guess he won't have much of a send-off.'

'Someone from here should go,' said Elizabeth. She looked at the warden nervously.

Cynthia returned her gaze with a grave smile. 'It'll be an honour to attend the funeral as a representative of the Maples. I'll be there to say a last farewell.'

Last person to see him alive. The only witness to his death. And the one to say a final goodbye. Flora shuddered. For the warden of a retirement village, Cynthia wasn't exactly what you'd call warm.

The warden rounded the reception desk and held up the wooden flap for Flora. She gave Elizabeth a little wave, then followed Cynthia out of the main doors.

'Oh, by the way. There's something I need to tell you. I'm so sorry to have to break this news but I'm afraid we won't be needing Shakers' services for our residents anymore.'

'Pardon?' Flora stared at the warden, her mouth hanging open. 'You don't need our services?'

'That's right. We'll see the contract out as agreed under its existing terms, which is two weeks' notice from either party. But we don't have any new residents moving in – or out – in the next fortnight, so this is it I'm afraid.'

'But ... why?'

The warden smiled, and for the first time in the last hour her smile looked genuine. 'We got a better price elsewhere. We're in a recession, you know. We have to get the best deal for our residents.'

By the time Flora could think how to respond the warden had gone. She stood by the glass doors, the wind whipping around her bare legs, her stomach churning at the thought of telling Marshall. Ditched. Their main contract – practically the only thing keeping Shakers afloat – gone.

There was only one explanation.

Rockfords.

***

Flora found Joy in her unit, packing. She was kneeling on the floor, half-heartedly throwing photo albums into a ratty-looking cardboard box.

'I need to make a start,' she told Flora. 'Otherwise I just won't have the heart for it.'

'Come on.' Flora held out her hands and pulled Joy to her feet. 'Leave it for now. Let's go for a walk.'

Positioned on the side of the River Severn, the Maples had its own rocky stretch of bank with wooden handrails and a platform to let wheelchairs get up close and personal with the ducks. Flora guided Joy to a silvered wooden bench and pulled out the packet of biscuits she'd grabbed from Joy's kitchenette. While her friend drowned her sorrows in custard creams, Flora filled her in on what she'd gleaned about the mystery man in black.

'He's a solicitor?' Joy sprayed a few stray crumbs over her lap in surprise. 'What, and the warden doesn't know who he is?'

'So she says.' Even as Flora said the words she realised it didn't ring true at all. Joy also looked sceptical.

'Maybe he's using a different name?'

'Maybe.'

'Well, there must be a way to find out. Are you absolutely sure it was the same man?'

'One hundred per cent. There can't be many people who look like him.' Flora took a biscuit and munched it thoughtfully. 'Did you know the Captain's real name?'

'Solomon, but everyone called him the Captain. He liked it. He was proud of his military background.' Joy looked out across the river. A pleasure boat, half-filled with optimistic tourists, cruised past. A child with a bright green sun hat waved a chubby hand from the riverboat but Joy didn't wave back. 'He sacrificed a lot for his career. Family. Hobbies. But he was happy, and he didn't even mind being on the third floor. Although ...'

Flora stopped munching and looked up. 'What?'

'The last few weeks he had been a bit down. I just assumed it was getting to him after all, even though he said he liked all the routines up there.'

'He seemed like a man who loved routine.' Flora thought about his room, the organised rows of belongings, the hospital corners on the bed.

'He was taking some kind of antidepressant, you know. All the residents on the third floor have them. They dish them out like sweets up there.'

Flora grimaced. 'The warden was in a tizzy about the police, said they've been asking questions about medication. That's who you've got to thank for your dawn raid, I reckon.'

Her friend shrugged. 'Doesn't matter now, does it? I'm still rumbled.'

But Flora wasn't listening. 'I've just had a thought –

what if the postmortem showed up something in the Captain's blood? Like, maybe he'd taken too many tablets or taken the wrong ones or something. Joy, that could explain everything. He got dizzy, disorientated, that's why he fell. And the warden, she's all over it because she's worried about the Maples' reputation and doesn't want it to get out.'

Joy had become very still. 'There's another explanation, Flora. One I've been trying to avoid even thinking about.'

'What?'

'That the Captain took his own life. That he just didn't want to live anymore.'

She pulled a crumpled tissue from her sleeve and blew her nose. Flora gave her a minute to compose herself, then slipped her arm around Joy's hunched back.

'I don't believe he killed himself, Joy. When I was studying psychology I volunteered with the Samaritans for a while. Of course, you can never tell for sure, but the Captain didn't seem suicidal. Didn't you say yourself that he was happy here?'

Joy nodded. 'I guess.'

'Anyway, this is all conjecture. There's no way of knowing what it said in the postmortem report. But I do intend to try and find out who might have benefited from his death. I think that's all we can do now.'

'It'll be Aubrey.' Joy sat back, her eyes alight. 'I just know it will.'

'How can it be?' Flora sighed. 'Weren't you listening to what I told you about that day at the library? It's not him, Joy. Mr Felix and Aubrey are not the same person.'

Joy's expression was mutinous, but she kept her lips tightly shut. Flora packed up the biscuits and held out her hand.

'Listen, if I prove to you that Mr Felix definitely didn't have anything to do with the Captain's death, and that he absolutely can't be Aubrey, will you let all this go and be happy again? I miss you. I feel like I haven't seen the real you since the day we went to Bridgnorth.'

'It's our anniversary on Friday,' Joy said softly. 'I'd love to go back there again.'

'Then we will. I promise. But think about what I've said, okay? And when this is all over you'll be able to have Otto back. You must miss him terribly.'

'Cramping your style, is he?' Joy shook her head when Flora protested. 'I'm only joking. I know you're getting attached to him, you just can't help yourself. Which is just as well.'

'What do you mean?'

Joy tipped up her chin, trying – and failing – to stop her lip from trembling. 'We can't have pets on the third floor, Flora. If I go up there I'll never be able to have Otto back.' And with that she turned and trudged back up the path, refusing to let Flora come along. 'I need to get used to being on my own,' she said. 'Besides, you've got work to do.'

Flora watched her go. She hadn't managed to convince her friend of Mr Felix's innocence, but she reckoned she'd planted the seed. Which was a start, at least. And if she could find out something concrete in the next few days, and if Joy's new medication started to work quickly, maybe they'd find a way to stave off the third floor move after all. It was worth a try.

She relaxed in the sunshine for a few more minutes, then made her way back to reception. Something Joy had said was playing on her mind, and aware that her welcome at the Maples was fading fast, Flora knew this might be her last opportunity to ask one final question.

Elizabeth was still sitting behind the reception desk. Flora leaned on the counter and smiled her most engaging smile.

'You know, I think I'm a bit of a scatterbrain.'

172

The receptionist grinned. 'You're not the only one! I've had to retype this letter three times already – my mind keeps drifting. I've got a date tonight,' she added, sotto voice.

'Really? Well, good on you. Is he gorgeous?'

Elizabeth nodded. 'Met him at the gym. He's really fit. And I don't mean in the literal sense.'

Flora joined in her raucous laughter, although she wasn't entirely sure what they were laughing about.

'Well, I'm in a dizzy daydream today too. That man I was talking about earlier – I think I got his name totally wrong. In fact, I can't remember what it was now at all.'

The receptionist's laughter faded. 'I can't give you information out of the visitor book, Flora. Cynthia will kill me. I'm not kidding.'

'Oh, of course! I don't want you to tell me anything confidential, far from it.' Flora smiled and gave a little shrug. 'Joy thinks she knows who this man is, that's all. She thinks he's an old friend. And of course, with her being so upset now the Captain's gone, I'm just trying to help her out.'

Elizabeth was nodding, but still looked wary. Flora made her expression vague.

'So, what I was thinking was, if I just describe what he looks like, you can tell me if you've seen him around. Not when, or who he was visiting, or anything like that. Just if he's been here. That's not confidential, is it?'

'No. I guess not.' Elizabeth looked at her nails, then back up at Flora. 'Okay, shoot. What does this old friend of Joy's look like?'

Flora began to describe Mr Vasco in graphic detail, but she'd only got as far as the beard and the hollow cheeks when Elizabeth began to nod vigorously. 'Oh yes. Of course I've seen him. He's been here a few times. Odd fella, but not unpleasant. Always says good morning.'

'So you've spoken to him?'

'Well, not really. In fact, no. I haven't.'

'But you signed him in? He must have said his name?'

The receptionist shook her head. 'He's got a pass. Signed by the warden herself. Comes and goes as he likes, doesn't need to sign in.' She smiled at Flora. 'So you got the right person, but the wrong name. Happens to me all the time.'

'How do you know I've got the wrong name? If you've never signed him in, I mean?'

'Well, because Cynthia said she didn't know who he was, didn't she? And she must know him if she's given him a pass.' Elizabeth pulled a face at Flora and made a "duh" sound. Flora forced a smile and nodded.

'I'm not the sharpest tool in the box today, am I?'

'I guess you're just worried about your friend. But Joy will be fine, you'll see. All the residents love it up there once they've settled in. All their meals cooked for them, room service twenty-four hours a day. I'd love it!'

Flora doubted that very much, but she kept her thoughts to herself. Instead she said thanks and turned to walk away. Elizabeth called her back.

'Don't suppose you've got any change on you? I'm collecting for the Six Wishes Foundation and I've only got a ten pound note. I suppose it's a bit mean of me, but I gave last time. I only wanted to put in a fiver.'

Flora dug out her purse. 'I've only got loose change, sorry.'

Elizabeth sighed. 'It's for a good cause, I guess.'

'I've heard that name before. Six Wishes – is it some kind of charity?'

'It was a favourite of one of our residents, Ida Smith. Did you know her? She left her entire estate to the foundation. It's coming up to what would have been her birthday so we're having another whip round.'

'Sweet.'

'Expensive!' Elizabeth gave her girlish laugh. 'But she

was a lovely lady. Heart of gold. I don't mind, really.'

'Good luck with your date tonight,' Flora said, winking.

She left the receptionist staring into space and headed back into town, dodging the midday shoppers who barged past with their elbows out, never bothering to say sorry. 'Don't mind me,' she snapped at a fat man with a baseball cap and about thirty carrier bags hanging off his arms. He didn't even register her existence.

There was no putting it off any longer – Marshall would have to be told about Shakers losing the Maples' contract. So much for Rockfords not being a threat. But Flora was almost looking forward to wiping the smug smile off Marshall's face. Getting pally with the enemy might be the transatlantic way of doing things, but it looked like Marshall had a lot to learn about doing business over here.

Chapter 13

Hello? Earth calling Flora Lively. I could do with some navigating here.'

'Sorry.' Flora shook herself and looked down at the directions Marshall had given her. 'I can barely read your writing. You write like a five-year-old.'

'Know many five-year-olds, do you?'

'Sitting next to one right now.'

'So funny. It's down here somewhere, I'm sure of it. Check where it says Tern Hill roundabout.'

'Reads. It reads Tern Hill roundabout, it doesn't say it. Directions can't speak, can they?'

'I wish they could, Flora, because they'd make a lot more sense than you. Will you ditch the attitude and just read the directions?'

Flora smiled to herself and held the piece of paper up to hide her face. 'Okay, at Tern Hill take the third exit – I think it's a three, it might be an eight – and then go about two kilometres. We kind of work in miles over here, Marshall.'

'Well so do we, miss clever ass. I just wrote what they told me. I thought it was another of your Britishisms, like "roundabout". What's wrong with traffic island, anyway?'

'Well, you go round it. It's a roundabout.'

'Ha. Quaint.'

'I've no idea how far two kilometres is, you know.'

Marshall glanced across the cab in astonishment.

'Really? No idea at all?'

'Nope. Is it the same as two miles?'

'You're just yanking my chain, right? No one's that dumb.'

A sharp retort died on her lips as Flora spotted the sign for the new housing development. 'There it is – Cherry Tree Heights.'

'And that's another thing,' Marshall said, steering the pantechnicon into a lay-by, 'these crazy tree names you give everything. Cherry Tree Heights, the Maples – you Brits are obsessed with nature.'

'Why have we stopped?'

Marshall tapped the clock on the dashboard. 'Not supposed to turn up until contracts are completed. It's only five of eleven.'

'Five to eleven,' Flora corrected. Marshall grinned.

'You still sore that I got us this new contract?'

She was, but she had no intention of admitting it. Marshall's reaction to the news that Cynthia was pulling the plug on the Maples' removals had been far from what she'd expected. He'd shrugged and said, 'No worries. It was a depressing gig anyway.'

Turned out he had his own news – he'd landed Shakers a deal with massive local builders Spearhead Homes, to offer removal packages to new homeowners.

'We're doing a trial this morning,' he'd told her, holding open the office door to shepherd her out. 'They were let down by their existing firm. It's a no-brainer for them. We do a good job and we're in.'

Flora's feelings were mixed. She was relieved, and not a little impressed, but also mightily pissed off. Marshall always came up smelling of roses, no matter what. Mind you, there was still the Rockfords' situation to be resolved. She wasn't letting that go without a fight.

'I wish you'd tell me what you and David Rockford were discussing on Saturday.'

177

Marshall smirked. 'I know you do.'

'I saw you shaking hands with him. That's not normal behaviour with our biggest competitor. That's not how *we* do things over here.'

'Now, what confuses me is this – you say you saw me shaking the guy's hand, but I saw you walking into the car park after he'd driven away. Which makes me think you were spying on me, Miss Lively. Is that the way it was?'

Flora huffed. 'No, that's not how it was. If you must know, I was waiting for him to go.'

Marshall waited for her to go on, eyebrows raised.

'Okay, I didn't know who he was, but I had seen him before. He … I was spooked one day, walking in from town. He was there, he seemed nice, concerned.' She stopped when she saw the look on Marshall's face. 'Oh, don't act the innocent with me. You were rubber-necking down at us. And you must have known who he was even then. He'd obviously been to see you.'

She got nothing but another infuriating grin.

'Will you tell me what you two were talking about?'

'Nope.'

'Was it me?'

The minute the words were out of her mouth, Flora could have kicked herself. Marshall was as sharp as one of Elizabeth's nails, and she'd just given far too much away. She searched around for a change of subject.

'I wonder why Rockfords didn't pitch for the Spearhead Homes deal?'

'Don't guess they knew about it. I've been developing my contact there for a while now.'

'"Developing your contact"? Is that code for dating the secretary?'

'Ha, good one. Speaking about dating, how you getting on with your little librarian?'

Flora whipped her head up. 'How do you know

about Heston?'

'Heston, is it? Real manly name, that. What car does he drive? One of those super-minis, I guess.'

Flora was saved by an incoming text. 'It's the Roberts. They're on their way. Let's go.'

Marshall fired up the van and pulled out, still smirking. She read out the directions and they arrived at the new development in ten minutes flat.

'Characterful place,' Marshall commented wryly.

Flora ignored him and jumped down from the cab. He could scoff all he wanted – there was nothing wrong with new estates. Well-planned, dinky little houses with their own integral garages and postage-stamp-sized gardens. Not that Flora would actually want to live in one herself. She'd be stuck for transport, for one thing. Unless she finally passed her driving test, which was unlikely with her record.

Which reminded her. 'Where's Richie today?'

Marshall joined her at the back of the van and began unstrapping the doors. 'He's busy doing other stuff.'

'What stuff?'

'Have you only just noticed he's not here? You're losing it, Flora. I've been driving all morning and you've only just realised that our driver isn't actually driving.' He laughed and slapped her on the back. Flora winced, but she wasn't fooled.

'He's skiving again, isn't he? And you don't want to admit it. You were purposely changing the subject the whole way here to keep me from asking. Well, come on – what was it this time?'

'How's that little dog of yours? Tonto, isn't it? Getting on okay?'

'Otto. And don't think you're getting away with it so easily, Marshall. Next time there's any hiring to do, I'm all over it. You've proved yourself rubbish at judging someone's character.'

Marshall jumped into the van, clearing the four-foot gap like an athlete. 'We might as well let him go now, anyway. Steve can come in as and when, and it's not like we need to worry about keeping the Maples' warden happy, right? Not now you've lost us the contract.'

'I didn't lose it, it just–'

'But I tell you what,' Marshall said, grinning. 'Now you're back in charge of hiring and firing, you can give Richie the good news.'

Fuming, Flora stalked towards the black car that had just pulled up outside Plot 21. The young couple inside looked exhausted, but radiantly happy. They stepped out and held hands, gazing up adoringly at their little slice of suburbia. Flora's anger dissolved instantly.

'Congratulations on your new home. You'd better tell us where you want everything to go.'

The woman smiled and shook Flora's hand, then promptly sneezed all over it. 'Sorry. Hay fever. Better grab some tissues.' She disappeared back inside the car. The man fished out a set of keys, attached to a Spearhead Homes key ring.

'Lead the way,' said Flora, wiping her hand on her jeans. She looked back and saw Marshall leaning against the side of the van, watching her. He smiled and stuck out his tongue. Flora's face creased into a grin. Sometimes she just didn't know whether to hit him or hug him.

***

'What are we doing here again?'

Flora whispered in Marshall's ear. 'You know perfectly well. Now shut up and look like you've got every right to be here.'

They were hovering outside Mr Vasco's offices in School Gardens. Yesterday, after they'd unloaded the Roberts' furniture and about a hundred boxes, Flora had told Marshall about the reading of the Captain's will. He'd pointed out, quite reasonably, that Flora still didn't know for certain whether Mr Vasco had actually been the Captain's solicitor, but Flora brushed his objections aside. Somehow, she just knew. The funeral was at two o'clock, and she planned to be outside Vasco's office by at least two thirty. If she was wrong, she'd be happy to have wasted her time. But if she was right, she wanted to make sure the once-dodgy solicitor had definitely left his shady past behind him.

When Marshall offered to go with her she was stunned into accepting. But afterwards she figured it might be good to have him along for the ride. Marshall was good with people. Not her, of course, but he could turn it on when he wanted to.

For once, he'd dressed up for the occasion: stone-coloured cords, soft at the knees, and a chambray shirt looked the height of elegance compared to Marshall's usual attire. Flora had swapped her patched jeans for the pair of black linen trousers she'd last worn at her dad's funeral. This, and the fact that they were now so loose on her, she tried to put out of her mind.

'What are you doing?'

Marshall was digging inside a carrier bag. He pulled out what looked like a handful of brightly coloured hair and an old man's tweed cap.

'Disguises!' He held out the hair for Flora to take, shaking it at her when she refused. 'Go on. It's a brilliant idea. Just in case he recognises you from the Maples.'

Flora took the wig and inspected it. 'He barely saw me, Marshall. And I am not wearing this. It looks like it's got fleas.'

'I resent that. It happens to belong to my mom. That wig was her pride and joy when she was younger.'

'Oh. Sorry.' Marshall could be touchy about his mum. Flora lifted it up and gave it a little brush through with her fingers. 'And the cap's for you, is it?'

Marshall was already ramming it on his head. 'Good morning to you, my fine fellow. I'm here to partake in the reading of the last will and testament of my uncle Solomon Wares.'

Flora giggled. 'Your English accent is dreadful. And I don't think you should pretend to be his nephew. It's too close. Make it more distant.'

'Get your wig on, then.'

'I'm not wearing it, Marshall. I don't need a disguise. No one will know who I am.'

'Really. What about her?'

Marching up the hill towards them was the warden. She'd swapped her usual uniform of combats and walking boots for a pair of black trousers and shoes with heels. Obviously uncomfortable, her gait was uneven over the cobbles. Flora slipped behind Marshall, grateful for his size.

'Pull your cap down over your face,' she hissed. Marshall did as he was instructed.

'If this was a movie, I'd take you in my arms right now and kiss you.'

For a moment, Flora thought she'd heard him wrong. 'What did you say?'

'To hide. You know, in movies when the hero and heroine are trying to avoid being seen the guy pulls the girl into an embrace.' He laughed. 'Usually she waits until the coast is clear before stepping back and slapping him. Which is why I didn't try it.'

Flora could feel her face heating up. She was suddenly aware of how close he was standing, of the heat coming off his body. Her heart was hammering.

'Ha!' she managed. 'I bet you did, alright.'

What had she just said? Did it even make sense?

'Well, at least that confirms we're in the right place. Let's go.' Marshall took a step forward, but Flora held

182

him back.

'Hold on. We can't just waltz in there now, can we? Not now she's here.'

'I wasn't planning on waltzing, but if you insist.' Marshall tried to take her hand in a dance position, but Flora pushed him off, irritated. Maddening man. Why had she let him come? She just couldn't think with him around.

'Wait. No. I don't think it's a good idea. She's already really pissed off with me. She thinks I'm a busybody. She thinks I'm interfering, getting in the way.'

'She's got a point.'

Flora whacked him on the arm. 'Shut up. We need to think of another plan.'

But Marshall was already walking towards the Vasco offices. Flora ran after him.

'What about our disguises?' he said.

She held up the tatty wig. 'You really think this is going to fool someone like Cynthia Curtis?'

'Hmm. Maybe not. Well, let's try anyway.'

And before she could stop him, Marshall had pushed open the frosted glass door and marched right in.

'Here goes nothing.' Flora followed. The Vasco offices were bigger than they looked from the window. There was a large desk in front of a partition, with the main room swelling out behind. Two shabby-looking couches were pushed against the far wall, and on one of these couches sat the warden, deep in conversation with none other than Mr Vasco himself. There were two more people milling around: a woman with wispy grey hair holding a notepad and a man with a bald head so shiny it reflected the strip light overhead. The woman looked across at Flora and smiled. The man ignored them completely. Flora turned to whisper to Marshall, but he was no longer standing by her side. Instead he was crossing the room and holding out his hand to Mr

Vasco.

Flora followed, arriving in time to hear the warden's gasp of surprise and her sharp, 'What are *you* doing here?'

Marshall's answer was not what they had rehearsed. 'We've come to make sure the Captain's will is in order, Mrs Curtis. Flora here has some reservations about it and we wanted to reassure ourselves that it's all being handled properly.'

What the hell did he think he was doing? This wasn't the time for the damn truth.

'Oh. She does, does she?' The warden turned her icy glare on Flora. 'I suppose that's what all your snooping around has been for. Not so worried about poor old Joy, after all.'

Flora's mouth dropped open. The nerve of the woman! 'Actually,' she said, thinking on her feet, 'I'm here on Joy's behalf.' She gestured towards Marshall and laughed. 'My colleague has got the completely wrong end of the stick. Elizabeth mentioned there might be something in the Captain's will for Joy, who was a close friend. Joy asked me to come along to the reading as she's too sick to come herself.'

The warden glared. 'She looked fine to me when I saw her at breakfast.'

'You'll be rethinking her move to Special Care then, if she's fine.'

Marshall cleared his throat. 'Ladies. Let's not forget what we're here for.' He nodded towards the solicitor, who was staring at Flora through narrowed eyes.

'Right.' Flora looked from Mr Vasco to Cynthia and back again. 'By the way, this is the man I was asking about yesterday. I believe you have met before after all.'

'No.'

'Of course we have.'

Flora glanced at Marshall. That the warden had given

one response and Vasco another didn't surprise her at all. These two knew each other alright. The question was, why had Cynthia lied about it?

Mr Vasco stood, and Flora was surprised again by his height. He even towered over Marshall. 'I'm afraid only designated parties can attend the reading, young lady. But rest assured if there's anything in Captain Wares' will for your friend – what was her name?'

'Joy Martin,' said the warden quickly.

'Right. Well, I'll be in touch with Mrs Martin in due course if necessary. But now, if you'll excuse us.' Mr Vasco turned and waved the man and woman over. Flora and Marshall had no choice but to head for the door. But once they were outside in the sunshine, Flora went on the attack.

'What the hell were you doing in there? What was all that "Flora has reservations" nonsense? That's not what we agreed.'

Marshall shrugged. 'I was improvising. Anyway, it's true, isn't it?'

'True is not the way to go here. We needed a cover story. Good job I was on the ball.'

'Oh yes, your cover story got us in there home and dry. Look at us, sitting at the reading.' He did a mock double-take. 'Doh! How did we get out here?'

Flora slumped against the wall. 'It's really frustrating. I bet you a hundred pounds what's in that will would go a long way to reassure Joy about the Captain.'

'Done.' Marshall spat on his hand and held it out for Flora to shake.

'Yuk!' She pushed it away. 'Anyway, why are you here, exactly? I hope it wasn't just to sabotage it for me, Marshall, because this happens to be really important.'

'You've sure got a great opinion of me.' He shook his head. 'Why is it so important to you, Flora? Why do you care so much?'

'You wouldn't understand. I just want to find out what's in that will. I can't explain it, I just need to know.'

'Your investigator instinct?'

She shrugged off the joke. 'You go back to Shakers. I'm going to hang around here a bit longer, see if I can quiz the warden when they come out. You never know, she might take pity on me and spill the beans.'

'Like hell she will.' Marshall turned to go, then stopped and looked back. 'Flora?'

'What?'

'Nothing. Later, alligator.'

'In a while.'

Flora didn't watch him leave. She'd already had an idea. She jogged down the terrace and slipped into a narrow alley between two three-storey town houses. The alley, she was pretty sure, led to the back of the offices on School Gardens. And from there, if memory served her correctly, she might just be able to sneak a peek into the back of Mr Vasco's office. As she ran she pulled out the wig she'd shoved in her pocket earlier. Why not? She pulled it on her head, laughing. The reflection of a red-headed stranger glanced back at her from a dark window. Maybe this new person would have better luck as an investigator, because Flora sure wasn't doing such a great job so far.

Chapter 14

Mr Vasco's voice was easily discernible, droning on and on in legalese. Flora, perched on top of a huge metal dustbin, was almost glad she wasn't inside the stuffy office instead. She'd climbed up and risked peering in just long enough to check she was in the right spot, then settled down close to the open window. She was just starting to worry that she'd missed the meat of the reading when Vasco's tone changed.

"'I, Solomon Wares, residing in Maples Retirement Village, Shrewsbury, hereby revoke all former wills and testamentary dispositions made by me and declare this to be my last will and testament on the seventeenth of April two thousand and twelve.'"

The sun didn't reach the alley behind School Gardens but that wasn't why Flora shivered. Hearing the Captain's own words read out like that was spooky enough, but the date made it even worse. This will was written the day before he died.

"'I appoint William Vasco to be sole executor of this will, and my estate should be distributed as follows.'" Mr Vasco cleared his throat. Flora was hardly breathing. "'I give absolutely all of my real and personal property, whatsoever and wheresoever, to the Six Wishes Charitable Foundation.'"

Flora's head jerked up. The Six Wishes Foundation? The Captain had left everything to the same charity as Ida? How odd. Hadn't there been anyone at all, no distant relatives or close friends? She forgot about her theory that the beneficiary might be behind the Captain's death and mourned his aloneness. At least her mum and dad had her to carry on after they'd gone. How tragic to leave behind no one at all. To be reduced to naming a charity for every penny you'd scrimped and saved and worked for, for your whole life.

Although what about Joy, and all the other friends he had at the Maples? What about his medals? She listened to Mr Vasco drone on about witnesses and probate, but there was nothing else of interest. No small bequests at all. Maybe Joy was right – maybe he really had been depressed.

So much for proving the third floor was a safe and happy place to be.

She began to climb down from the bin, gripping on to the window ledge for support. In a way, she was relieved. At least this meant there was nothing untoward about the Captain's death. No one benefiting meant no motive. She'd cleared up the mystery, even if it wasn't much of a mystery at all. Judging by the warden's new-found overzealous attitude to medication, it was most likely the Captain had taken some kind of mis-dose of his medication and suffered a dizzy spell at the top of the stairs. Maybe Cynthia really did see him fall and just didn't reach him in time. Flora suddenly became aware of how ridiculous she must look, clambering over a dustbin, listening in at windows, Marshall's mum's scraggy wig perched on her head. All for nothing. Her overactive imagination was only half the problem: it was Joy's she needed to deal with.

She planted her feet safely on the ground and brushed the dust off her backside. As she stuffed the wig in her bag she noticed a shuffling sound coming from a pile of cardboard stacked further up the alley. Rats, no doubt. Flora remembered hanging out behind the library buildings as a teenager, being teased mercilessly by the tough-nut guys who found – and chased her with – a dead rat. She grimaced. Horrible things. Keeping her eyes on the towering stack of discarded packaging, she edged towards the end of the alley. The sun had disappeared behind a cloud, and the narrow space, dingy enough to begin with, was bordering on dark now. Especially in the shadows cast by the looming walls overhead. She'd have to creep past the rat to get out to the lane. She pushed her hand through her itchy hair and took a steadying breath.

Just then the cardboard began to move. Flora watched as piece after piece fell away from the wall, and out from behind it emerged a low-crouched figure. She screamed – a strangled, breathless sound – and flattened herself against the wall. Not a rat but a man. A man who was running now, reaching the end of the alley and turning left, out of sight, leaving Flora stunned and shaken.

A man wearing a dark blue hoodie with the hood pulled low over his face.

Had she disturbed a tramp? She didn't hang around to find out. Flora jogged to the end of the alley, glanced left to make sure the coast was clear, then headed right, as fast as she could, back towards the safety of the shoppers on the high street. She looked over her shoulder two or three times to make sure neither Mr Vasco nor the warden had seen her: they must have heard her scream outside the office window. Hopefully they'd put it down to teenagers. High jinks.

It wasn't until Flora was seated in Caffè Nero, nursing a reassuringly frothy latte, that the full implication of what had happened in the alley dawned on her. The man she'd seen fleeing the mound of cardboard had not been a tramp at all. It was obvious, whichever way you looked at it, that he had been watching her. Spying. The discarded packaging provided the perfect hiding place, the ideal vantage point to see what she was up to.

And what had she been up to? Spying on Mr Vasco, listening at an open window to the private reading of a will inside a solicitor's office. Her face burned with shame. What crazy idea had brought her to this? For all she knew the hooded man was plain-clothes police – she could be in real trouble over this. She'd been hanging around the retirement village, asking questions about the Captain ... Her hand flew up to her mouth as a horrible thought struck her. Cynthia had said the police had been all over the Maples: maybe the postmortem had proved his death was suspicious and now they were keeping tabs on their suspects. After all, this wasn't the first time she'd been followed – couldn't the man from the alley be the same as the person who'd trailed her through the back streets of Shrewsbury a week ago? Maybe they'd been watching her for a while.

Flora took a sip of coffee, wincing as it burned her throat. The queue in the cafe was right out the door now; a draught blew in and flapped at the hem of her linen trousers. She thought about it again then shook her head. No, that couldn't be it. The police didn't operate that way. An officer would have told her to step down from the bins back at Vasco's office and demanded to know what the hell she thought she was doing. But soon her relief turned to anxiety again: if not the police, then who? Why would anyone be spying on her? Unless ...

The heat in the latte did nothing to counteract the chill that crept over her skin. She watched the hairs on her arms lift up. Suddenly every detail seemed distinct: the veins on the backs of her hands, like a pale blue-green road map; the freckles that spotted her skin. And as her eyes focused in, then out again, Flora saw the glaring fact that had been missing from the picture all along.

Someone was following her for one simple reason: she was on to them.

***

'I'm sorry, Dad. I know I'm letting you down here. But I'm pretty sure if you were still around you'd be just as curious as I am.'

Flora smiled up at the photograph on the noticeboard then wiped her eyes on her sleeve. The truth of what she'd said lifted her heart a little – hadn't Peter and Kitty brought her up to be fascinated by people, inquiring and interested, determined to look deeper than surface explanations, no matter what the situation?

Sometimes she'd been interested to the point of being irritating, of course. A memory made her smile again: herself aged eleven, trying to solve the "mystery" of the strange noises that came from her parents' bedroom on a Saturday night. She'd been so sure it was a ghost she'd spent hours at the library trying to trace the history of their house on Windmill Lane. Maybe an old mill worker, cut down in his prime, was trying to speak to the living?

She'd driven her parents crazy with questions. Not content with the explanation offered – extra-loud snoring – she'd stayed awake one night and crept in, torch in hand, to find out for herself.

'That made for an interesting conversation, didn't it?' she said to the photo. Her dad stared down at her, his proud gaze fixed forever.

The computer fired up, slow and clunky. Flora filled the kettle while she waited, too edgy to sit for long. The past twenty-four hours had seemed interminable – she'd been worrying at the Captain situation from all angles and sorely needed to find a resolution.

Fact: she'd made a bit of a nuisance of herself after

191

the Captain's death and someone – either at the Maples or connected with someone there – must have overheard. Fact: someone had been following her, almost certainly trying to find out what she knew. And if that was the case, there must have been something suspicious about the Captain's death after all.

Fact: if she was on to them, and they – whoever *they* were – knew it, then she may well be in danger too.

In the middle of another disturbed night, Flora had started to wonder about the Six Wishes Foundation. Wasn't that the only thing that linked the Captain and Ida *and* Mr Vasco? Two deaths and a dodgy solicitor – there had to be something there. A clue. The rest of the night she'd held Otto tightly, sleeping in fitful snatches, dreaming of dogs tangled up in a never-ending string of bright red liquorice that moved on its own and grew tighter and tighter every time the poor beasts struggled.

Marshall broke her reverie with a cheerful, 'Hey, there,' and a request for coffee.

'There isn't any.' Flora held out the canister to show him. 'Someone's emptied it and didn't bother to get any more. Typical.'

'Well, it wasn't me. What's eating you today? Oscar keep you up again?'

'It's Otto, okay? Is it so hard for you to remember a simple name? Got too much on your mind have you? Like secret assignations with our rival and nemesis.'

'They're only our nemesis if they actually manage to bring us down, Flora.' Marshall smiled and threw himself into a chair, spreading his hands wide. 'Last time I looked, we're still here.' He was back in his usual combo of worn jeans and college T-shirt but somehow he seemed better put together than usual. Flora inspected him surreptitiously from the other side of the room. He'd had a haircut. And his pale green T-shirt looked freshly washed and possibly even ironed. Then she noticed his

192

shoes: black and white Converse. She smiled.

'Got a date later?'

He pulled a puzzled face. 'What makes you say that?'

'Nothing.' Flora laughed and sat down at her desk. The computer was fully operational now, flashing messages about viruses and updates and emails waiting to be read. She ignored them and pulled up Google. Typed *Six Wishes Foundation* into the search box and hit enter.

'That's so weird.'

'Huh?'

'Come and look at this.'

Marshall rounded the desk and leaned over her. She could smell his natural scent of heat and something spicy, with faint notes of cologne on top. Definitely a date. She felt his chest pressing against her shoulder and shifted away.

'"The Six Wishes Foundation",' Marshall read. 'Isn't that the charity you said the Captain left all his money to?'

Flora nodded. She pointed at the screen. 'But it doesn't say anything here about servicemen and women.'

'Should it?'

'That's what I overheard. When Vasco was talking after he'd read the will he called it the "Six Wishes Foundation for ex-servicemen and women". But hold on.' She clicked on the menu then shook her head. 'No, nothing. Marshall, this is really weird.'

He turned around and sat on the desk. 'Go on.'

'Okay. This is the charity that Ida – the old lady who died at the Maples at Christmas, remember? – this is who she left all her money to, right? But Joy said Ida was a cat lover, and that she'd left it to a charity for sick animals. I remember reading about it. It was in the papers.' She shook her head again and pulled a face. 'But I heard Mr Vasco myself, and he was reading directly from the Captain's will. Ex-servicemen and women, he said. How can it be the same charity?'

'Search again. Maybe there are two with the same name.'

'There aren't. I checked just now. And look, Marshall. There's nothing on the About page to say what the foundation does. Don't you think that's odd?'

Marshall said nothing. He pursed his lips and gazed at the screen. 'There's a donate button. Pay through PayPal.'

'So?'

'So, if you donated something it would take you through to their merchant account and give you an email address at least.'

Flora raised her eyebrows, impressed. 'Okay. But I'm only donating a fiver.'

'You're all heart.'

Marshall watched while Flora filled out the online form and waited for it to process. She sighed. 'There's nothing. Six wishes dot org, that's it.'

'Shove over – let me have a look at that website.'

She huffed as Marshall practically sat on her lap, and vacated the chair. 'What do you think?' she said, chewing on a nail.

'I think this strap line – "help make wishes realities" – is so vague it could apply to anything.' Marshall sat back and looked at her. 'This Vasco fella – was he Ida's solicitor too?'

Flora cast back to her conversation with Joy. 'You know, I'm not sure. I just assumed he was because Joy said this mysterious man in black had visited her on Christmas Eve. Is it better or worse if he was?'

'No idea. But we should find out.'

'How?' Flora looked out of the window for inspiration, but Marshall was tapping away at the keyboard, and then he picked up the phone.

'What are you doing?'

He tipped his head to the side and winked. Flora sat on the desk and slipped her hands under her thighs.

'Hi there. Can you hear me okay?' Marshall spoke into the phone from a distance of about a foot, putting on an American accent totally unlike his own. Flora rolled her eyes, but she leaned in to listen all the same.

'Is that the Marples care home? Oh, Maples, right. I'm trying to trace my mom's cousin's aunt's grandma – her name is Ida …' He looked up at Flora and mouthed, 'Last name?'

'Smith.'

'Ida Smith. My mom's pretty sure she's been staying in that there care home of yours in – where are you, Shrewsbury?' He pronounced it Shrew-wus-berry. Flora smiled. What a loon.

'What are they saying?' she whispered.

'Ah. Oh, right. Ah my. Okay, then. And do you have a number for them? Thank ya kindly. Have a nice day, now.'

By the time he ended the call, Flora was shaking her head in despair. 'Marshall, you are incorrigible. This is serious, you know.'

'Well, I know that! I was doing my bit for the investigation.'

'"Have a nice day now." What are you like? Was it Elizabeth who answered? You're lucky she didn't recognise you.'

Marshall's expression turned serious. 'Ida Smith, she was very sorry to tell me, died of heart failure on Boxing Day last year. My mom's cousin's aunt's grandma was a very generous lady who donated all her worldly goods to charity, and I have the number of her legal representative right here if I need more information.'

Flora and Marshall stared at the number he'd written down on a scrap of Shakers headed paper. Flora shrugged. 'Go on then.'

Marshall dialled and held up the phone. They bent their heads together, listening to it ring out. Flora inhaled Marshall's spruced-up scent again and closed her eyes briefly. A woman answered.

'Vasco and Co solicitors. How may I help you?'

Flora reached down and pressed the End Call button. She looked at Marshall.

She was close enough to kiss him.

Startled, she jumped away and headed to the opposite side of the room and the empty coffee canister. Where the hell had that thought come from? She was overwrought, was all. All this so-called sleuthing was starting to take its toll on her nerves.

'You know something? All this – it's not okay, is it?'

Flora looked over her shoulder and met Marshall's eyes. For a minute she thought he was talking about them. She shook her head. Because it wasn't okay. Working together with all this tension and sniping was very far from okay.

But then she realised he was merely voicing his thoughts about the Vasco situation. She berated herself silently then spoke with her back to him.

'Two residents of the Maples get a visit from a solicitor – who we know is dodgy, or has been dodgy in the past, because Max told us all about him. Both of the residents die within days of his visit. One of them we know made a will – a new will, almost certainly, as it's reasonable to assume an eighty-nine-year-old man would have made one already at some point in the past – and he made this new will literally the day before he died. And both of them leave everything they own to the same charity.'

'Which is either supporting sick animals or ex-service people, depending on whose will you happen to be reading,' Marshall added.

Flora sighed and turned around. 'What am I missing, Marshall? Or is there nothing here at all? Is it just a coincidence and I'm making too much of it?'

She flicked the kettle on to reboil. Might as well make a cup of tea, although a strong coffee would go down a damn sight better right now.

'I'm gonna nip out and get us some coffees,' Marshall said. Flora smiled wryly. Helluva time to start reading her mind.

'Make mine a double shot,' she told him. He stopped at the top of the metal stairway and gave her a look.

'What? *What*?'

'Nothing. Just don't go getting your knickers in a twist while I'm gone, okay?'

She made a wafting motion and told him to get lost, then she abandoned the kettle and took up her position at the computer again. Marshall had brought up the Maples' website to find their number, and Flora moved the cursor to the top of the screen to close the page. But then she stopped. She clicked on the tab that showed the Six Wishes Foundation and stared at it hard. Then, on impulse, she opened another tab and typed "Vasco and Co Solicitors Shrewsbury" into the search box. A single business-card style page opened with the familiar curly V she recognised. She clicked back through them in order, alternating, then randomly. Was she seeing what she thought she was seeing? Or was it just more paranoia?

'Having fun?'

Flora jumped so high she banged her knees on the underside of the ancient desk. Richie was standing right behind her.

'You nearly gave me a heart attack! What did you do – levitate up the stairs?'

She turned off the monitor as she stood. Richie had his iPod plugged into his ears as usual, and was nodding his head to a beat Flora thankfully couldn't hear. She gestured for him to take the headphones out.

'Richie, where have you been? It's gone ten o'clock.'

'We got a job on? I thought that was tomorrow.'

'It is tomorrow, but you're a full-time employee. You still need to come into work for the hours we're paying you for. There might be … other tasks and duties.'

'Like?'

She wracked her brain but couldn't come up with a single thing. Which was annoying because she knew damn well there had been loads of stuff that needed doing on down days when her dad had been in charge. She gave Peter Lively's photo another silent apology. It was no good hiding from it: she really was letting him down.

But then she remembered her conversation with Marshall on Monday and sighed. No point being hard on the kid when they were about to lay him off anyway. And that was definitely a job Marshall could do himself – he wasn't going to delegate it to her just because it was unpleasant.

The clattering of footsteps on the stairs announced Marshall's return.

'Hey, Richie. How's it going?' Marshall was carrying three take-out cups, and he handed the spare to their driver. Flora inhaled the delicious aroma and took a grateful sip.

When she looked up again, Marshall was staring at her meaningfully. She stared back and he opened his eyes wide, nodding towards Richie, who was sitting against the far wall, rocking back on his chair. Flora shook her head. She made her face confused and shrugged her shoulders. Marshall rolled his eyes.

'Richie,' he said. Flora sat up, interested.

Richie took one earplug out and dropped the chair legs back on the floor with a crash.

'Shame about the Maples contract. I guess you've

heard from your aunt, right?'

'No. Heard what?'

Marshall gave Flora another look, then turned back to Richie. 'Shakers lost the contract, bro. I thought she'd have told you. Means things are gonna be a bit tight around here for a while.'

Richie shrugged. 'She never said nothing.'

'I guess she didn't realise how it would affect you,' Flora put in. 'I'm sure she'd have said something if she did.'

'How will it affect me?'

'What Flora's trying to say is, we're gonna have to make cutbacks. Until things pick up again.'

'Didn't you just land that contract with a big building firm, though?'

Richie, thought Flora, might not seem all there at times, but when it came right down to it he was sharp enough. She said, 'We did, as a matter of fact, and we had to do a test move for them on Monday. And you were where on Monday, exactly?'

Marshall coughed into his hand, hiding a grin.

But Richie ignored her question and turned to Marshall.

'How much notice you giving me then?'

Flora felt her face grow hot. She opened her mouth to answer but Marshall got there first.

'Two weeks. And if you turn up on time every day, Flora here might even write you a decent reference as well.' Marshall's voice was uncharacteristically cold. Flora flashed him a half-smile, then turned to Richie again, only to see him strolling out the door. His feet clattered on the metal stairs and a few seconds later they heard the outside door slam shut.

'He's pissed,' said Marshall.

'For the hundredth time, over here that means drunk. He's pissed *off*, is what you mean.'

199

Marshall grinned. 'Not the only one, by the looks of it.'

'Well, just marching out like that. And totally blanking me, when I'm supposed to be the one in charge.'

'Except you're not, are you?'

'Excuse me?'

'Nothing.'

Flora fiddled with the hem of her cut-offs. She knew exactly what he meant. But it wasn't a conversation she felt like having right now.

'Strange, though.'

'What? What's strange?'

'That Richie knew nothing about the Maples' contract. I thought those two were pretty thick.'

'You mean thick as thieves, right? Not stupid?'

'Dumb? Well, in Richie-boy's case that too.'

Flora downed the rest of her latte in one go. The caffeine hit was starting to take effect and she felt oddly upbeat. 'Well, I guess she doesn't tell him everything. Why would she?'

'I've got a theory.'

Flora groaned. 'Are we going to get any work done at all today?'

'What work is there, Flora?'

She waved in the direction of the warehouse below. 'How about trying to drum up some business?'

'It's all in hand, boss. So, back to my theory.'

'Fine. Whatever,' she added with a mock-American twang. Marshall grabbed a rubber and threw it at her chest. 'Hey, watch it.' She picked it up – it was heart-shaped, pink, off the end of one of her pencils.

'I'm thinking that the warden hasn't got a better price at all,' Marshall said, not taking his eyes off her.

She pulled a face. 'Crazy theory. Why would she sack us then? We've been doing a great job, haven't we?

We've moved twelve residents in so far and not had a single complaint.'

'*We've* been doing a great job. But you – well, let's just say I think you're holding the bag.'

'What?'

'Let's just say you threw a wrench in the works. You've been on the warden like a bird dog, and it's a clearly a hot button.'

'Marshall, I am going to ram this rubber down your throat if you don't stop talking in idioms and just tell me your stupid theory.'

'I think I'll take the fifth, ma'am.' He stood up and pointed to the heart Flora held in her hand. 'And that's an eraser. If you were shoving a rubber down my throat you'd be doing something very different indeed.'

She threw it at his head, but he ducked and the rubber bounced off the wall just below Peter Lively's photo. Her dad looked down on them indulgently. Flora sighed. 'Despite the riddles, I think you're dead wrong. Besides, I haven't been meddling that much. And why would the warden blow us off just because of that? No, I'm sure it's because Rockfords have undercut us. Your friend David is behind this. What?'

Marshall was smirking at her. He shook his head. 'You're just really funny sometimes, that's all. Anyway, I can tell you for a fact it's got nothing to do with Rockfords.'

'How do you know?'

'I just know. But you can ask David yourself, if you like? He's popping in about eleven.'

Flora's eyes nearly bulged out of her head. She looked up at the clock. It was five to. 'Here? Why? What the hell's he coming here for?'

'Business.'

'What business?'

'Wait and see.'

She grabbed her tote bag and slung it over her arm. Not likely. David Rockford had never been on her list of people to spend time with, and that was before she actually met him and realised he was drop-dead gorgeous as well as super-rich and slick as an oil spillage on a wet road.

'Oh, leaving already? What about all that work we've got to be getting on with?'

Flora glared. 'I've got an appointment.'

'At the hairdresser's?'

'No. What's wrong with my ... Oh, funny. You're a funny guy. Have fun with your pal, won't you. I'll see you tomorrow.'

She ran down the steps and raced across the warehouse, emerging into the sunshine, blinking. Still running, she scrabbled around in her bag for her sunglasses. It was the beginning of May, inclemently warm, but the prickling of sweat on her back had a lot more to do with avoiding David Rockford than the sticky weather. She found her glasses, stuck them on, then circumnavigated the car park and made it to safety just as the red sports car swung in. Flora kept her face averted lest David recognise her. Not that he would – he probably didn't even remember that first meeting.

He certainly wouldn't remember it in as much detail as Flora.

Heading into town, Flora tried to get rid of the image of David Rockford's green eyes by thinking about the three websites – there was definitely something strange going on there. She veered into the coffee shop for another shot of caffeine. Maybe it would clear her head. While she waited in the queue she rested her bag against the counter and pulled out her phone.

'Uncle Max? I need to come and see you again. As soon as possible. Yes, it is important. Really, really important.'

Chapter 15

Flora always enjoyed travelling by train. She loved the sense of movement, of getting somewhere fast. Unlike her fellow passengers, she never read during a journey. In her tote bag Flora carried a paperback novel, but it was only for any serious waiting around. So far, so good. The train to Crewe from Shrewsbury was bang on time and Max had agreed to meet her at Wem station.

If he was surprised to see her again so soon he kept it to himself. She jumped into the Land Rover and tutted at the door, which still wasn't fixed. But her uncle got off without any serious ribbing. Flora had other things on her mind.

This time, however, she had remembered to bring wellies. She picked her way through the chicken poo and settled in Max's rustic kitchen, tapping her fingers on the worn oak table while he made coffee.

'You've turned your back on your roots,' he said, spooning in a measure of instant.

'Come again?'

'All this coffee business. Marshall's rubbing off on you, Flora. There's nothing wrong with a nice cup of tea, you know. Plenty of caffeine in tea.'

'You sound like Joy.' Flora reached for the cup and took a sip. Not brilliant, but not bad either.

'How is she doing? Any more incidents to report?'

'May I?' She put down her coffee and pointed at her uncle's iPad, which sat on the kitchen worktop surrounded by bits of tractor engine, unwashed mugs and plates and pans, unopened envelopes and piles of coins. Max nodded. Flora quickly opened up three tabs and typed in the web addresses she'd memorised.

'Look at these. Anything about them strike you as odd?'

Her uncle pulled up a rocking chair with five missing slats. He peered at each screen before tapping on to the next. When he was done he sat back and rubbed his chin.

'Flora, I thought I told you to stay away from Vasco.'

She said nothing.

'I promised your dad I'd look out for you, and it hasn't been a difficult promise to keep. But now … I just don't understand why you're getting involved. You've always had a talent for trouble, but it's never been anything too serious.' He looked at her arm – it was the merest glance, but Flora knew he was remembering when she'd got that particular tattoo, and how devastated her mum had been.

There was no point dwelling on all that right now. She lived with the guilt, and she wasn't about to let Max rub it in any further.

'I'm not looking for trouble, Max. And I'm not "involved" in anything. I'm just looking out for a friend. Trying to do what's right. You can understand that, can't you?'

He pursed his lips. Flora took that as a Yes and pointed at the iPad. 'So, does anything jump out at you, looking at those three websites?'

Max's brow creased as he stared at them again in turn. 'No. I'm sorry. Obviously I recognise Vasco's name here – his site looks a bit basic for a hotshot solicitor, perhaps. And this one, isn't this the retirement home where your friend lives? And the other – what's that, some kind of charity?'

'A charitable foundation. Are you absolutely sure you've never heard of it?'

When Max shook his head Flora's shoulders slumped. She'd been convinced her uncle would know something about the charity. In fact, she'd been banking on it. To her eyes, all three websites looked suspiciously similar – the same layout, similar fonts, almost identical menus. The theory she'd developed overnight was that there was some connection between Mr Vasco and the charity. Maybe he'd taken up web design as a sideline and offered to do the Maples' site too. At the very least, they'd all used the same service. Maybe that was how the three were linked, and there was someone else behind the charity who was using – paying? bribing? – the solicitor to coerce the residents into leaving all their money to Six Wishes.

As theories go it was thin, but to Flora it felt close to being right. She'd spent half the night trying to find the origins of each site, to no avail. And she was no computer whiz. If Richie hadn't proved himself to be worse than useless she might have asked him – Marshall had said he'd done computer science at the Technology College. She looked at Max and sighed.

'You know they're moving Joy up to the third floor tomorrow. She's in such a state about it, won't even let me visit her. She's still paranoid about that Mr Felix fella, and I'm persona non grata because I haven't somehow managed to magically make him disappear. Meanwhile, I'm so sure that there *is* something weird going on over there that I've made things even worse for Shakers, losing the contract because of my meddling is what Marshall thinks, but I think Rockfords are behind it. I know the Captain's death has got nothing to do with Mr Felix and I'm positive your Mr Vasco is involved, but I don't know how. And I want to make sure it's safe for Joy. More than that, Max, I want to be able to *prove* to her that she's got nothing to fear. Her asthma is really bad – she's deteriorated so fast recently. It was only a few weeks ago I took her out to the funicular railway and her asthma was fine then. Totally under control, with her medication and her inhaler. But now ... I just don't know what's going to happen. How can I reassure her that the Maples is a safe place to be when I'm convinced that the Captain's death – and maybe another death too – wasn't by natural causes? She's too ill to stay in her unit alone, but moving up to Special Care might kill her anyway, she's so stressed about it. And there's this charity, and the Captain's will, and is it sick animals or ex-service men, or–'

Max laid his hand on Flora's arm. 'Calm down, kid. Take a breath. Never mind Joy, what about your stress levels? You look like you're about to have a heart attack.'

They were both silent for a moment.

'Sorry, Flora. That was insensitive.'

'It's okay, Uncle Max. It's just a figure of speech, you didn't mean it to be upsetting. But you know, I do think about dad a lot in all this. You know what he was like, his sense of justice, of doing the right thing. If there was the slightest chance that someone hurt that old man intentionally, dad wouldn't have wanted them to get away with it.'

'No one would. I think you can rest assured of that.' Max sipped his mug of tea and stretched out a booted foot. 'Look, why don't you just start at the beginning. Tell me everything. Let's see what you've got.'

Flora started with Joy, going all the way back to the day of their Bridgnorth trip. She even mentioned the bunch of daffodils and the postcard of the Roman goddess. As she spoke, Max listened carefully, interrupting her once or twice with a question, but mostly just taking it all in. When Flora got to the part about the hoodied figure who may or may not have been following her, he tensed and clenched his fists. And when Flora told him about the Six Wishes Foundation, and Ida's and the Captain's different ideas of what the charity's main function was, he sat forward and slammed a fist on the table.

Flora jumped and looked at him in alarm. 'What's wrong?'

'That's what it was. The lowlife, disgusting … Flora, tell me again about this charity. Everything you know.'

She did, and they looked at the website again on the iPad. Max rubbed his chin, massaging the stubble with grimy hands.

'Vasco, he had his fingers in lots of pies. Like I told you, he represented all sorts of criminals and most of them got off.'

'I remember you telling me about the councillor. And then he blackmailed him, right? Do you think Mr Vasco was blackmailing the Captain?' Flora tried to imagine what the solicitor could have had on an eighty-nine year old man but drew a blank. But then even Joy had her guilty secrets, and they were tearing her apart. Maybe everyone had something hidden in their past. Even someone like the Captain.

But Max was shaking his head. 'That's not what I'm saying. I remember a case early in Vasco's career, before I even got on the council. There was a woman who was charged with running a fake charity scam. It was absolutely disgusting. She netted thousands out of the generosity of innocent people, many of them elderly, and she walked away from it clean. Thanks to Vasco.'

Flora's ears had pricked up at the mention of a charity scam. If she was honest, that had been bothering her more than anything. It seemed so unlikely that anyone would fake a charity – it was so callous, for one thing – that she had tried to put it out of her mind. But the Six Wishes Foundation … there were just so many things about it that didn't add up.

Max carried on, with Flora hanging on every word. 'Do you remember those little envelopes that used to come around when you were a kid? Well, maybe they weren't so popular by then, but back in the late seventies and eighties it was the main way for charities to collect. They'd drop an envelope through your door and come back to collect it the following week. People would put in whatever they could afford. Ten pence or ten pounds – it was anonymous and very effective. I can't remember how she got caught, but the police started to investigate this woman – Cyndy, her name was. Cyndy Baker. Cyndy with a Y. Very affected, I thought. They found she'd been running this scam for five years, all over Shropshire, changing the name of the charity every so often, printing these little envelopes at a dodgy printer's in Birmingham. With so many victims it was a really tough case to bring to court. But they did.'

'And Vasco got her off? How?'

Max shrugged. 'I've told you before, he's clever. I guess he found some loophole or other, I don't remember the ins and outs of the case. But when you told me about that Wishes charity – what was it called?'

'The Six Wishes Foundation.'

'Right. Well, it struck a chord. Because that's really similar to one of those fake charity names. Different number, it might have been seven wishes, or eight or something, but the rest is the same.'

Flora stared at Max, her mouth dropping open. 'So you think Vasco remembered the charity scam and decided to set up his own? Maybe the name was subconscious, just hanging around in his memory from years ago.'

'You're the expert in all that subconscious psychology stuff, not me. But yes, I think you might be on to something. At the very least, it should be looked into. Someone with Vasco's past, and two old people leaving their money to a charity that doesn't seem very easy to pin down. I think the police would be interested, don't you?'

Flora agreed. She nodded when Max offered her another cup of coffee, feeling a weight lifting from her shoulders. Finally, she had something concrete. She could go to the police now with a credible reason for being suspicious. Not just that an old man like the Captain was unlikely to fall down a set of shallow steps. Not just a gut feeling. And if Max came with her, a former councillor and pillar of the community no less, they'd have to take her seriously.

'You know,' she said while Max hunted in the cupboard for some biscuits, 'at first I was quite enjoying investigating all this. I mean, it was horrible, of course, what happened to the Captain, and I'm not saying I enjoyed that side of it. But trying to work it out, solving a puzzle, it's kind of addictive.'

'I'm sensing a "but".'

'Too right. It's like this huge pressure, especially when you're the only one who thinks there's anything wrong. Everyone just believed the warden's explanation that the Captain tripped and fell and that was the end of it.'

'And that may still turn out to be the case, Flora,' Max said. 'All this, it's only a theory. Besides, even if there is something untoward about the old man's will, there's no reason to assume someone would kill him for it. It wouldn't really be necessary, would it?'

'What do you mean?'

'You said he was in some kind of special care. I think it might be safe to assume that his death was fairly imminent.'

'You're right. It's all too horrible to think about. Maybe they were just too impatient to wait for nature to take its course.' Flora frowned. 'Anyway, it's just as well I'm not really a private investigator. I don't have the stomach for it.' Max raised his eyebrows and she shook her head. 'Oh, nothing. Just Marshall, teasing me as usual. Saying we should open up a private eye branch of Shakers.'

'Well, I hope to God you're not seriously thinking about it.' Max looked horrified.

'You think I'm that rubbish?'

'No.' He set down her coffee and put his hand on her back. 'I think you're the only family I've got left. I need to know you're safe.'

'You've got Marshall too.'

Max smiled, but the smile didn't reach his eyes. 'You know what I mean. You just take care, okay? Promise me.'

They agreed that Max would be the one to phone the police on Monday morning. He had a contact there so he'd make the initial call. 'They'll probably want to come and see you, Flora.'

'Good,' she said. And she meant it. The sooner someone official was involved, the sooner she could wash her hands of the whole thing.

Now all she had to worry about was Joy and her imminent move.

An intractable old lady with a guilty conscience or a possible murder? It was hard to know which was the most difficult to handle, to be honest.

***

'Tickets please.'

Flora rooted around in her bag and pulled out the return ticket to Shrewsbury. She handed it to the conductor with a smile. He didn't even bother to meet her eyes. She noticed an enormous spot on the side of his nose and grinned to herself. Serves him right for being so grumpy.

She settled back to watch the scenery fly past. Fields, more fields, backs of houses, fields. She'd be glad to get back to the hustle and bustle of the town, the air filled with evidence of human life, even if it was just exhaust fumes.

She thought again about those little charity envelopes Max had talked about. She could picture one, red text on a white background, sitting on the hall table waiting to be collected. What kind of a person fakes a charity envelope and has the audacity to turn up and collect it? Unimaginable. What was her name? Cyndy-with-a-Y. Cyndy Baker. And she got away with it, too. Flora sighed. That was the real crime, when you thought about it.

For want of anything better to do with her hands, Flora reached into her bag for her notepad and pen. She laid them on the table in front of her and wrote: Cyndy Baker. She underlined the Y and turned it into an evil face with slanted eyes. A thought occurred to her, a thought so horrible and ridiculous she tried to dismiss it instantly. It refused to go away. She stretched out her legs, full of a sudden energy, and accidentally kicked the man opposite. He held his paper to the side for a second and looked her up and down. Flora forced a smile. The man nodded and carried on reading.

Flora looked back down at the notepad.

Underneath Cyndy's name she wrote another.

Cynthia Curtis.

She drew a circle around the two Ys.

Cyndy with a Y. Cynthia with a Y.

And then, her hand shaking slightly, she wrote: Richie Baker.

She underlined both Bakers twice, three times, four times, her pen digging deeper into the page. She wanted to jump up and run to the end of the train; she wanted to scream. Tucking her hands under her thighs she forced herself to breathe, to calm down. Her face was on fire, the back of her neck like ice. She tried to swallow but there was no saliva.

It was too much of a coincidence to be ignored.

She looked out of the window and watched a bird fly alongside the train. It swooped away, doubled back, then flew over the carriage and out of sight. She looked back at her notepad.

Cynthia Curtis was Richie Baker's aunt. If she was his father's sister, Baker would be her maiden name. Cynthia with a Y; Cyndy with a Y. One could easily be a shortened version of the other. The name, and the connection with the Maples, and by association the Six Wishes Foundation, plus the Vasco factor. She had it. Flora felt a shift in her consciousness, as though a curtain had suddenly been lifted to expose a whole new world. Cyndy would be an affectation the warden had distanced herself from, with good reason if she was once again involved in a fake charity.

Was that why Cynthia had needed the solicitor involved? To play it safe, keep them from suspicion? She thought about how well protected the people behind Six Wishes were. In almost two days of searching, Flora had failed to find so much as a name to connect to it. Could the warden have done this alone? It was impossible to say. Flora wrote Vasco's name alongside the others. He must be in this up to his scrawny neck, taking care of the residents' wills once they'd somehow been coerced into leaving their estates to Six Wishes.

Just how did they manage that, anyway? Flora felt her stomach turn over as another piece of the puzzle fell into place. Guilt, that was how. Playing on their kindnesses, the causes they had spent their lives supporting. For Ida it was cats. Flora could just imagine the warden telling her about a brilliant charity doing wonderful things for sick animals, probably producing pamphlets and all sorts of other materials to support it. Six Wishes would need a website – the elderly residents of the Maples were pretty handy when it came to the internet. Someone thinking of donating their life savings to a charity would want to look them up first. Flora wondered if Cynthia had involved anyone else in the scam. Photos of rescued pets; a phone call from the so-called president of the foundation, perhaps, thanking her for her generosity. And then Mr Vasco to make it all official. Nothing to do with the retirement village, a complete outsider, to maintain the illusion it was all above board. Perhaps he offered his services for a discount, via a leaflet or a card the warden would leave lying around in their rooms …

Guilt. And perhaps a touch of psychology. Why leave all your money to some nameless distant relative who never visits, who in all probability doesn't even know you exist? Why not do something good with your nest egg, something worthwhile? For the Captain it was a no-brainer, as Marshall would say. Ex-military, no family, he'd devoted his life to the service of queen and country. The warden was perfectly placed to know exactly which buttons to press.

And then, just sit back and wait for them to die. If all your targets were in Special Care, you could be sure, as Max had pointed out, that you wouldn't have to wait too long.

The train slowed down and stopped just outside Shrewsbury's centre. Flora sat on the edge of her seat, chewing a nail. The man opposite was still reading his paper; she envied him his innocent calm. Looking across the backs of industrial units, two thoughts hit Flora simultaneously.

One: the warden had been lucky that both Ida and the Captain had died so soon after she'd secured their signatures on the wills.

Two: surely this luck was a coincidence too far?

Had Cynthia progressed beyond fraud and turned to murder as well? Flora felt sick at the thought of it. Cynthia, too greedy and impatient to wait for them to die naturally, easing them on their way. The Captain – how exactly had she managed that? A sleeping tablet slipped in with his breakfast, banking on his insistence on walking down all those stairs, perhaps. Or had the warden been walking with him, helping him ... helping him on his way with one well-timed shove?

Flora swallowed and wondered how many more there had been, or how many were already set up and ready to be dispatched. It made her blood run cold. Maybe Joy's fears about the third floor weren't so farfetched after all.

Joy. Who was herself about to be moved to the third floor due to poor health. Sitting on a healthy sum after Eddie's death last year, no family to speak of, already depressed and demotivated. Not to mention holding a guilty secret that coloured her view of everything she saw. Wasn't she an ideal target for the warden's evil scheme? Flora suddenly remembered Cynthia appearing behind them the day Joy confessed all about the Joan of Arc club. How long had she been there, and how much had she heard? If she knew everything, all she'd have to do would be talk about a wonderful charity for bullied children – or better still, bullied children from poor families who really loved dogs. She could make up whatever she wanted, and the Six Wishes would be back in business with a new incarnation, ready to receive its latest bequest.

Chapter 16

E lizabeth? I'm sorry to be a pain, but can you do me a favour and find Joy?'

Flora had jumped on a bus outside the station, impatiently dialling Joy's mobile again and again. But either Joy was ignoring her or she wasn't near her phone, so Flora had called the Maples' reception instead. Figuring it would be quicker to catch the bus to the other side of town than go on foot, Flora was now hovering near the door ready to dash off as soon as they reached her stop.

'I don't think she's here, Flora. Bear with me, I'll just go and check.'

'Hang on a minute,' Flora shouted, but it was too late. She could hear Elizabeth's shoes click-clacking along the corridor. Flora glared at the phone in her hand.

'Damn it.'

A woman with a toddler on her lap looked up at her disgustedly. Flora pulled an apologetic face and turned back towards the front of the bus. Traffic was heavy and progress maddeningly slow. The car in front of them – an ancient Ford with smoke billowing out of the exhaust – indicated and stopped to let out a passenger. Right in the middle of the road. Flora bit her tongue to stop herself from swearing again. She looked at the phone, willing the receptionist to return. If she could just talk to Joy, tell her not to speak to anyone about Aubrey – and more importantly not to talk to any solicitors, or indeed the warden – it would buy them enough time to get the police involved. But she needed to see Joy for herself. There was something inside her, some pressing weight on her chest, that wouldn't ease up. Flora didn't even want to think about what it was trying to tell her.

But when Elizabeth came back she had bad news. 'Joy's not here, sorry. I didn't think she was, to be honest.'

Flora could have strangled the woman. 'Okay, no worries. Did you check her unit?'

'No.' Elizabeth laughed. 'I got halfway there and remembered. What a dizzy Lizzy I am.'

The bus started up again, almost throwing Flora off her feet and into the lap of the woman behind, which was already occupied by the howling toddler. 'Oh, my goodness! I'm so sorry.' She gave the distressed boy a gentle pat on his arm and his mother drew him back as though Flora had tried to hit him. Passengers two or three rows behind were starting to stare at her now. She looked away, her face burning.

'Elizabeth, could you just tell me where Joy is? I really need to know.'

'Oh, sure. She's gone off with the warden to visit her solicitor. Said something about signing her will. Poor old dear, this moving up to the third floor really has upset her, hasn't it? You were right about that. I saw her at breakfast and she kept talking about doing the right thing … I was a bit worried about her, to be honest.'

Flora was only half listening. 'When did they go?' she shouted, cutting Elizabeth off mid sentence.

'Oh, I think they left about an hour ago. Or maybe less. I'm not sure. By the way, Flora, there's something else I need to tell–'

'Thanks, Elizabeth. Bye.' She ended the call and stepped up to the driver. 'I need to get off right now.'

'No can do, missy. Not a scheduled stop.'

In a fair imitation of the child behind her, Flora stamped her foot. Hard. And then she stamped it again. The driver looked at her like she was crazy.

'Listen, you jumped up, pompous, barely out of high school little git. I. Need. To. Get. Off. This. Bus. Now!'

He slammed on his air brakes, almost throwing her through the windscreen. Flora swallowed and pushed herself off the warm plastic dash, then brushed herself down and stepped from the bus with as much dignity as she could muster.

'There's no need to get personal,' shouted the driver, closing the doors behind her. She only just managed to pull her bag out of the way before they shut with a hiss and the bus pulled out. Faces pressed against the window; Flora fought the urge to stick up two fingers. She hooked her bag over her shoulder and began to jog back up the hill towards the library. Back towards the offices of Vasco and Co.

***

'Where is she?'

Flora burst through the door, confronting Mr Vasco who was bending over a filing cabinet in the corner.

'Excuse me?'

He turned and straightened. After a quick glance around, and finding the rest of the office empty, Flora marched across the room and stood in front of him, almost toe to toe. She just about reached up to his chest.

'Listen to me, Vasco. If you've done anything to my friend I will personally see to it that you rot in jail and never see the light of day again. I know she's been here, with your old pal Cyndy. Where is she? Where?'

Emboldened by her spat with the bus driver, Flora could hardly believe the words that were coming out of her mouth. Inside she was shaking, but whether it was with fear or pure rage, she couldn't say. Mr Vasco, however, was not so easily intimidated. He looked down at her and laughed. It was not a nice laugh.

'I've got no idea what you're talking about. But I do recognise you – you're the annoying girl from that removal company. Shakies, or something equally silly. The warden at the retirement village told me all about you the day of Captain Wares' funeral. She said you were a pest.' He sucked in his already hollow cheeks and his face took on the appearance of a skeleton. 'How dare you come in here shouting the odds to me?' he hissed, bending at the waist so his face was level with Flora's. 'Don't you know who you're dealing with?'

She took a step back. Come on, Flora, don't wimp out now. But the solicitor's menacing demeanour was hitting the alarm button on her sense of self-preservation. She stepped back again.

'Just tell me where Joy is and I'll leave. I know she's been here. Unless …'

Flora whipped her head around to look at the door. Maybe Elizabeth had got her timings wrong and Cynthia and Joy were yet to arrive. Or maybe they'd stopped for a cup of tea on the way. When she looked back again, Mr Vasco was sitting on one of the worn sofas with one knee crossed over the other, regarding her thoughtfully.

'What name did you say earlier?'

'What?' She took another step towards the door. There was something about his expression she didn't like at all. 'Joy? My friend Joy, from the Maples.'

'No. Another name. You came charging in here and said you know all about me and some old pal of mine. Who did you say it was?'

Vasco smiled, and the effect was more terrifying than his grimace.

'Sally,' Flora told him. It was the first name that came into her head. 'Your old pal Sally told me that Joy was coming here today. To ... to ask about her tax returns,' she added, grabbing the idea from an Inland Revenue poster on the wall behind his head.

'Tax returns? But I thought she was retired?'

Flora laughed. It was a high-pitched hysterical sound she barely recognised herself. She'd messed up big time: what she really needed to do right now was get the hell out of here. Maybe she could hide out across the street and watch for Joy and the warden. But what if they'd been already? She needed to know one way or the other. She looked around the office desperately, her eyes finally lighting on the open diary on Vasco's desk. It was one of those massive page-to-a-day affairs, open at Friday 4th May, and with only a glance Flora could see that Vasco wasn't much in demand. There was only one appointment booked: *11:00 – Joy Martin. New LWT.* And next to it was scribbled *6W?*

Six Wishes question mark. And LWT obviously stood for last will and testament. Flora swallowed hard. The appointment was ticked off in red pen.

She was too late.

She took another step back. 'Well, I guess I must have got the day wrong or something. I'll go home and call her. If you do see Joy tell her I was looking for her, won't you?'

Flora reached the door and swung it open, dashing outside just as Mr Vasco's expression cleared and he jumped to his feet. She started down School Gardens, almost knocking over a thin guy in a cream suit.

Oh, Jesus. It was Heston.

'Flora? What are you doing? You nearly sent me flying!' He glared at her, brushing invisible dirt off his slacks. 'You do have a habit of knocking people over. You really should learn to be more careful.'

Flora groaned. Heston was the last person she wanted to see right now. But she knew Vasco would be hot on her heels so she linked arms with him and began to march across the square past the library. Glancing over her shoulder she saw the solicitor watching from his office window. He was talking on the phone. Damn it. She'd totally given the game away, blurting out Cyndy's name like that. He was probably calling the warden right now, warning her.

And what exactly would that mean for Joy?

If they knew their scam was about to be exposed, would they see Joy as one last chance to get some cash in the charity's coffers? After all, if she'd already signed the will …

Flora increased her pace, all but dragging Heston along with her. He wasn't coming quietly.

'Where are we going? I've already finished my lunch break. I need to get back.'

Not: Are you okay, you look flustered? Or even: I've missed you.

As soon as they were out of sight of School Gardens, Flora dropped Heston like a hot brick.

'See you around,' she said, taking off down the hill at a pace.

'Wait! Can I see you again soon?'

'I'll call you.'

She rounded a gaggle of tourists and shook her head. There was no way she was going to call him. He might recall her existence when she was ploughing into him on the street but he'd clearly not thought about her all week. As she ran along the pavement, dodging shoppers and prams and determined tourists, the only regret Flora had about Heston was that she'd have to find somewhere else to relax in town. The library would be off-limits for a while.

But right now she had other things on her mind.

She had to find Joy.

Empty. Flora peered through the window. All she could see were boxes and stripped furniture. So they hadn't moved her yet, but it was clearly imminent. She hammered on the door again just in case Joy was in the bathroom. Her mind was working overtime, figuring out the next place to try.

'She's not here.'

Whirling around, Flora came face to face with Mr Felix. He wasn't on his mobility scooter today, but had his orthopaedic crutch rammed under his right armpit. He shuffled back as he took in Flora's wild appearance.

'What happened to you? You look like you've been in a fight.' Mr Felix looked her up and down unpleasantly. 'Been attacking old people in the library again, have you?'

Flora tried to calm her breathing. No point getting irate with him – it wasn't his fault Joy had gone AWOL. 'Do you know where she is?' She was already heading for the main building, with Mr Felix hobbling behind.

'No idea. I saw her go out a while ago. And I found this.'

In his hand he held a blue inhaler. Flora stopped, stared at it hard, then walked on.

'Where did you find it?'

'I found it on the path near her unit. About half an hour ago. She must have dropped it.'

Not good. That meant wherever Joy was, she was even more vulnerable. Hopefully Flora would find her sitting in the communal area with Vera or one of the others. Hopefully the trip to Vasco's had been nothing more than a primer – maybe they'd told her all about the wonderful charity and asked her to think about it. "6W?" might have been a code for a preliminary meeting. Besides, even if she had signed something, there would be plenty of time to undo it. Make a new will, or invalidate the old one. Flora was sure that once the police got involved all Mr Vasco's dealings would be looked at in great detail.

In some ways, it might be good if they'd coerced Joy to sign a new will. It would certainly give them more evidence. But not if Vasco had put it all together and figured out that Flora was on to them. Why had she mentioned Cyndy? Stupid. She just needed to see Joy for herself, was all. See she was fine and then find a way to protect her. She'd already decided to ask Joy to come and stay at the bungalow until the Maples got the all clear. Her parents' old home would be perfect for Joy, and Flora couldn't cope with the stress of worrying about the old lady for another minute.

They reached the main building and Flora pushed against the glass doors. They didn't open.

'What's going on? Are they locked?'

Mr Felix shouldered past her and produced a key card from his trouser pocket. 'New security system. Apparently someone has been asking questions about the Captain's death, talking about mystery visitors or some such rubbish, so now we've got all this to contend with. As if life wasn't awkward enough for some of us,' he added, manoeuvring himself inside the building while trying to hold the door open for Flora one-handed. She hid her face so he couldn't see her expression.

Elizabeth's face paled when she saw Flora with Mr Felix.

'Oh, my. I'm not sure you should be … The thing is, Flora–'

'I need to know where Joy is. Have you seen her since they came back?'

The receptionist looked startled. 'Came back? Oh, they haven't come back yet. They won't be back for hours.'

'What?' Flora leaned over the desk, her palms flat on the polished wood surface. 'You said they'd popped into town to see a solicitor.'

'I know. And I really shouldn't have told you even that, Flora. You see, the warden, she said–'

'I'm not interested in what she said, Elizabeth. I just want to know where Joy is.'

Mr Felix cleared his throat. Flora ignored him.

'Well? Do you know or not?'

Elizabeth nodded. 'It's more than my job's worth, though. I'm so sorry. Cynthia said, well, she specifically told me not to talk to you at all.' She dropped her voice to a whisper, looking around as though she feared the warden might materialise any minute. 'And that's not all she said.'

Flora looked directly into the older woman's eyes. 'Listen. This is massively important. If you know where she is you must tell me. Is your job more important than the safety of an old woman?'

The receptionist whimpered and opened her mouth, but then closed it again and shook her head.

Mr Felix cleared his throat a second time.

'What?' said Flora, rounding on him.

The old man raised his eyebrows. They were bushy and ginger, sprouting from his freckled forehead like two surprised caterpillars. 'If you'd like to step outside with me, I might be able to help.'

With a withering look at Elizabeth, Flora followed Mr Felix back out into the quadrant. He was maddeningly slow, shuffling along at a snail's pace. Once they were outside she took out her phone and checked for messages. Nothing.

'Well? You said you could help.'

'I said I might be able to.'

'Please, Mr Felix. I know you and I didn't get off to the best of starts, but could you just tell me what you know. You can see I'm at the end of my rope here.'

'You're worried about Joy.'

'Yes. Yes, I am.'

'Well, she's fine. That's what I was trying to tell you. She went off earlier with the warden, quite safely, and I heard them say they'd be back in time for dinner but not before.'

Flora looked at the time on her phone. 'But it's after two. Dinner was ages ago.'

The old man tutted. 'Lunch, young lady. Dinner isn't until six o'clock. Your breeding is showing, my dear.'

Breeding? Flora shook the insult away. 'So you heard them say they wouldn't be back until six? You definitely heard that?'

He nodded.

'Anything else?'

'Something about an anniversary. But that's all, I'm afraid. It was only later I found her inhaler on the path. She must have dropped it in her excitement.'

Flora perched on the arm of a nearby bench and tried to think. Something was tugging at her memory, something triggered by Mr Felix's words. She jumped up again and grabbed his arm.

'Why did you say that?'

'What?'

'That she dropped it because she was excited? How do you know she was excited?'

'I don't know. She just looked sort of … animated. She's been a little down lately, you might have noticed, and it was nice to see her more upbeat.'

Flora could have hugged him. 'I know exactly where she's gone with the warden.'

'You do?'

'Oh yes.' She pulled Marshall's number up on her phone and pressed Call. 'I've been so distracted,' she told Mr Felix while it rung out, 'I totally forgot that it's Joy and Eddie's anniversary today.'

'Eddie?'

'Her husband. Come on, Marshall, you useless lump. Where are you?'

'She's married?'

'Widowed. But today is – would have been – their anniversary, and Joy wanted to go to the railway again. The fourth of May, three weeks exactly since our trip there.'

And I promised to take her, thought Flora with a stab of guilt. I've let her down. And because of that she's gone with the warden instead, who has God-knows-what ulterior motive.

She gave up on Marshall and turned to Mr Felix. 'I've got to get to Bridgnorth right away. Ideas?'

A smile crept over the old man's face. 'As a matter of fact, I have a great idea.'

Chapter 17

'Y ou drive quite fast, don't you?'
Flora was clinging to the inside of the passenger door and had her feet planted wide apart to steady herself. Mr Felix swung the Fiat around another corner at forty miles per hour and laughed.

'Quite fast for an old fogey, you mean?'

If the cap fits, thought Flora. She just smiled. More than anything, she was grateful for the favour. Mr Felix had surprised her with the offer of a lift, and now he was surprising her even more. Not only was he a crazy driver, he also seemed touchingly concerned about Joy's wellbeing. *And* he was a really good listener.

They'd been travelling for about half an hour, and so far she'd told him pretty much everything. Not about Joy's conviction that he was in fact the much abused caretaker's son, of course, but all about Mr Vasco and her suspicions about the warden and the possibly fake charity that had so far benefited from not one but two huge bequests. And probably had another from Joy on the way.

Mr Felix listened in silence, occasionally shaking his head.

'I'm glad I've got no money,' he told her when she reached the part about Joy's visit to the solicitor that morning. 'No one would be interested in me as a target. You know, it never occurred to me as odd before, but now you come to mention it there's something else that fits your theory.'

Flora sat forward, keeping her hands braced to either side. 'What?'

'There was this questionnaire when I moved in to the Maples. I'm renting my unit, can't afford to buy a place outright like Joy, so I just thought it was a kind of security or financial check.'

'Like a credit rating?'

He nodded. 'You had to list all your assets, and then at the end there was a section about family. Your emergency contacts and all that, but also beneficiaries.'

'Really?' Flora thought about it. A perfect way to assess incoming residents for suitability – and vulnerability. She shuddered. The warden was even more calculating than she'd imagined.

'And speaking of charities, there was a section on any charities I might support. Ongoing direct debits, things like that.'

It all fitted. Flora was sure of it now. If this pressure in her chest would ease off for a minute she might be able to think more clearly, because now there was something else niggling at her. She sighed. It was no good. With Mr Felix rabbiting on – who would have guessed he was so chatty? – and throwing her around in the car like a ragdoll, it was all she could do to keep focused on the job at hand.

Find Joy. Make sure she was okay. Tell the warden to take a hike, then keep Joy safe until the charity scam was exposed.

That was all she could think about right now.

'So I wrote down that there was nothing and no one, of course. A life of work and nothing to show for it. That's just the way it is for people like me.'

'What did you do before you retired?' Flora looked over at him. His colour was high. She remembered Elizabeth telling her he was obsessed with vitamins. She had to admit, he looked the picture of health.

'I was a chemist. Worked in university labs.'

'Did you enjoy it?'

He shrugged. 'What's to enjoy? A job's a job.' He glanced over at her, his smile wide. 'I suppose you're one of those feminist types, are you?'

'What makes you say that?'

'You're a young woman running a business that traditionally belongs to men. And you're friends with Joy, of course.'

Flora laughed. She saw the sign for the funicular railway and told Mr Felix to turn left. 'I'm no feminist. If I was I'd be following my own dreams, not carrying on someone else's.'

Mr Felix was silent then, and Flora looked out of the window, embarrassed. He sure was easy to talk to, but she'd said far too much already. She pushed the feeling of melancholy away and craned her neck for that first stunning view of Bridgnorth. And there it was, rising up on a cliff, the beautiful architecture and domed church of the High Town looking majestically down on the valley below.

She directed him to the bridge, then asked him to pull over.

'But the Severn Railway is further on.'

'What?'

'I thought you said she wanted to go to the railway?'

Flora laughed. 'Not that railway. This one.' She nodded towards the arched entrance to the cliff railway and Mr Felix shrugged.

'Well, good luck. Do you want me to hang around and give you a lift back?'

Flora was torn. They would need to get back to Shrewsbury somehow and it was getting late for a bus. Marshall still wasn't answering his phone. But Joy would no doubt refuse to travel in Mr Felix's car, even if her life depended on it.

The old man seemed to understand her dilemma. 'Tell you what – I've got a bit of shopping to do, so how about I meet you back here in half an hour. If you want a lift, fine. If not, no problem.'

She nodded and told him to meet them at the top, in High Town. 'It's easier to park up there.'

'Okay, then. I hope you find her.' He smiled and strapped his seatbelt across his body.

'Thanks, Mr Felix. You're a star. And listen, I'm really sorry about what happened in the library the other day. It was all just a misunderstanding.'

He waved and drove away. Flora ran across the road, dodging traffic, and dived into the alley that led to the tiny ticket office at the bottom of the railway.

'We're closed.'

Flora came to a halt, practically running into the barrier. She looked at the opening times stuck to the window.

'No, you're not.'

The man behind the counter glared at her. 'Yes, we are.'

A shout pierced the air. The man's face took on a panicked expression and he moved to the rear of the cubicle.

'What was that?' Flora followed his gaze. On impulse, she slipped under the barrier to get a better view.

The two train carriages were sitting empty, one at the top and one at the bottom. The sight of them made Flora shudder. Good thing it was closed, when you came to think about it: she didn't really want another trip up the cliff face. But if it was closed, where might Joy and Cynthia have gone instead? The track led up and up: Flora followed it to the top with her eyes. Along the wall that overlooked the track and the valley, people were leaning over and pointing to something out of Flora's line of vision.

She edged forward a little further, pressing her nose right up against the glass.

'Crazy old lady,' grumbled the ticket man. 'Costing me money. No one ever thinks about that, do they?'

High above the top carriage, on the metal gantry that ran across the narrow track, stood a solitary figure. She had white fluffy hair that whipped around her head in the strong breeze. The sleeves of her pastel blue cardigan were pushed up to the elbows and her arms where ghostly white. Almost as though she was wearing long white gloves …

Flora took in a sharp breath and a strangled cry escaped her throat.

The woman on the gantry was Joy.

***

'Joy! Oh, my God.' Flora banged her fists on the glass. 'You have to do something. Can't you get her down?'

The man threw her a disgusted look. 'Don't you think we're trying? She's been up there for fifteen minutes. Crazy old bat. Hold on – do you know her?'

'How do I get up there?' Flora had dropped her bag on the floor and was looking around for an access door. Her eyes fixed on the carriage. 'Come on, open it up. You can send me up in that. It's the quickest way.'

'No can do. Health and safety.'

'Damn it! Joy, hold on. I'm coming.'

'You'll have to go on foot,' the man told her. He gave her directions. 'It's not far, just steep. You'd better run.'

She didn't need to be told that. Swinging her bag over her shoulder, Flora legged it out of the ticket office and turned left, heading for the cobbled street that would lead her to High Town. She could hear the cries on the wind, people shouting, trying to talk Joy down. What was she doing up there? Did she know about the warden already? No, that wasn't possible. Maybe it was the thought of moving to the third floor, of losing her independence forever. That must be it. The poor old thing, full of fear, unable to face life without Eddie, unable to cope with the shame and guilt of what happened all those years ago. Flora had been right all along – that was what was behind her friend's anxieties and stress. If only she'd tried harder to get her to talk about it, to resolve it. But she'd been too caught up with playing detectives. She'd let her friend down completely.

Her phone started to ring. Flora answered it, still running. Good job she was fit, although her breathing was starting to show the strain and her legs were already burning. It was Marshall.

'Flora, where are you?'

'I'm in Bridgnorth.'

'What? Me too! What are you doing?'

'What did you say? I'm in Bridgnorth.'

Marshall's voice sounded strained. 'Flora, I'm in Bridgnorth too. Listen, there's something going on with Richie. He took the van, the police called me about an hour ago, it had been abandoned just outside High Town with two flat tyres. Steve's just driven me down here to pick it up.'

Flora's eyes stretched wide. 'Marshall, I can't explain right now but I think Richie might be in on it with his aunt. He must have done it so we couldn't follow them here.'

She turned left again and started up a flight of steps, taking them two at a time.

'In on what? What's going on?'

'Where are you exactly?'

'We've had to wait for a mechanic so we've come into the town. I'm by a big supermarket next to a medical centre.'

Flora knew where that was. The thought that

Marshall was close by lifted her heart in a way she wasn't about to analyse. 'Listen, you have to get to the top of the funicular railway.' Her words were coming out in gasps now, running and talking was impossible. 'The cliff railway. Ask someone, just get there as fast as you can. Okay?'

'Sure. Flora, are you–'

She cut him off. She was nearly at the top. There was the ice cream shop she'd passed with Joy only three weeks ago; around one more corner and she'd be able to see the tea rooms with the winding gear up ahead. Her mind was working quickly, figuring it all out. Richie. Of course. He'd been spying on her all along. She remembered how he'd crept in on her yesterday – and she'd left the websites open on the screen, had only turned off the monitor. It would have been easy for him to come back later and see what she'd been doing. It must have been him following her too, reporting back to the warden exactly what she was doing and who she'd talked to.

She ran along the walled walkway, heading for the crowd that had gathered at the end. In her mind she said her friend's name over and over.

Joy, whatever you're thinking right now, just hold on. I'm coming. Just. Hold. On.

A high-pitched scream pierced the air. With tears streaming down her face, Flora lurched forward.

**

'It's okay. She's okay.'

Flora had pushed her way to the front of the crowd to where a man was fanning a woman's face with his hat.

'Oh, my goodness! I thought she was going to jump,' the woman said, leaning back against the wall with her hand on her chest. Flora took a step to the right and looked up at the gantry.

Joy was still up there. Which was good news, kind of.

'Joy! Joy, it's me. What the bloody hell are you doing?'

The old woman started and peered down. 'Flora? Is that you? What are you doing here?'

As if they'd bumped into each other shopping. A bubble of hysterical laughter burst from Flora's lips.

'You crazy old biddy. Get down! You're losing the funicular paying fares.'

Joy laughed. For a suicidal geriatric, she didn't seem too melancholy.

'Joy, what exactly are you doing up there?' Flora shielded her eyes from the sun. The wind was picking up now, blowing Joy's fluffy hair straight back off her forehead.

'I'm the king of the world!' Joy shouted, and she leaned against the metal barrier, holding her arms wide.

'Listen to me, it's not the bloody Titanic! Stop messing around and get down here. Someone's going to notice soon, you'll get us into a ton of trouble.'

'Ha! You're so funny, Flora. That's one of the things I love about you. Because I *do* love you – you know that, don't you? You've been like family to me these past six months.'

Flora edged closer to the wall. She closed her eyes for a second, trying to stem the sudden swell of nausea. It had to be here, didn't it? Joy couldn't have chosen somewhere not-high-up to have some kind of breakdown. She steeled herself and opened her eyes. And looked right into the eyes of the warden.

Cynthia was standing on the other side of the track, about five feet below. Judging by the tables and chairs around her, the warden was on the terrace of the tea rooms. She locked eyes with Flora, who recoiled in shock. So much hatred there. Any hopes she'd had of being way off the mark disappeared in that single frozen moment. Cynthia – Cyndy – already knew that Flora knew everything. With a final glare in Flora's direction, the warden turned her attention back to Joy.

'Don't listen to her, Joy. I've told you all about her. She only befriended you to get your money, she's done it before.'

What? 'Joy, that's crazy! It's her – she's the one after your money. Didn't she take you to sign your will this morning? Well, guess what? That charity she told you about, it's hers. All the money goes to her and her pal Vasco.'

The warden began to clamber up the wall that ran along the perimeter of the terrace. A gasp ran through the crowd. There was a fifty-foot sheer drop the other side of that wall, but the warden seemed oblivious. She spoke to Joy again, holding out her hands. 'See what I mean? What kind of a person would say something like that? I know what that cause means to you. I just want to help you do the right thing.'

Joy was still leaning against the barrier, her head twisting from one side to the other like she was watching a game of tennis. She started laughing, waving her arms. 'Wheee!' she said. 'Whooo!'

'Is she on something?'

'Probably drunk.'

Flora shot the people behind her a withering glance. 'She is not drunk. Or "on" anything.' But when she looked back at her friend she started to wonder. What on earth made her get up there in the first place? Could the warden have slipped her some kind of pill, something that would make her behaviour erratic, reckless?

She elbowed her way around to the narrow stairway that led up to the gantry. Joy would have had to climb over a gate marked No Entry to get up there. Surely she wouldn't have gone to such extremes just to see her favourite view? And now she was swirling around, taking imaginary dance steps with an invisible partner.

Or maybe he wasn't invisible to Joy.

With a shuddering sigh, Flora climbed over the gate and ran up the metal steps. She kept her eyes to the left, away from the so-called stunning view – stunning to anyone without chronic vertigo. At the edge of the platform she stopped and crouched low, steadying her breathing. She made sure she had a firm hold of one of the metal bars, then she reached out her other hand and called to her friend.

'Joy. Come on now. It's time to go home.'

Joy's ebullient mood evaporated instantly. 'I don't have a home anymore. You moved me out of it, remember? You moved me into that place, and that's where I'm going to die.'

'No. No, you're not. But you can't stay up here any longer either.'

Out of the corner of her eye Flora could see the bright yellow high-vis vests of the police, who were clearing the onlookers away from the wall. She kept her eyes trained on Joy's legs.

'You're right, Joy,' called the warden from the other side of the gantry. She was closer now: she'd climbed right up to the top of the wall and would be close enough to touch Joy's feet if the old lady moved to the far end of the platform. 'She was the one who made you leave your home. *She's* behind all of the weird things that have been happening to you. The flowers, that postcard, what happened to your lovely dog. All her fault.'

Flora shouted out in indignation. How dare she? 'Joy, take no notice of her. Come here. Come here right now. You know I hate heights. I can't believe I'm doing this.' She stood up and took a step towards her friend.

The gantry moved. It was the slightest shift, but Flora felt it beneath the thin soles of her sandals. She swallowed and took another step. It happened again. With a creak and an unmistakable lurch, the metal began to pull away from the wall.

'Joy! We really have to get off here.'

'It's not made for more than one person,' came a voice from below. Flora peeped out from behind her hands and saw the ticket man standing with his hands on his hips. He must have followed her up. Standing beside him, his wispy comb-over blowing off his freckly scalp in one piece, was Mr Felix. He was holding something up high and pointing at Joy. Flora looked closer. Then she looked back at her friend.

'Oh no!'

Joy had slumped to the back of the gantry and was clutching her chest. Her face had pinked and each breath was becoming more and more laboured.

'She's having an asthma attack! We need help up here.' Flora looked down at Mr Felix again. 'Can you throw me her inhaler?'

'No.' Joy was crawling away, heading for the other side of the gantry and the warden. The metal creaked sickeningly.

'Joy, what are you doing?'

'I don't trust him. He's put something in it. I'm telling you, Flora. He's trying to kill me.'

'He's not!' Flora thumped her fist against her thigh in frustration. 'Joy, he's not trying to kill you, he's trying to save your life.' She turned back to the old man. 'Throw it to me. Just hold on a minute. And you,' she told Joy, 'don't move so much as a finger. If this thing comes away from the wall we're both dead.'

Joy stopped crawling and looked up, terrified. The warden seemed about to climb onto the gantry, then clearly thought better of it. She threw a triumphant look at Flora, then began to clamber back down to the tea room terrace. She was going to get away, but there was nothing Flora could do about it now.

She wedged herself against the front of the rail and steeled herself to let go. She'd need both hands to catch the inhaler.

'Oh, hurry,' someone called from the walkway. Flora ignored them. She kept her eyes focused on Mr Felix. She nodded.

In the moment before he lifted his arm into an overhand throw, it occurred to Flora that if Mr Felix really was Aubrey this was his crowning moment. He could simply miss. He could fling the inhaler down the ravine and no one would be able to blame him. Stress. Pressure. Never any good at throwing, actually. Did his best and all that. She held her breath and watched the inhaler leave the old man's hand and fly, up and up, then down and down, never taking her eyes off it until it landed safely in her outstretched palms.

She gripped it tightly the minute it made contact, just like her old PE teacher had instructed, and rolled back down onto the gantry, holding it out for Joy. The watching crowd cheered. Someone clapped. Joy grabbed hold of the blue plastic tube and stuck it in her mouth. And Flora looked down at Mr Felix and smiled. He was smiling right back up at her, triumphant.

Chapter 18

You sure know how to find the action.'

'Marshall!' Flora fought the impulse to throw her arms around his neck, so pleased was she to see him. 'You took your bloody time.'

He smiled and reached out to touch her cheek. 'Take it easy, Tiger. It's all okay now.'

She ducked her head so he couldn't see the threatening tears. So, she could overcome her fear of heights, climb up onto a dangerous gantry and rescue an old lady, *and* see off an evil mastermind – but Marshall being nice reduced her to tears?

Figured.

She nodded towards Joy to divert his attention. 'She okay?'

'Fine. That is, her breathing's stable. The paramedics said she seems a bit hyper. I guess it's all the excitement.'

'I guess.' Flora watched the old lady sip from a glass. She frowned. 'Does anyone know what happened? I mean, how she got up there in the first place?'

Marshall shook his head. 'Best guess – and this is the police talking, not me – is that the gate was left open.'

'No way! That's so dangerous.'

'Wasn't it open when you went up there?'

'I didn't even try it. I just assumed it would be locked. Stop smirking! There's a great big No Entry sign on it. Who'd even think to try and open it?'

'Erm, Joy?'

'Very funny. But why did she go up there? How did she know it was open?'

'Again, guessing, they think the warden arranged it somehow, planned it as some kind of treat for Joy and Eddie's anniversary.'

'Joy would have loved that. The view, this place, it means a lot to her. And she's a right daredevil.'

'Not the only one, hey?'

Flora shrugged. 'I was terrified every second I was up there. It was one of the worst experiences of my life.' She thought for a moment. 'But only one of them.'

Marshall put an arm around her shoulders. She didn't move away. 'You made a pretty good catch too, I've heard. You'll have to join our baseball team.'

'Flora?' Joy was waving her over. Flora slid out from under Marshall's arm and made her way to the ambulance.

'How are you feeling?'

'I've been better.'

'Joy?' Flora knelt down and looked up at her friend. 'What were you doing up there? What was really going on?'

'What do you mean?'

The old lady sounded indignant, but Flora knew her too well.

'I can swallow the stuff about the view and it being your anniversary and all, but really? When I arrived you were going pretty crazy. And why wasn't the warden on the gantry with you, if it was her idea and all?'

'Big scaredy-cat, she was, just like you. Couldn't cope. She said she'd go and wait for me in the tea room, but I knew better.'

'What do you mean?' Joy's blanket was slipping off her shoulders. Flora pulled it back on.

'She thought I wanted to top myself. See – you're not even surprised. You expected it too. I'd become a burden to everyone, of use to no one. She took me to see a solicitor, got me to sign a new will. She said there was still time for me to do something worthwhile with my life, told me about this charity for women who've suffered multiple miscarriages. Did you know that was why we never had children, Flora? I just couldn't carry one to term. It was heartbreaking. As soon as I read all that wonderful stuff about that charity I knew I had to try and help someone else who'd been through it. It was another way I could make amends.'

Flora's jaw tightened. She hadn't known, but Cynthia had clearly done her homework well.

'Joy, there's a lot you need to know about the warden, and that charity. But now probably isn't the best time. What you must know, you have to believe this, is that you are not a burden or useless. You've got everything to live for, and once we've got you sorted on your new tablets you'll be absolutely fine.'

Joy smiled. 'I do feel better, you know. Those tablets the doctor gave me have done wonders for my eczema already. Look.' She peeled down a glove to show Flora her arm, which did look a lot less angry. But then Joy sighed. 'I just don't want to go into Special Care. Standing up there – something came over me, Flora. Some kind of euphoria. I thought I could be with Eddie instead. I could step off the edge of the world and dance with him for all time. That would be better than being sent to the third floor. Wouldn't it?'

Flora nodded. She swallowed over the lump in her throat. 'Joy, I think I can say with some certainty that you are not moving up to the third floor. The warden – well, I don't think we'll be seeing her again.'

'Really? That's good. She had some funny ideas, you know.'

'Miss Lively? We need to take a statement.'

Flora stood and nodded to the policewoman. She

called Marshall over. 'Could you take Joy home?'

'Sorry.' The sergeant shook her head. 'Mr Goodman is helping us with our enquiries too.'

'I'll take her.'

Four pairs of eyes turned to Mr Felix. Joy let out a sound that was half huff, half outraged laughter. Flora smiled.

'Would you? That would be so kind.'

'I've got the car just over there.' Mr Felix looked down at Joy nervously. 'I parked it in a disabled spot.'

'I am not going anywhere with that man,' said Joy, turning her head so far to the right it made Flora's neck ache just watching.

But Flora's patience had been stretched to breaking point, and the look on the old man's face made her feel ashamed. 'For God's sake, Joy. You just saw him save your life. If it wasn't for him we wouldn't even have had the damned inhaler! You dropped it back at the Maples. So could you just quit being so rude to the poor guy and give him a break? Please?'

Joy opened her mouth to protest. She got as far as 'But how …?' and then shut it again. She looked at Mr Felix, then at Flora and Marshall, then back to Mr Felix.

'Okay. Okay, fine. Come on then. Let's do it.'

'Finally!'

Marshall helped Joy across the road and into the Fiat. 'Drive carefully,' Flora called when Joy was safely strapped in.

Mr Felix winked at her. 'I always do. And you can bring her something nice when you've finished here. Maybe a bunch of flowers. Some narcissus, perhaps. She'd like that.'

'He doesn't seem like such a bad fella.' Marshall stood at Flora's side as they watched the car pull out into traffic.

'No.' Flora was chewing on a fingernail. 'No. That's

what I thought.'

'You shouldn't do that, you know. It looks real ugly. Aren't girls supposed to have like a French manicure or something? Your hands look like a boy's.'

Flora wasn't listening. She said, 'Narcissus.'

'Flowers, right? We can stop off at that supermarket and get some on the way back – Steve got the bus back to Shrewsbury, he's left the car there for us.'

'Right. Marshall, can we just sit for a minute? Somewhere out of the way?'

'Sure. What's up?'

They perched on a low wall overlooking a row of trendy cafes. Flora tucked her knees up under her chin.

'He just said "narcissus".'

'O-kay. And?'

She shook her head. 'Why would he say that? Get her a bunch of flowers, fine. But why those flowers? Does anyone even know what narcissuses are?'

'Narcissi.'

'Whatever. Listen, a couple of weeks ago Joy got a bunch of flowers left outside her door. She went totally crazy, refused to even have them in the house.'

'Weird.'

'They were just a perfectly ordinary bunch of daffodils, but she was stamping on them and then she picked up what was left and tore them into shreds. I mean, those flowers made her mad as hell. When she told me all that Joan of Arc club stuff she said the daffodil is a type of narcissus, which is also the name of one of the characters they'd studied – Roman or Greek or something. Someone who loved himself, I guess it's where narcissistic comes from. It's all really confusing, but I do remember that Joy was adamant – and I mean adamant – that Aubrey, the caretaker's son, was the only other person who would know the significance of sending her a bunch of daffodils.'

Marshall stretched out his neck. 'But this was a couple of weeks ago, right? And it is spring and all. Daffodils are a pretty common flower, aren't they?'

'Well, that was my argument exactly. But hearing him say it just then, it seemed so …'

'Left field?'

She nodded. 'And there's something else. Back there, when we were trying to get her to go home with him, she was about to say something and then she stopped. I think I know what it was.'

'What?'

'She was about to say "But how did he know it was my inhaler?" And you know what, Marshall? She had a point. How did he know? I mean, no one at the Maples knew Joy had asthma until a few days ago, not even their own doctor. It was one of the things we argued about – I thought it was really dangerous that she hadn't told them. Then on Monday I get a call from Joy and the warden's raided her unit and Joy's flushed all her tablets down the toilet.'

Marshall laughed. 'Raided? Boy, I do not want to get old.'

'But do you get my point? There's no way Mr Felix could have known it was Joy's inhaler. Unless he knew her before.'

'I dunno, Flora. Maybe the warden told everyone.'

'Ha! She controlled information like it was gold dust.'

'Maybe he just saw her using it one time. You said yourself she's been getting worse these last few weeks.'

'Mm. Ever since the day she got those flowers and poor Otto had his accident. And I'm thinking …'

'Don't you think you should stop thinking?'

Flora stood up and went to peek around the corner. The policewoman was still talking to the owner of the railway. The ambulance had gone.

'Marshall, I need to get back to the Maples. Right

now.'

'Something else to investigate, Miss Lively?'

He clocked her expression and the smile slid off his face. 'You're serious.'

'Deadly. If I'm right, we've just delivered Joy into the hands of someone even more dangerous than the warden and Mr Vasco put together. And judging by the look on his face as they drove away, he's got one more trick up his sleeve.'

***

'Flora Lively, desperado.'

'Ha, you're hysterical. Come on, Marshall, I thought you were supposed to be fit.'

'Some people think so.'

'Not the time or the place. Do you think they've noticed yet?'

Flora looked over her shoulder at Marshall puffing along behind her. He didn't answer. She wasn't too worried about the police – they knew where to find her for a statement. Joy's wellbeing had to come first.

'Marshall, I'm not being funny but you really need to keep up. They've had a fifteen minute head start already, and I'm telling you, that Mr Felix, or Aubrey or whatever his name is, he's one crazy-fast driver.'

'You're right,' Marshall said between breaths. 'You're not being funny.'

They made it to the car in three minutes and headed out of Bridgnorth, grateful the rush hour traffic had yet to kick in. Flora pulled out her phone and dialled Joy's number.

'No harm in trying,' she said with a shrug. But Joy didn't answer. Flora couldn't even hazard a guess at which of Joy's foes had dispatched the old lady's phone. She tried the main reception. An automated voice told her it was currently unobtainable. She stared at the handset angrily.

'Do you think they'll find the warden? And Richie, what about him?' Richie had been in on it from the start, she was sure. He'd been Cynthia's inside man: it was quite brilliant, really. Shakers would be obliged to give him the job, and then he'd be free to check out the clients as they moved in, looking for anyone with lots of money and no family, someone who might make a likely target. Perhaps even checking through their stuff to find their weaknesses – injured animals, sick children, a son or daughter lost to cancer – so Cynthia could play on it with her fake charity scam.

'They'll find them,' said Marshall darkly.

Once they were clear of the town, Flora told Marshall what was on her mind.

'She kept saying the tablets weren't working anymore, and I remember now her talking about being confused because the latest batch seemed bigger, or tasted different or something. I wish I'd taken her more seriously. Marshall, what if Mr Felix swapped them for something else? What if he got into her unit and swapped them for something that looked like her real medication but was just a harmless vitamin? It could have been the day Otto had his accident.' She pulled her knees up to her chest and hugged them. 'Which would mean, of course, that Otto's accident might not have been an accident either.'

Marshall looked dubious. 'If he meant her harm, why not swap them for something dangerous instead?'

'He wanted her to suffer. He wanted to *see* her suffer. Otto, the flowers, that postcard. He's been biding his time, playing with her, probably laughing at how everyone's saying her deterioration is down to stress and old age. But he'd know stress makes her condition worse, and that the tablets that are supposed to help are just placebos.'

'She'd notice.' Marshall overtook a lorry, then tucked back in again smoothly. He glanced at Flora. 'Wouldn't she?'

Flora gave him a rueful smile. 'He was a chemist. Before he retired, I mean. He'd know exactly what kind of tablet to give her, and would be able to choose one that mimicked her medication closely.' She remembered something and slapped her knee with her palm. 'Of course! He'd been having loads of deliveries. Vitamins, she said it was. I bet he was trying to find the right one to replace Joy's medication with.'

'A chemist? Wow.'

'Wow indeed.' She pushed her hair back from her forehead and rubbed her eyes. They felt gritty, like she hadn't slept in days. 'I bet he was really pissed off when he found out she'd started getting proper meds again. He'd have to come up with a plan B.'

They drove in silence for a while, Flora turning it all over in her mind. As the lush fields gave over to housing estates, she looked at the phone in her hand.

She would so rather not have this conversation in front of Marshall, but there really wasn't a choice. She had to find out what Mr Felix might be planning, and she had a pretty good idea how to do exactly that. Unfortunately it meant doing something that went totally against the grain.

'May I speak to Heston, please?'

Marshall didn't look over, but she could see by the way he kept his face dead straight he was suppressing a grin. She turned away from him and waited.

'Flora? I can't talk long, I'm doing claimed-returns.'

Whatever that was. 'Heston, I need you to do me a favour. It's a biggie, I'm afraid.'

Silence. If they weren't still at least ten minutes away from the retirement village, Flora would have been tearing her hair out. As it was, she could afford to let him think about it for a moment or two.

'What is it?' he said quietly. Resignedly.

'I need you to look up the library records for a Mr Felix.' She told him how she'd seen the Maples' resident writing in a medical text, hoping Heston's outrage would overcome his reluctance to break the library's strict data protection rules.

Her gamble paid off. 'He did what? Hold on, I'll just pull up the right screen.'

Marshall slowed down for traffic lights on the town's perimeter. He cleared his throat. Flora ignored him.

'In medicine, you say? No, he doesn't have anything out from six ten.'

Flora shook her head, annoyed with herself for being so dense. 'He put it back. I remember now – after I'd knocked over the trolley he got up and put the book back on the shelf. Heston, it's really important. I need you to go and find it and have a look. It was definitely something medical, and it had a green cover.'

'Flora, I can't go through every page of every medical book to see if–'

'He put it back on the wrong shelf! Heston, look in six three five. Look there for a mis-shelved medical book and I bet that will be the one.'

'Gardening? Okay, hold on.'

The wait felt interminable. Marshall had started humming. It was driving her crazy.

'Say nothing,' she told him.

'Exactly what I am doing.'

Flora chewed a fingernail. What if the library staff had already tidied those shelves, put Mr Felix's book back where it should be? How would Heston find it then? They reached the park and ride on the outskirts of the city centre. Flora looked at the clock on the dash. Joy and Mr Felix would have been back for at least twenty minutes now. Long enough for anything to happen.

If he'd even taken her home, of course. If not, they could be anywhere.

She pushed the thought out of her mind. Heston's voice came back on the phone.

'Got it!'

Flora let out a puff of air. 'Has it been written in?'

'Sure has. This is terrible, Flora. If you're sure you saw him do it I might have to put a note on his record for someone to talk to–'

'Heston, I don't mean to be rude, but will you just tell me what it says?'

'Nothing.'

'What?'

'Well, it's just doodles, really. In the margins. No words, just symbols. Which makes it harder to prove it was him, of course. No handwriting.'

'But the margins – what pages has he marked up?'

'Let's see … Wow, quite a few. He must have been at it for some time. You know, I'm not surprised he didn't want to take this one out on his card. But he could have had the pages photocopied.'

Flora's shoulders drooped. She'd been so sure there would be something, some clue, in the book. Something to help keep Joy safe. If only she'd listened to her friend, believed that Mr Felix really was Aubrey, she could have looked at it herself sooner. But then Heston's words filtered through her fog of guilt. She sat up straight.

'What did you just say?'

'This book – it's on our watch list. We have to inform the police if anyone takes out a book that could be linked to possible terrorist or criminal activity. You know, like serial killers, bomb making, that kind of thing.'

They stocked books on bomb making at Shrewsbury library? That was news to Flora.

'And poisons,' Heston continued. 'Which is what this

book's about. Your fella at the old folks' home has been reading up on mould.'

'Mould?'

'"Natural Poisons", it's called. "Mould: The Secret Killer". Interesting stuff, I might have a look at it on my tea break.'

Flora hung up. She looked at Marshall. His face was grim now, all traces of humour wiped away.

'My aunt Lorena, back in Oregon, she nearly died after sleeping in a damp basement for a week. She had asthma too.' He turned and met Flora's eyes. 'It was the mould that did it. Mould can be fatal for folks with asthma.'

Flora sat back and closed her eyes. It was the only way she could contain the hysteria that was building up in her chest. She fixed an image of Joy in her mind – her odd-shaped humpy back; the fluffy perm; the way her eyes crinkled up when she was being mischievous – and held it there. As long as she could see her she'd be safe. And she pressed her foot hard on an imaginary accelerator, willing Marshall to get there as fast as he could.

She could only hope it wasn't too late.

Chapter 19

You can't go in there. Stop!'

Elizabeth had been waiting for them under the arched hedge. She seemed flustered, twisting her hands in her long hair and looking anxiously over her shoulder. But when she tried to block their entry, Flora rounded on the receptionist with venom.

'Just get out of my way. I know what you're going to say, what you've been trying to tell me all day. I'm barred from the Maples, right? Big deal. I've got news for you – your boss won't be coming back here anytime soon, so you're taking instructions from the wrong person.'

Flora took a step forward and Elizabeth jumped back with a cry. 'No, that's not it at all! The police are here, Flora. They're all over the place. They've got the computer and the phone line's down and they're interviewing the staff. It's a nightmare. I've got no idea what's going on.'

Marshall put a steadying hand on Flora's arm. 'Why are you out here then? Why aren't you in there being interviewed with the others?'

'I'm waiting for you. They sent me to gather the residents together, and I saw Mr Felix and Joy coming in.'

Flora's heart lifted. Joy was here.

'How long ago was this?'

'I don't know, twenty minutes or so? I told them what

250

was happening, and Mr Felix said to wait here for you. He said he had something to tell you, and if you came in you'd get caught up in all this police business, so I'm to go and get him and bring him out here to you.'

Flora took in a sharp breath. He was clever all right. Keeping them out here, just in case they were starting to get suspicious – giving him enough time to get on with whatever he was doing uninterrupted.

Whatever he was doing to Joy.

'Come on.' Flora and Marshall raced past a protesting Elizabeth and ran across the grass towards Mr Felix's unit.

Flora turned the doorknob: it was locked. Marshall pushed her gently to the side, then shouldered the door clean off its hinges. They rushed inside, adjusting their eyes to the gloom. Joy was sitting on a worn brown sofa, holding a cup in her hand. The room was so crowded with books and pictures and overlapping pieces of furniture and unopened boxes that Flora couldn't see the carpet at all. In fact, the room looked exactly the same as it had the day Shakers had moved the old man in. She turned her head towards a movement in the far right corner. Mr Felix was walking out of the kitchenette, his face wearing an astonished expression.

'What's going on? What … what the hell happened to my door?'

Marshall was tense by her side. She tried to take it all in: the teapot in Mr Felix's hand; the cup Joy was even now raising to her lips. His querulous tone at the library: *I know all about herbal medicine. I brew up a mean cup of herbal tea. You should try it sometime …*

At the library where he'd been researching poisonous strains of mould.

'Joy, no!' Flora threw herself across the room, reaching out for the cup. But it was too late. Joy lifted the teacup clear and took a long sip. Then she placed it carefully on its saucer and sat back with a satisfied smile.

'Joy, what have you done?' With an agonised cry, Flora grabbed the cup out of her hands and thrust it at Marshall. He held it away from himself, his lips curling in disgust.

'We need to get her to the emergency room,' he said. 'Right away.'

Flora nodded. She made to help Joy off the sofa, but the old lady pulled back and gripped the dirty-looking upholstery hard. 'I'm going nowhere. Not until I've finished this for good.'

'Would someone mind telling me what is going on here?' Mr Felix had rearranged his face into an expression of mild amusement. 'First that scatty receptionist starts rabbiting on about the police, then you burst in here, you break down my door, and now you're suggesting my friend here is in danger from some herbal tea! Are you quite insane?'

'I'm not your friend.'

Joy's voice was so low Flora had to strain to hear it. Marshall pushed past a stunned Mr Felix and disappeared into the kitchenette, hopefully in search of something to contain the suspicious tea.

'What did you say?'

'I said, I'm not your friend. I was once, a long time ago. But not now. You've made sure of that, Aubrey.'

Mr Felix pulled a face. 'My name's not Aubrey. It's Albert. And I don't know what you're talking about, for sure.'

Joy laughed and threw up her hands. She'd taken off her gloves, and Flora noticed that her skin really was almost completely free from tell-tale welts. She was getting better. And her breathing seemed calmer too. Her relief was short-lived.

Her friend had just drunk tea that was almost certainly poisoned with some strain of mould, brewed up

252

by the former chemist.

'I know you want to do this now, Joy, but we really should get you checked out. How much of it did you swallow?'

'I drank most of the tea, Flora, and it was quite the most disgusting thing I've ever tasted. Herbal tea, my eye! You can't beat a nice cup of English breakfast.'

Mr Felix grinned. He looked at his watch: a theatrical gesture, bringing his wrist up to his eyes, as if to tell them Joy didn't have long anyway so there was no point rushing her off to the medical centre. 'Well,' he said, 'let's have it then. If there's something you need to say to me we might as well get it over with.'

Flora pushed past him and ran into the kitchen. 'Marshall, I don't care if you have to pick her up and carry her, just get her out of here now.'

He nodded. But as they started back into the lounge, Mr Felix blocked their way. 'Don't be so hasty. You're forgetting who I am. The only person who can save her now is me.'

An antidote? Flora mouthed the word to Marshall.

'I don't think so,' he said, grimacing.

Mr Felix wasn't listening – his attention was refocused on Joy.

'So, you finally admit it.' Joy's voice was calm, unwavering.

'Well, of course I'm him. You knew it as soon as you saw me, I know you did. Couldn't stand it, could you? Being faced with the results of what you did all those years ago.' He held up his right leg, lifting it with both hands. 'Crushed, it was. Left me a cripple. While you and your cronies got off scot free.'

Joy's voice was strained. 'I never stopped thinking about it, Aubrey. I've lived with the guilt my whole life.'

'Oh, my heart bleeds. Look at you, with your comfortable nest egg and your friends and all this luxury. I can't afford to be here, they wanted to send me to the council place instead. But I had to come once I saw you. I recognised you straight away too, Joy Stevens. You'd managed to get your horrible skin condition under control, although I admit that threw me for a while. I had to be sure it was you. But as soon as I found your medication I knew.'

'You swapped it, didn't you?' Flora couldn't help herself, she had to know if she was right. Mr Felix's eyebrows danced on his forehead.

'Why, you're a clever little thing, aren't you? Yes, I knew you were on to me that day at the library. But it didn't matter, I'd already decided on my final move.' He looked at his watch again. A shadow passed over his face.

'Not dead yet? Is that what's bothering you?' Joy smiled and reached down the side of the cushion. 'You shouldn't leave your old sample bottles lying around, you know,' she said, wrinkling up her nose. 'Although thankfully this one was empty. Flora, have you ever seen anyone living in such a disgusting state? Really, men do not fare as well as women when they're on their own. They lack a certain pride, don't you think?' She held up a small cylindrical bottle, half full of a dark brown liquid. 'Herbal tea, anyone? Although I don't think you'd want to try this. It really is disgusting. This particular batch was meant for me, of course, so I'm sure it's got a little something special in it. Arsenic, perhaps? Some kind of opiate? I'm sure the police will be able to tell.'

Mr Felix made a lunge for the sample bottle, but Marshall was one step ahead. He wrapped both arms around the old man's waist, holding him off the ground while his good leg pumped frantically at fresh air.

'Mould,' Flora said, taking the bottle out of Joy's hand and pulling her into a hug. 'And you, my friend, are completely crazy.'

'And brave, though. Come on, admit it – you're impressed.'

Flora looked into Joy's pale blue eyes and smiled. 'You're the bravest person I've ever met. I'm so sorry I didn't believe you.'

'No one will,' cried Mr Felix, as Elizabeth arrived at the door, even more flustered-looking but now with two uniformed policemen by her side. 'No one will believe you because it's all lies. I've done nothing wrong.'

Marshall marched over to the doorway, still carrying the wriggling man in his arms. 'He's all yours,' he said, setting him down.

'Wait!' Joy struggled to her feet and held out her hand. She picked her way across the room and stood facing a furious Mr Felix, who was now flanked by the policemen with Marshall positioned behind. 'Aubrey, there's something I need to say to you. Something I've wanted to say for over sixty years.'

'I don't know who this Aubrey is,' Mr Felix said loudly, waving his hands. 'She's completely lost it. Drugs, you know. There's a lot of it about.'

'Save it, fella.' Marshall's voice was laced with ice. 'Listen to what the lady's got to say.'

Joy took a shaky breath and held Flora's hand tightly. 'Aubrey, I'm sorry. For what we did to you all those years ago ... and for Jack. I'm truly sorry.' She leaned into Flora's arms and sighed. 'I'm glad I had the chance to say it at last.'

One of the policemen led a protesting Mr Felix away; the other looked around the room and raised an eyebrow. 'Does anyone want to tell me what's been going on here? Does this have anything to do with your missing warden?'

Joy turned to Flora. 'Yes, what exactly has been going on with the warden? You and her were having some kind of battle of wills up there at the funicular. What was all that stuff about the charity?'

'We were fighting for you, Joy,' Flora said with a weary smile. 'But I had no idea you were so capable of fighting your own battles.' She linked arms with her friend and nodded to the policeman, Elizabeth and Marshall. 'Come on. We've got quite a story to tell you. But I think we should do it over a nice cup of coffee.'

'Oh, I prefer tea,' said Joy, wrinkling up her nose.

'Really?' Flora gave a shaky laugh. 'I'm not sure I'll be able to look at a cup the same way ever again.'

Epilogue

'One thin and crispy with salami, one deep pan with spinach and egg.'

The waiter laid the two plates on the small round table. Flora eyed Joy's pizza with her lip turned up. 'I don't know how you can eat salami. It's gross.'

'Ha! Says the girl who thinks having a fried egg on top of a pizza is normal fare!'

'It's on the menu, Joy. It can't be that weird.'

'Well, we'll just have to agree to disagree, won't we?'

They tucked into their lunch in companionable silence. But after only three mouthfuls, Flora laid down her fork.

'I'm so sorry, Joy.'

Her friend sighed. 'Not this again. You have to let it go, Flora. Believe me, I know all about holding on to something you feel guilty about.'

'I can't let it go.' Flora reached for Joy's hand. Clear-skinned and ungloved, her eczema was healing up fast. 'I can't forgive myself. The whole time you were suffering, struggling with it alone, I just thought you were imagining it all. I thought … well, it doesn't matter now.'

'No, go on. What did you think? Maybe if you tell me you'll finally be able to shut up about it.' Joy tucked into her pizza cheerfully. The new medication was giving her a healthy appetite.

Flora took a sip of water and looked at her glass.

'Well, I suppose it was the guilt that threw me. Guilt can be a terrible, confusing, messy thing. I figured you felt bad for how you treated that boy all those years ago, so guilty you never even told Eddie about it, and you'd lived with that for years.'

'And you thought the guilt made me imagine that Aubrey had come back to find me, ready to exact his revenge?'

'Yes. I thought it was just your guilty mind playing tricks on you. After the stress of losing Eddie, and then what happened to Otto … Well, you can see how it might have seemed.'

Joy smiled. 'It's great to have Otto back. He misses you though.'

'I miss him too.' Flora had taken him over to Joy's that morning. She couldn't imagine how empty the bungalow was going to feel when she went home.

'Anyway, I should have believed you. The truth is, I think I was channelling my own guilt, looking at it through my eyes, not yours.'

Joy stopped chewing. With her mouth full of pizza, she said, 'What on earth do you have to feel guilty about?'

'When I was fourteen, my parents told me I was adopted. They'd been agonising over it for years, trying to work out the best time to tell me. It was a shock, and I was at that age where you think your parents are everything and nothing, you know? Invincible, but also mortifying. They pulled the rug out from under me – I would have given anything to have known nothing about it, to have gone on for ever thinking Peter and Kitty Lively were my real parents. My annoying, wonderful, flawed, crazy parents.'

'It must have been hard for them. Trying to do the right thing.'

'Well, I know that now. But I was a teenager. I was

angry. I told them both that I hated them, that I wished I knew my real parents, wished I lived with them instead. I said some terrible things.'

Joy shook her head. 'They wouldn't have minded. They probably expected far worse.'

'I know. They were saints, the best parents anyone could wish for. But I said it, don't you see? And even though they never brought it up again, I still knew I'd hurt them.'

'And you always felt guilty?'

Flora swallowed. Did Joy need to hear all this? Did she even want to?

'I went totally off the rails. I got my ears pierced, started drinking, hanging around with a bad crowd. I got a tattoo – Mum hated it. She was so disappointed. Said I'd ruined my looks.'

'I had wondered about your tattoo. It's very – surprising.'

Flora smiled. Good job Joy didn't know about the other one.

'The day before my mother died, she told me she loved me more than anything else in the world. No matter what.'

'Ah, that's lovely. For you and for her. It must have given her great peace.' Joy speared a slice of salami and popped it into her mouth. Her eyes were full of kindness.

Flora remembered it so clearly. The bedroom had been unnaturally quiet – no kids shouting outside, no dogs barking or hedges being trimmed. The machine that regulated her mother's morphine dose hummed gently next to her bed; every movement her mother made, every rustle of the sheets, made Flora wince. The morphine only managed the pain, dulled it into something bearable. She knew her mother was suffering, despite the brave smile.

'Flora,' said Joy, pulling her out of her reverie. 'I

doubt she even remembered your teenage years. Not in the way you think, at least. She had twenty-seven years as your mother, and half of them came after the day they told you the truth about your birth. She was a lucky woman. I would have given anything for a child, Flora, especially one as caring as you. No, don't brush the compliment away. You're far too self-deprecating, but that's an issue for another day. You need to let it go. She loves you more than anything else in the world and always will, no matter what.'

It was a while before Flora could speak again. She dried her eyes on a serviette and smiled weakly.

'I should be better at this stuff, don't you think? I do have a degree in psychology.'

Joy brushed her words away. 'They teach you nothing at school or university. Life is the only educator we need. You were looking at my situation through the filter of your own experiences – I imagine it's very common. Anyway, I really did have reason to feel guilty. What we did to Aubrey was terrible. It was right for me to be called to account. And I guess I'd always been expecting it to happen, one day.'

'Not like that though,' Flora objected. 'You didn't deserve to be terrorised. You didn't deserve to die for it!'

'No, maybe not.' Joy shrugged and picked up the dessert menu. 'But there you go.'

Flora was struck again by her amazing resilience. 'You really were sure all along, weren't you? You were sure Mr Felix was Aubrey because–'

'Because he was,' Joy finished wryly. 'I recognised him alright, but you weren't the only one to second-guess it – I couldn't believe my own eyes at first. I passed him in the dining hall and I was ninety per cent sure. He looked at me and there was something in his expression. Not hate, nothing as extreme as that, it was more like pleasure. Recognition and pleasure. Like he'd been waiting for this moment and was happy it had finally arrived. I should have marched right up to him and said, "Hey, you're Aubrey, aren't you? The caretaker's son. I'd know you anywhere. And there's something I need to tell you, Aubrey. I treated you appallingly and I'm really, truly sorry. There's not a day in my entire life that I haven't felt bad for my part in what we did to you and I hope you can forgive me."'

'I wonder what would have happened if you had?' Flora doubted it would have changed anything. Mr Felix was clearly a bitter old man on a mission.

'I was too afraid. There was something about him, don't you think? Something menacing?'

Flora said nothing. She didn't want to admit that she'd found Mr Felix about as menacing as a caterpillar. Which didn't bode well for her skills as an amateur detective. Not that she was taking Marshall's suggestion to heart. If this fiasco was anything to go by, Flora's investigative acumen was hardly likely to be in demand.

'You did work out what the warden was up to,' Marshall had pointed out. 'And you rescued Joy from Aubrey.'

'She rescued herself, after I'd sent her off alone with a man hell bent on revenge after convincing her he was totally harmless,' Flora had countered.

'Do you think it would have made a difference?' Joy asked softly. Flora looked up at her friend. She was gazing at a point beyond Flora's shoulder. 'Do you think he'd have left me alone if I had just acknowledged him and said sorry?'

'I don't know, Joy. He was pretty twisted. Look at what he did to Otto.'

'He swore it was an accident. The police said he told them Otto had been trying to bite his leg when he was swapping my medication and that in the kerfuffle he'd got tangled up in the blind cord somehow.'

'Do you believe that?'

And had he really used the word "kerfuffle"? Some master criminal he was. But at least he'd confessed all, relieving Joy of the burden of a long-drawn-out investigation. The police had been lucky with the warden and Vasco too, getting to their respective offices in plenty of time to unearth all the evidence they needed to prove their involvement in the charity scam. Thanks to Max. There wasn't much of a chance they'd be able to prove the pair had been responsible for the Captain's or Ida's deaths, Max had told her, but at least they could make sure they'd never hurt anyone else.

Flora would just have to be content with that.

'Your eczema's better, I see.'

Joy grinned. 'Well, I can't wear those gloves for ever, can I? Makes me look like a villain in a Bond film.'

'You're more Bond girl than villain, I think,' teased Flora. Joy gave a guffaw and slapped Flora's arm.

'I was right about the third floor, wasn't I?'

'Poor Captain. The police think they've got enough evidence to send Cynthia and the solicitor away for a very long time.' She gave Joy a sideways glance. 'So now there's nothing to fear from moving into the main building, right? Now there's a new manager?'

Joy grimaced. 'You'll never get me in there, Flora. I'll throw myself off the roof first.'

'Joy! Don't even talk like that.'

'Oh, don't get your knickers in a twist. They've said I can stay in my own unit now, provided I look after myself properly.'

Flora cut a piece off her pizza and put it in her mouth. It was cold, but not as bad as she'd expected. 'And do you think you can do that, Joy? Can you look after yourself properly?'

The old lady just grinned and sipped her tea, a mischievous glint in her eye.

Flora walked Joy back to the Maples, then cut back across town to Shakers. What she was about to do would be tough, but it was entirely necessary. If she'd learned one thing in the last three weeks it was that life was too short to spend it doing something you didn't love. She needed to find a way to satisfy her dad's wishes, but also live her own life too. And she thought she had a pretty good idea how to do just that.

'Hey. How you doing?' Marshall was in the warehouse, sweeping up. Busy work. 'How's Joy?'

'She's fine. Really. It's amazing how resilient she is.'

'Did you take the dog back?'

She nodded.

'And you're feeling sad about that, right? Why not get yourself a puppy? I never had you pegged for a dog lover, but it might do you good. Otto certainly seemed to soften out your edges a bit.'

'No can do. Well, not until I'm settled, anyway. I might end up somewhere that's no good for pets.'

Marshall looked up in alarm. 'What do you mean? Settled where?'

'Don't get your hopes up, I'm not leaving the country. But I am selling Mum and Dad's place. That bungalow is not me. I miss my old flat – I'm going to look around for something similar.'

'Wow. Any more bombshells for me?'

She laughed. 'It's hardly a bombshell that I'm moving house. At least it'll put some business our way.'

'I'll give you a very competitive quote.'

'Thanks. I might get one from Rockfords too. Do a bit of mystery shopping.'

Her face reddened at the thought. She pictured David Rockford sitting in her parents' lounge drinking coffee. Not a good idea, even as a joke.

Marshall put the broom against the wall and bent down with the dustpan and brush. 'No point asking them. They're not in the market for domestic removals at the moment.'

Flora did a double-take. 'What did you say?'

He looked up at her and grinned. 'Yeah, it's weird. Not only did they pull out of the lease on the Battlefield site, I heard they're not bothering going after boring old house removals in this area at all. Turns out there's not enough money in it. They've got some newfangled idea about commercial storage instead. Apparently,' he said, stretching out the word, 'it's the hot ticket right now.'

She pulled up a crate and perched on it, planting her chin on her upturned hands. 'Marshall, are you saying what I think you're saying?'

'Well, that'd depend, wouldn't it?' His eyes twinkled. There was a charge in the air, like electricity. Flora swallowed.

'Did you give your business idea to David Rockford? Is that what all those secret meetings were about?'

He nodded. Flora looked up to the ceiling. 'Marshall, you idiot! I was just about to give you the go-ahead for that.'

'Really?'

'Right now. Today. I figured I'd had my chance to run it the way Dad wanted, now it was time to do it differently. Besides ...' she tailed off. There was no point telling him she'd been thinking of doing something else for a while, leaving him totally in charge. That could wait for another day.

'This is totally left field, you know,' she said, smirking.

'Finally she gets a saying right!' Marshall threw an imaginary ball into the air. 'Slam-dunk.'

'Oh yeah. A bit of a curve ball, in fact.'

He gave her a look. 'You're overdoing it now.'

She grinned, but then her smile slipped. 'Are you sure it was the right thing to do, Marshall? That business plan, it was your baby.'

'Well, I'm not really a family kind of guy. It'll keep them off our backs for a while, give us a chance to regroup. Maybe do some advertising of our own, brainstorm some ideas with your uncle.'

'Thank you.' She leaned forward, just a tiny bit, enough to smell Marshall's warmth and his spicy scent. He tipped up his head, rocking forward onto one knee.

'Flora, you know, there was a good reason why I did it. I wanted to–'

'Hello? Hello, is this where – ah, Flora! There you are! I've been calling you for days. Is everything okay?'

Heston. Perfect timing. Flora got off the crate with a sigh.

Marshall sat back, his eyes darkening. 'I'll leave you two to it.'

She watched him go. There was so much she wanted to tell him. Like, even though he drove her crazy he'd been there when she needed him and she wouldn't forget it. That it was only going to take about five minutes to send Heston away – she had already rehearsed the exact words she was going to use to let him down gently. But mainly that she knew. She knew he'd done it for her, and that he stayed around for her. Because Shakers was as much his business as it was hers. It wouldn't be the same without him.

Marshall reached the top of the metal steps, his shoulders drooping, then disappeared inside the office. Flora's heart felt heavy. Heston moved around to stand in front of her. He looked nervous. She sighed and gestured for him to sit down on a crate. She took one last look up at the office window. Marshall was sitting in her chair with his legs up on the desk, looking down at the two of them and laughing. Behind Heston's back he pulled a face, mocking the smaller man's wan expression. He sucked in his cheeks and rolled his eyes, then slapped his thighs in delight. Flora glared up at him balefully. Impossible man.

And to think she'd been just about to soften. Ha! Not a chance.

'Flora? Flora, what are you looking at?'

'Nothing,' she told Heston with a kind smile. 'Nothing at all. Come on, let's get out of here. There's something I need to tell you.'

THE END

Acknowledgements

I'd like to thank the following people who contributed to the writing and production of this book: Jez Phillips, my wonderful husband, whose continued support makes writing a joy; Jude White for her brilliant proofreading and editing; Chris Howard for another wonderful cover; and finally my amazing Beta Readers: Emma Harrison, Sherry Meyer, Pauline Wiles, Rachel Owen, Marina Sofia, Emma Dellow, Kathryn Michaels and Kate Frost. I'd also like to thank my readers – without you none of this would happen at all. Know that every time you download, buy or borrow one of my books you make my world an even brighter place.

To find out more about my books visit me at www.joannephillips.co.uk where you can sign up to my mailing list and hear about new releases, giveaways and special promotions.

Coming soon …

The Flora Lively Mysteries: Book 2

A Date With Death

Also by Joanne Phillips

Can't Live Without

The Family Trap

A Life Unpredicted and other stories

Lightning Source UK Ltd.
Milton Keynes UK
UKOW04f1849010715

254453UK00004B/171/P